Laughter Behind The Tiers

TO MY FAVORITE
MALE HANDLER. THANKS
SO MUCH FOR BUYING
MY NOVEL. YOU ARE
A WEALTH OF KNOWLEDGE
AND THIS BOOK WILL ONLY
ADD TO IT.

Mel Slew

3-4-21

SGT. MIKE SZABAN

LAUGHTER BEHIND THE TIERS

2007

Laughter Behind The Tiers

A SPECIAL THANKS TO EVERYONE WHO DIDN'T MIND ME SITTING ON THE COUCH FOR SIX MONTHS;

KATHLEEN MCKINNON

ALBINA CORMICK-BARRE

FREDDIE SZABAN

MATT, JOHN, SYDNEY, HANNNAH

KARLNESTLEBERGER@YAHOO.COM

MY INTRODUCTION
A MUST READ

B e careful what you wish for. It just might come true. How many times have we heard that? Wishing for a regime change sealed my fate only three years from retirement at forty-three years old. This is a story about the corruption, politics, affairs, and callous humor of life in prison—not through the eyes of some ex-junky rapist, murderer, or wannabe gangster, but of a regular Joe, an all-American man who worked for seventeen years inside the walls of a county jail where everyone from murderers to shoplifters are held. There are some truly crazy stories when dealing with caged criminals and some of the staff and the politicians who run these institutions are no better than the cons they guard; they are just playing on another level. The names have been changed to protect the guilty as well as the innocent.

I was forced into resignation to avoid termination, forced out by the new sheriff to whom I had devoted a year of my life—and my eighty-seven-year-old grandmother—campaigning. We had fistfights in the prison's locker room between the old administration's people and us, the people who wanted change. Now I'm out, looking in—not because of the numerous assaults, affairs with secretaries, union activities, or anything else that occurred in a prison atmosphere, but because of my unwillingness to pay or bribe the newly elected sheriff. I could have given Sheriff Gobi a large donation, or begged and groveled as so many of my peers had done. But the newly elected sheriff had promised to do away with that. Instead, he was running the jail just like his campaign—on donations. Shame on me for believing his campaign promises; I should have listened to my dad who said," Once a politician, always a politician." I have always told my fellow officers to watch the movie *Braveheart* and decide which side they were on—the side of the true freedom fighter or the side of crooked politicians who have no business running a prison or any law agency for that matter.

I was shocked to see how quickly the people I stood shoulder to shoulder with on picket lines, not to mention saving lives and breaking up gang fights, turned and just wanted to be on the inside of the glass house looking out. But why did they put on such an act? They could have bribed or "donated" to the previous sheriff. I know now that most people are not freedom fighters, but cowards. They were forcing me out because I didn't pay tribute to the "king." Sheriff Gobi didn't even have the intestinal fortitude to speak to me himself. He met with everyone he hired, fired or squeezed out. He especially made it a point to meet, and meet again, the pretty ladies that he hired. But he had his sloppy, Big-Bird shaped real-estate lawyer/friend/warden deal with me for him. The man was teary eyed, knowing that he couldn't intimidate me like the others by putting on a façade of being tough. He had two years on the job with no prior experience in any phase of law enforcement or correctional facilities. In fact, none of the top three men in the Sheriff's Department had any military experience or any type of police academy under their belt. They were just Gobi's friends. But they made me resign. They knew that I wouldn't sell out like so many others just fighting for scraps from the commonwealth's table.

CHAPTER ONE
THE BASICS

Sergeant Mike, this punk just threw piss on my face!"
I heard the radio transaction come over my radio, but I had to look down from the booth window into the dayroom of the segregation block to be sure of what I just heard. Officer Hartwell, a stocky but doughy officer with a baby face, was looking up at me with his arms outstretched and a mortified look. From the booth some fifty feet away, I could see the liquid dripping off the shocked officer.

The segregation block is like a large two story gymnasium with cells on three sides and eight shower stalls with cages to shower the inmates who make it to the "hole" or "seg" on the fourth side. This building wasn't designed to hold the worst of the prison population, but it sure as heck held one hundred of the worst prisoners. The officers who worked here were mostly good guys on somebody's shit list. A lot of them were strong or athletic, and some had an unusual amount of testosterone.

Officer Hartwell was picking up food trays after feeding the inmates through the slot in the solid cell door when Inmate Westbrook threw a cup of urine into his face. I ran out of the booth and down the metal stairs with Officer Bousquet to the cell door. Officer Bousquet was a Frenchman who grew up in an Irish neighborhood, on an Italian street, and owned a dojo. He was a martial arts expert, very stocky, and bald with a goatee. He looked intimidating and rightfully so. But he was French and spoke like he was one of the Sopranos.

From the moment you are out of that observation booth, you are on stage. One hundred convicts are watching your every move from the keyboard-sized window in their cell, and the noise is louder than an NFL game. They get excited like dogs in heat when action occurs. Any type of fight fuels their inner criminal minds. If some inmates started going off the hook, we'd have to wrestle or subdue them also. Then we'd have more work to do. In essence, they act like caged dogs; when one starts barking, the rest follow.

I had to move and move fast. The black leather gloves are always on when you work the seg block. Fights, feces, germs and the blood that is almost a daily occurrence in prison are just a few of the reasons for the water resistant black leather gloves. Officer Gardella was with Hartwell and ordered the cell door opened. Gardella tackled Inmate Westbrook around the knees and I dove like a kid into a pile of leaves on top of the two. Westbrook, who looked surprised, was on the gray concrete floor, facedown with my knee in his back. We handcuffed the kid and Frenchy and I carried him up the stairs. At least that's what the report stated. I actually had such an adrenaline rush that Frenchy was being swung around along with the inmate. I was carrying the con by the hair and the seat of his pants up the metal stairs to the high-risk tier, and Frenchy was the caboose holding onto the punk's legs. The high-risk tier was where the suicidal cons and staff assaulters were placed. When a prisoner throws body fluids or assaults staff, we place them on the steel bunks and restrain their arms and legs. It seems barbaric, but when you've gone through this time and time again, you know it is for everyone's protection, not for punishment—at least, that's what we were officially told.

The assaulting con was placed on the bunk, Frenchy ripped off the con's clothing to his underwear and Officer

Gardella brought us the restraints. The kid spent the next day lying on his back, stripped, chained and face up wondering if it was worth it.

During the incident, the rest of the inmates were laughing, banging on the metal doors or yelling things like, "Who's pissed off now?" "You must be pissed, Hartwell!" " Ur-ine trouble, Westbrook!" I had Hartwell, who stood in the middle of the dayroom traumatized, escorted to the infirmary; they thought that he should go to the hospital as a precautionary measure against infectious disease. We later found out that the kid threw the urine on Hartwell as an initiation into a Spanish gang. They had played Westbrook. They were never going to take this scrawny white kid into their gang. They just used him for entertainment, and he ended up getting an extra nine months on his sentence.

***

Why on God's green earth did I stay working at this hellhole? Was the money worth it? Power trip? Benefits? I still have no clue. How many fights had I seen? How many inmates did things to staff or other cons? What was my first encounter?

I can remember walking through the metal detector and the old steel gate for the first time. It can be quite intimidating, especially if you have an ounce of claustrophobia. The floors and half of the walls were battleship gray. Dim lighting and the smell of rust, dirty gym clothes, and paint made it almost a good setting for a horror movie. Old fashioned gates were everywhere. Long, narrow corridors led to many different cellblocks, each block had its own personality, smell and comfort level. There was a glass bubble, so to speak, in the middle of the jail that controlled all the staff and inmate traffic in and out of corridors, other cellblock booths and exits to the jail itself. This was central control. All movement outside the prison housing areas was controlled by the staff that worked there. The windows were supposedly bulletproof, but I noticed a lot of nicks and scratches on the booth windows. Bulletproof?

No pistols were allowed inside the jail. That's for the movies. If officers have pistols, the prisoners will get them. I felt a mix of emotions: wanting to be tough, as I was one of the bigger recruits, as well as curiosity and a little intimidation. The first inmates I saw walk by me during orientation were a group of about eight kitchen workers. An officer was kicking the sole of an inmate's foot who was lagging behind, apparently not thrilled about going to work. The officer kept saying, "Move it along, Gilligan!" The little con did resemble the silly first mate from *Gilligan's Island*. This casual encounter put me a little bit at ease. I also noticed that a couple of officers were kind of small and meek looking. I figured that if these guys could work here, then I should be just fine.

The sheriff's academy was kind of a joke for me. I had been in the military, and this was their first official academy. Previous recruits had been sent to other counties or the state run academy. The sheriff's academy was run by three people: an older lawyer, a politician and a man who worked in the cell blocks for a week and was going to quit, but had been talked into staying by a relative that had donated some cash to the sheriff in exchange for a job away from the cons. A specialty job. None of these guys had any military experience and they were trying to teach us how to march and do physical training. Hmm...

The recruit class had about thirty rookies in it. I, along some of the other military veterans, helped them with the physical training and marching. The six week academy went by quickly. Only about four people dropped out due to academic problems. We were all excited and yet nervous about our assignments. Would we be working first shift in minimum security or would we be on third shift in maximum security? It all boiled down to politics. There was a union at that time, but Sheriff Smith had them in his pocket. There was no such thing as seniority or job bidding and posting. It was pure cronyism. As a matter of fact, the man who bargained the contract for the union was promoted after each contract that he sold us. Eventually that caught up to the bargaining committee leader and newly elected Captain when he had pressure put on him by his brother who was in trouble. The Captain had to represent his brother. Sheriff Smith felt that he had promoted him to Captain and that his loyalty should go to the administration instead of his brother.

I was a little proud when the graduation ceremony commenced, looking forward to having my picture taken with bigwig politicians and other high-ranking officials. This was a wonderful publicity stunt for local politicians who wanted their pictures in the paper for looking tough on crime. I was still young and naïve. My assignment: first shift and medium security. I lucked out.

As in all new jobs, my first few weeks were spent getting to learn the routine, the staff and all the buttons, switches and lights. The control board for a single housing unit looked like the Christmas tree at Rockefeller center. Each cell door and gate had a red and green light on an accompanying switch in the block's control booth. Now on top of learning this, I had to get to know the inmates. This was where my training came into play. These men were cons. Most would sell their mom out for a pack of smokes. If anyone was around, they'd fight you for saying that; but in private, they'd be reaching for the smokes and handing over their mother.

Most convicts sit around and plan how to get something—anything—from you. There is a booklet handed out in the academy called "Downing the Duck." It warns that the inmate will try to establish a familiarity with you. "Hey, don't I know you from Joe's pub?" or "Where do I know you from?" They get the smallest detail and work it until they know all about you. Then they might ask you to mail a letter to their mom because it's her birthday and they missed the mailbox. Eventually you spend more time talking to the cons than you do your own family. If you think about it, you are spending eight plus hours with these guys with no place else to go. So, you are stuck hanging with these dudes like you are one of them—albeit you are wearing a uniform and are the boss. Sometimes they get someone to mail that letter, then they may ask you for a pen, then it is a pack of gum or something. The more an officer does, the more the con wants. Eventually you say no, and they drop it or offer you a favor or even try to blackmail you into giving them more. They may work their way up so the officer ends up lugging drugs or whatnot. Some officers have fallen into the trap of bringing in too much. I've seen some officers get set up by cons with nice looking women on the outside, meeting them for drinks or sex and bringing in a package of something illegal for the convict. When the con gets mad or is disciplined in any way, he rats everyone out. And most of the cons, though not all, end up ratting. Hence the saying, "There is no honor among thieves." That's how most cons think. So I wanted to walk a fine line between being well-liked and not crossing any contraband lines.

As I said, I was working in medium security, which meant three separate cellblocks. This one in particular was set up like a college dorm with two wings (east and west), each with two floors. There were community showers and toilets and a laundry facility. The rooms were not cell doors, but wooden ones just like in a dorm. The doors did not have locks since the bathrooms were at the beginning of the tier. It was tough if not impossible to keep an inmate in his cell. The dayroom was in the middle with a T.V. and a pool table. You can see the problem with a pool table in a prison setting, can't you? So these inmates were never really locked in their rooms. This block was generally quiet as a lot of these guys had maintenance or kitchen jobs that kept their minds off of their problems and made time go by faster. A busy inmate usually stayed out of trouble.

One Sunday morning, I noticed an inmate out of his room staring at Officer Lou Cafarelli. Lou was a loud, roid-rage type of guy. He was good to have on your side, but he gave us officers a bad rap. His biceps must have been twenty-two inches and he was only five feet six inches tall. Lou, myself and my ex-wife's cousin Ray Garabedian were all sitting in the booth this morning. Usually this was a no-no, but it was Sunday and the cons were supposed to be in their rooms until breakfast. Lou normally worked three to eleven, but he had opted to work a rare overtime shift that day. Easy money—so why not?

One of the inmates, Nikos, was staring at Lou. The design of the building was wrong, as the inmates could look down into the booth from the top tier—a psychological advantage for the con. Lou walked out onto the tier and told Nikos to get back in his room. Nikos said," No" and "Fuck you"! Lou told him one more time to get into his room and he refused. So Lou told him that he was locked in for another twenty-four hours now (a small, routine punishment for minor infractions, where the con stays in his room/cell for twenty-four hours and has his meals brought to him...no big deal—unless it's visiting or canteen day). Lou came back into the booth and told me to watch the door while he went up, as there were two doors with broken locks. Officer Garabedian was manning the panel in the control booth. Lou picked up the phone and called his buddy Hooker from maxi (maximum security), another juicer with a bad temper, a square head and the typical cop bowl type haircut. Hooker was so excited at the chance to beat someone down and drag him off. This was probably one of the few times he got wood. He arrived with Officer Sanchez, a good officer who was married to a deputy's niece. (Just for the record, the rank structure goes officer, sergeant, lieutenant, captain, deputy, warden, and then sheriff.) Sanchez was more into keeping the block clean and quiet than looking for a battle.

I watched Lou, Hooker and Sanchez go up the stairs to get Nikos. Watching the action from below, I felt that this was going to get ugly and I had only been here a couple of months. Nikos was huge. He weighed in the vicinity of three forty and was about six feet three inches tall. Just a big, big man. But my two juiced up coworkers and Sanchez were going up to bring him down.

I heard Hooker say to Nikos, "Turn the fuck around, you're going on the taxi to maxi!"

Nikos yelled back, "Get the fuck outta here, punks!"

Hooker grabbed Nikos' arm and twisted it while Lou grabbed him around the neck and pulled the group to the ground. That almost always works in favor of the officers. Sanchez had the leg irons and two sets of handcuffs. By now some inmates started coming out of their rooms and drifting towards the action. My juiced up coworkers were not well liked by the inmate population. It's what they call "king of the hill syndrome." If you are bigger and stronger, people want to knock you off the hill. You can relate to it by being the super bowl champs. Everyone brings their "A" game to play you the next season. I heard a lot of grunting and swearing coming from the pile and realized it was taking these guys way too long to handcuff Nikos. So I decided that I was not going to be the doorman any longer. When I got to the stairs I noticed a considerable crowd at all the stairwells. The inmates were getting angrier and angrier. Sanchez went to place the leg iron on Nikos' leg and I heard Lou yell, "That's my fuckin' wrist, stupid!" I went up the stairs and hollered at Nikos to just put his hands behind his back and end this bullshit. He yelled, "I can't, these stupid fucks are lying on my arms!" My coworkers looked like they were running out of steam and the crowd started throwing books and toilet paper at us. This was getting ugly real quick. I radioed the booth to get more help and to announce on the PA system for the inmates to return to their cells. But Officer Garabedian looked like he was in shock. I guess we were on our own.

I moved one of the officers' legs off Nikos' arm and cuffed it; the Hooker then passed me his other arm and we got it cuffed. Then a small Spanish inmate pushed Sanchez and he almost went down the stairs. Sanchez grabbed a railing with one hand and dropped a pair of handcuffs. Lou was screaming at me to get the restraints, which I knew would make a nice souvenir for any inmate—or worse, a tool to be used on us. Hooker and Lou picked up Nikos and proceeded to bring him down the stairs. Near the bottom, Nikos decided that he didn't want to walk anymore, so they all fell and went into the wall. I spread my arms out to keep the inmates from passing me and getting to the action. They were on the landing and I was just trying to keep them back until they got Nikos out of the building. "Let's get these fuckin' cops!" and "Fuckin' pigs!" were among the choice phrases hurdled my way. One chubby white kid got past me; I kicked his foot over to his other leg and he fell. I tried to joke about being careful because the floor was slippery.

Now the officers were dragging Nikos out of the building by the shoulders and the inmates were in a frenzy. Books were flying by the officers, and then I saw a pool ball. Oh my God! This could turn into a riot. Crash—glass breaking. The TV was just thrown on the floor. They were lighting the books on fire and pool balls were being thrown at the booth. I saw a couple of shattered windows. Great! Now the inmates had more weapons with the shards of glass. The convicts were yelling at Hooker and Lou to fight them. I know my coworkers would have beaten half of them, so why did it take so long to handcuff Nikos? The natives were going crazy.

They finally got Nikos' 340-pound frame out of the building. Just then I realized I was the only officer left. I tried to speak rationally to the cons, agreeing that the situation was handled poorly, but that Nikos was at fault. They seemed to be surrounding me. I spoke to a couple of the ones I knew, but I was still a cop in their eyes. I felt like taking my shirt off and saying, "I quit! Let's get those fucking cops!" half joking, half trying to ease the tension. But that would have been wrong and my safety was still at stake.

I looked into the booth; nobody was there. The booth door was not locked but jammed and I was trapped inside with no officers in sight. I was alone with one hundred and nineteen inmates. Although I enjoy a good fight as well as the next person, there was no way I could win a fight like this. And I didn't want this to end up like a gay gangbang movie. It was then that I realized that I needed some more diplomacy. I told them that Nikos could have avoided this whole thing by going into his room and speaking to the captain later. A couple of them agreed. Then I distracted them a little by making notice of the TV. Finally Pee-wee, a skinny older black inmate, whom I knew from the streets, told the cons that I was cool and that this situation would never have happened if I was in charge. Pee-wee commanded a fair amount of respect from the cons' point of view due to the amount of time he'd done; he was a well known drug dealer who had some second rate strippers working the streets for him.

I heard dogs barking. The inmates were running around lining up bars of soap and squirting baby oil on the floor near the booth. I guess they didn't want anyone else to come in. This was a small-scale riot, but they weren't really holding me as a hostage. Still, I couldn't reach the door due to the cons surrounding me, and now there appeared to be a lot of activity outside of the building. I was hoping that someone remembered I was still inside. No pepper spray or rubber bullets for me.

It seemed like an eternity passed until the door opened and I saw Deputy O'Malley. The inmates and the officers loved him. He gave everybody a break. If you screwed up, he would yell at you and that was it. No more. But on the same aspect, he would cut the cons the same break. He was the same guy all the time. He looked at me and said in his Joe Pesci voice, "Who's in charge here? I thought you knew better than this." I told him that I wasn't sure, but he'd find out the whole story in a few minutes from the cons. The inmates all went over to him like he was Santa Claus. The deputy spoke and listened for a good twenty-five minutes. When they'd all said their piece, the deputy had them go back to their rooms and some of the officers came in, taking out the few troublemakers without any further incidents. Then Deputy O'Malley told me to get a couple of inmate workers together and clean the block up. The place was back to normal by the end of my shift. You wouldn't have known that there was a mini-riot unless the walls could talk.

The next day Lou was transferred to the lowest security level, watching inmates play cards and watching TV. I wanted that job, but it was a tough transfer for a man with that much testosterone. A week later the deputy told me I would be working the medium "C" block. "You're a young buck. You should be in the main part of the jail: we could use a little young muscle there." More responsibility. Huh...only nineteen years and ten months to go until retirement.

All the blocks or housing units as they were called were designated with a security level and each security level had several blocks. Now, the medium "C" block was what I pictured prison to be like: cold, battleship gray steel bars and gates everywhere, rumbling with a metallic clink when opened or closed. There were two tiers or levels each about two hundred feet long and dimly lit with twenty-six cells on each side. The top tier had bars for cell doors and the bottom tier had a solid steel door with a small window about the size of a dictionary on edge. The control booth for medium "C" was positioned in between the two levels at the front of the block so that you could see door to the two corridors. The top tier inmates could still look down into the booth, while the bottom tier had to look up.

The noise factor on a cellblock is something that takes a long while to get used to. Everything echoes or is magnified. When sound bounces off the walls it has only one way to travel: towards the booth. And in this case, the booth wasn't clean either. Very rarely did someone actually take the time to clean or mop the place up. Coffee stains, dirty windows—and the toilets were like the Port Authority bathrooms on 42nd street of New York City. You didn't even really want to walk in there to take a quick leak. The only time it was embarrassing was when a female employee came in, whether a social worker or an officer. The booth was as far as social workers or other civilians could go. Most of the officers hung around in the booth and proceed to make their rounds ensuring that the inmates were somewhat honest. Actually, the only reason that most officers left the booth was to cover their own asses. Most of the time, the jail might not be quiet, but it was uneventful. Which was supposed to be a good thing, but it could get very boring, routine, or lull you into a false sense of security.

The officers who worked this block were older, seasoned officers, a sergeant and a lieutenant. They liked to sit around and discuss "the good old days."

"Remember when we kicked Marty down the stairs for throwing a turd on the booth window?" the barrel-chested Sergeant Percy inquired one morning as five of us sat in the booth together. "Yeah….and how about the tomato man?" Another officer chimed in. Everyone in the booth froze and looked at Charlie, the lieutenant, an older pot-bellied man, bald and just waiting for his last year or two to pass for retirement. We were all waiting for a radio transaction from the kitchen officer that the watered down oatmeal and half a grapefruit was ready to be served in the chow hall. They served oatmeal at least three mornings a week. The cons hated it, as did the staff. The oatmeal just never seemed to be right. It was usually very runny with lumps. I guess when you are feeding thirteen hundred people quality isn't at the top of your list. Anyways, Charlie was hesitant to tell the story and even Sergeant Percy seemed a little freaked out as well as the others. I must have been the only one who had not heard this story before.

The tomato man. Apparently this guy was semi-famous. He was a small town tomato farmer who was supposedly possessed. There was even a book published about him and he was on all kinds of talk shows. Even later on in my career, I told people about him. Quite a few people had never heard of him, and yet the semi-famous man was from our own area. I never read the book and was a little leery and maybe a tiny bit scared to read it.

Finally Charlie proceeded to tell the story. The others listened attentively as did I. But I could not help but wonder at these grown older veterans of a prison, some who had seen everything look like little kids listening to their dads' ghost stories around a campfire.

"We had in this block a man who was possessed," Lieutenant Charlie began. "When he became angry, his eyes would bleed, and a small cross would appear in the middle of his forehead. We had to move him out of the block and have him put in county lockup by himself because the inmate population was freaked out by him. There were always sounds coming out of his cell at night; when the staff looked in there, he was sound asleep and still they heard noises, distant groans and occasionally prayers. Lieutenant Gazzo was doing a wind one night and shined the flashlight on the tomato man; he was floating six inches off of his steel bunk. Other people have seen it, but they choose to not think about it.

"One day the man's wife came to visit him and Gazzo had to ask her about him. The wife told him that she feared for her husband. He was out mowing the hayfield on their farm when she yelled and waved her arms to signal that lunch was ready; when she turned he was in the bathroom shaving. She also said that when he shaved, the reflection in the mirror was sometimes laughing. Ten years later or so the man committed suicide. The poor prick." Charlie finished his story and the guys in my booth, who must have heard it, many, many times looked as though they had just heard it for the first. As for me, I was very skeptical, but part of me was scared. I was thinking that this guy was from only a few towns over and he had been in this prison cellblock, right where I was working.

***

As time went on the veterans showed me how to chase the inmates out for chow, the universal prison language for breakfast, lunch and supper. I also learned how to conduct counts, run canteen or commissary, do the paperwork, and supervise the cleaning of the living area, which was done by inmate workers, also called trustees or runners. The workers had a few benefits. They received cigarettes, got to stay out of their cells more often, and were given a little leniency if they violated any facility rule. There were workers in every block. They mopped the floors and painted, which the jail did frequently. As a matter of fact, the officers always joked that the hallways had been a lot bigger when they started. Besides, sometimes it was easier to cover up dirty walls and floors with paint than to clean them.

The state was funding a huge complex of new cellblocks for the jail—the mods, short for modular units. This complex was designed to hold three hundred prisoners, but at the end of my tenure, it was holding well over six hundred. The staff was always gossiping about who was getting transferred down to the mods, who was getting promoted and all the new hires. The jail was on a huge hiring spree. Anybody who knew a politician, a high ranking police or fire department official had a job if he or she so desired. The job was based on who you knew and promotions were given based on who you blew—or more accurately, by donations given. They always said that there were tests and qualifications to be met; but if there were, I missed them, too. I guess I was lucky, being hired and sent through the academy six months before the mods opened up. I also had a little seniority from being hired when I was.

That year the jail must have hired around one hundred and twenty-five officers. When you met a new hire, you always tried to find out where they were from and who they knew to get hired. Then the mods were opening up and staff started receiving their orders. The higher ranking people were notified first as they went down to the mods to try out the new area and be the first to notify their superiors of any glitches. I guess they wanted to justify being supervisors; if they showed their superiors that they were always finding things wrong, they were supposed to be good leaders.

One by one, the staff was sent down the mods. Days, weeks and then a month went by before a single inmate was sent down there for a real trial run. Most of the guys I was working with were sent, and with all these transfers came promotions. There were about twelve sergeant positions, six lieutenants and two captains. One of the new captains, Dumas, was a gym officer. Later he was nicknamed Dumbass—mostly behind his back. He was tall, a karate and diving instructor, and a pretty boy, at least in his mind, with his slicked back hair. But he was never a sergeant or a lieutenant. Apparently he was on the wrong side of the last election and the sheriff didn't want to promote him. But he gave enough money and did enough ass-kissing to keep his cushy gym officer job. The whole jail knew about him and his partner Mike Greenberg, running into the sheriff's office as soon as Smith was elected, giving an envelope with an undisclosed amount of cash and begging for forgiveness. They were both on the losing side of the former sheriff being voted out. They were known for yelling at the men and women holding signs for the soon-to-be elected Sheriff Smith. They tried to scare those officers and threatened them with terminations and suspensions for holding signs for incoming Sheriff Smith. But that election was years ago and way before my time at the jail. So since money makes the world go 'round, Greenberg kept his day shift as a lieutenant and became promoted when the mods opened up. Dumas kept his rankless gym job where he could work out, read the paper, or nap if he so desired. Dumas also was promoted when the new buildings were opened. It must have been a large envelope since he, too, was promoted—not to sergeant or lieutenant, but to captain. Gym officers did not have to wear uniforms; they pretty much made up their own schedule within their own department and only had to supervise the cons playing hoops, handball and lifting weights. The cons loved the gym. They rarely ever screwed around there, as they didn't want to lose that privilege. So the gym job was cushy, but very political. Or you might call it, very monetary.

My daily routine was becoming second nature. You ended up in a very mundane routine. The days turned into weeks and the weeks into months; and before you knew it, a year had passed. I would come in, take a count, make sure that the animals were alive, feed them and send them off to their programs. Then run the canteen, make sure that there were no love affairs going on and try to prevent any problems from escalating.

There were some days that I was in charge, when the sergeant was off and I answered to the lieutenant. One morning I had just finished up with the after breakfast count when one of the older Spanish leaders, Davey Ortiz, approached me and whispered to me that there was a problem with one kid who was half white and half Spanish. I asked Davey what the problem was and he said, "Wait here, I go get him." Ortiz was very muscular, short, about five foot five, and around fifty years old with enough tattoos to pass for a biker. *Sleeved* is the term bikers use when your arms are covered with tats. Davey was also a worker and the muscle for one of the dominant Spanish gangs. Whenever there was a problem with a punk inmate, Dave was the guy we could go to and there would be no paperwork and no questions from the inmate population; the issue would be resolved quickly and quietly. Of course, nothing is free. He would ask for one of his buddies to come out of his cell and help him clean, or we'd let someone use the phones when they were supposed to be shut off, or occasionally move one of his buddies up on the workers' waiting list.

Today I had another officer, Michael Anderson with me. Davey brought the kid out of the block and into the hallway behind the booth where we were out of view from the rest of the inmate population. Anderson said to the kid, "Aren't you O'Brien? You're the kid who diddled the old lady at the nursing home?" The kid didn't say anything. His look said it all for him. He shouldn't have been in this block to begin with, I thought. He molested an old lady in a nursing home where he worked; why was he in general population? Most of the sex offenders go into PC (protective custody.) PC also houses known rats, informants, and/or whistleblowers. And believe me, there are plenty of rats in prison. Later in my career, that term was replaced by "special needs" inmates. That was given to us by the politically correct—another acronym for PC. But the officers and inmates alike called them *skinners*. There were many other funny names for them: diaper swiper, booty bandit, and many others that escape my mind at this moment.

But this kid, O'Brien, shouldn't have been here. Maybe he signed off on a release form that keeps relieves the staff from being responsible if the inevitable happens. Maybe he had a lot of drugs and bought his protection from a gang. The prison population has a different caste system. Skinners or sex offenders are the worst. If a con ever gets the chance to beat one up or stab him, they do. And they are looked on as a hero after taking out a skinner. On the other hand, if a con is a cop killer or known to assault staff, the rest of the population places him on a pedestal. *Instant street credit* is what it's called today.

Davey said, "Go ahead and tell Mike what happened." Dave either had a soft spot for this kid or the kid was out of drugs and favors. Probably his protection money had run out. The kid just stood there and shrugged his shoulders. So I said, "I will help you. Do you need to check in and go to protective custody?" With that, he tried to push by me and head back for the housing unit. I grabbed him by the shirt, threw him up against the booth wall and said, "Look O'Brien, I'm hear to help ya. Tell me what the fuck is going on!" O'Brien took a half assed swing at me, missing my head by a good six inches. It was more of a cry for help than anything else. I shoved him up against the wall with one hand at the base of his neck. He was in tears now.

Davey said, "Look, Mike is cool; he's trying to help you. Tell him." The little punk took another swing at me; I partially blocked it and the rest of it hit my shoulder.

Officer Anderson said, "That's it, motherfucker! You're outta here!" I spun the kid to the ground with ease as Anderson pulled O'Brien's legs out from under him. Davey stayed put. I heard him reaffirm me, "You tried COs(correctional officers); you tried, Mike." He kept repeating it as if he was on my team. Maybe he was. Maybe he just hated O'Brien.

I grabbed O'Brien's wrists forcefully and placed the handcuffs on him. As we were hoisting him to his feet he shrieked out like a little girl, "Ya wanna know? Ya wanna know? Ya wanna know what they did? They shoved a toothbrush up my ass! They shoved a fuckin' toothbrush up my ass! Do you like that? Do you like that, fuckhead?"

Anderson manhandled the kid down to see the nurse, then off to protective custody where he belonged. I felt angry with the kid for having swung at me when I was trying to help him. But he was a low-life skinner, so maybe he should have gotten more of a manhandling. Then again, this was jail where inmates are supposedly innocent until proven guilty. But they are in here for a reason: probable cause from a jury or judge. And now I had to write reports. Damn! Probably an hour's worth of reports for three minutes of talking and thirty seconds of action.

When I radioed Officer Anderson, I said, "Where's Anal B going?" I heard a chuckle on the receiving end of the radio and then he said maxi-block then protective custody. O'Brien was now known as Anal B, the toothbrush tester. That became more popular than his molesting a lady in a nursing home. Neither one was a good thing to be remembered by.

More and more weeks passed. During some absolutely nothing would happen, while other times it would be hectic and the phone in the booth would be ringing at least twice a minute. Social workers needed to see Johnny so-and-so. The infirmary had to check Jose's tuberculosis test. The special services unit always needed to question someone about something and they thought that they were too good to come to the block and escort the cons. The school teachers had to call the cons down just to hand them homework and the substance abuse workers believed that the inmates really wanted help. Maybe a few did, but most inmates were only in those programs for the good time credits. The recidivism rate was in the eighty percent range when I started. You'll hear that most crimes are drug related, and they are. Drug related crimes could amount to just about anything from O'Brien molesting the old lady in the nursing home because he was high, to breaking and entering someone's house to get a VCR to sell to pay for drugs, to killing someone because they have cocaine on them or it's a territory issue. It's sad that these crimes are committed, but they tie almost every one of them to drugs. It seems like an excuse for them. Cons can use the word *drugs* to justify any crime they commit. We've all done drugs in high school and college, or at least prescription drugs at one time or another. That shouldn't give anyone a justification for why they did such and such. But that's for the experts, judges and lawyers to hash out. That isn't something a jail guard, or CO to be examining.

***

One fine Tuesday morning, Sergeant Percy was running canteen and I was assigned to the lower tier to make sure that no one sneaked over to see what the inmates on the upper tier were buying. Canteen is one of the better privileges that the inmates have. It's a little store where the inmates hand in a slip and check off what they want for the week. The items are priced cheaply and they can spend sixty bucks a week. The inmates buy items such as cookies, chips, candy bars, hygiene products, and a small radio and, yes, TVs. It seems like a good deal for them. Sometimes the bigger inmates or gangs take tribute from other weaker inmates. The rule of the jungle, I guess. We try to prevent as much thievery or extortion as possible, but that is just the nature of the beast in the big house.

One of the big rackets in jail is two-for-ones. Let's say that you want a candy bar, so you borrow one from some big con who has a lot of snacks, a "store." On canteen day, you have to give him back two. That's the vig or interest. If you do not pay it back, you get beat up by his sponsors. In all actuality, the big guys or gang leaders may own the "store," but they usually have a puppet or punk hold it for them so the officers can't accuse them of running an inside business. Some cons do a lot of two-for-ones just before canteen, and then purposely get into trouble so they get moved out of the block and don't have to pay back anything. I guess you could equate that with going bankrupt on purpose by running up your credit cards.

So here I was on the bottom tier all by myself. The lighting was a dim yellowish, kind of like what you'd expect to find on a submarine on low power. I did see Officer Doucette sitting at the end of the block on a plastic dayroom chair looking down my hallway. A very well built, Spanish bodybuilder type walked past me from the upper tier and headed down the lower tier. I called after him, "Hey, you gotta go back to your tier." The inmate looked at me and made a face as if to say, "Who does this bitch think he's talking to?"

I ignored his attitude and said, "Go, get outta here." He put his back up against the wall diagonally across from me with one leg up and his huge biceps flexed and crossed, looked at me and went, "Pppppffff." I was stunned. What did he think I was, a bitch? I was trying to be decent and he was disrespecting me in front of all cons.

The inmates were watching me to see how I'd react. This would set quite a tone for the rest of my career. I'm no stranger to fights or brawls, but I have to be professional in uniform. I walked over to the con and firmly said, "Get out of here or you will get d-boarded!" A d-board stands for disciplinary board. There are three people that hear the inmate's charges/case: a social worker, a classification person, and an officer not from that area. They determine if you are innocent or guilty and the amount of time in the segregation unit. Inmates can also lose privileges like visits, gym, and canteen time and have to stay in their cells except for showers for anywhere from three to thirty days. Sometimes it can be even longer depending on the severity of the infraction.

As soon as I said *d-boarded*, he pushed me across the hallway and pinned me against the wall. I look down the hallway and Officer Doucette looked at us, got up and left with his chair. I couldn't believe my eyes. What a friggin' coward! The inmate had his hands under my armpits holding my triceps out to the side so I couldn't grab him. He also had one knee against my inner thigh. I tried to out-muscle him, but I was caught off guard fast, and this guy was strong. No doubt he had done this before. I would have kneed him in the balls, but his knee was pressing my inner thigh out and I would have fallen. And to be honest, I was worried about getting kneed in the groin myself. I was hoping for and at the same time not wanting help to come around the corner and see me wrapped up like this.

Then I remembered something my dad told me. If you are ever in a full Nelson just go limp and let your legs go out from under you. The attacker now has to decide if he wants to expend a lot of energy and hold you up, let you go, or fall with you. I decided to drop with one little variation; I would clench my arms into my side and keep his hands immobile. It seemed like we fell in slow motion. I landed fairly hard with this muscular guy on top of me. He seemed confused, so I wrapped my legs around his stomach and squeezed. I just wanted to wrap him up. Sergeant Percy must have heard the commotion because he came around the corner. His three hundred and twenty pound body dove onto the back of my attacker who was partially on top of me. Percy's impact was tremendous. The weight was crushing me. But for some reason the body builder-attacker was no longer aggressing, the will to fight sapped out of him. His grip under my arms was now feeble and Percy had him handcuffed in no time. When the sergeant picked the guy up, he pulled me most of the way up off the floor as my legs were still wrapped around the con's waist. Then Percy brought my attacker down to the maximum security area. I never told anyone about Doucette, but Percy questioned him and Doucette was transferred the next day to the famed third shift. Good! No room for his kind in here.

A short time later Sergeant Percy was transferred to the segregation block. I learned a lot from him; he was one of those people who knew everything about his job. He knew all the cons, their games, and the institution, and he lived for the job. He remained in the segregation block for years—way too many years for anyone. It took a toll on him. His supervisor friends kept him in there, never realizing what they were doing to him. They were just glad that Percy made them look good. He had over twelve years in the jail and never left his seg. unit. He thought that if he left, it would not run without him. He didn't even eat in the chow hall. He stayed there all day long. The only reason he ever left was to go home. When you spoke to him, you'd think that he would have liked to stay around the clock and work there. He absolutely loved his job. He liked it better there than he did at home.

His friend and newly promoted captain, Greenberg, left him in there all the time without giving him a break or recognizing that he was starting to lose it. Greenberg just wanted to look good to the administration. Then one day there was some shitbag with a shank. A shank is a makeshift knife made from a disposable razor or toothbrush filed down. There are many, many ways to create shanks. So this shitbag is looking out his little window in the segregation block and was making threats towards staff. Percy tried to reason with him, to no avail. I would have thought that Percy would have opened up the cell door and bitch slapped the kid, taken the shank and proceeded with his routine. But Percy called the tactical team. The institution was trying to keep up with the times by implementing new safety procedures to avoid officers getting hurt. These officers were some of the biggest ass-kissers, but they were suited up with pads, helmets and all kinds of protective gear. It was a fairly good system to use, but when you called them in, they were in charge, not you. They were apprised of the situation and they quelled the problem.

Another good part is that they had to write the reports. So Percy gave the team leader the run down and he stepped into the booth. The tactical team is dressed in black, with helmets and a shield, and they can look quite intimidating. The inmates usually all start yelling and kicking the cell doors when they enter. They know that someone is getting a beating if they try to fight these guys. The last man in the tactical team films the incident. They proceeded up to shitbag's cell and ordered him three times to come to the door to be handcuffed. This gives the inmate one last chance to do the right thing. Most of the time the convicts turn around and "cuffs-up." This kid didn't. The team leader sprayed three short blasts of pepper spray, but the kid blocked it with his mattress and was prepared for a battle. He had poured baby oil all over the front of the cell where the tactical team was coming in, he had covered his mouth and nose with ripped sheets, and he had a shank. When the last order was refused, the tactical team rushed in the cell and slipped on the oiled floor. One of them still managed to bring the kid down to the floor. Percy, seeing the action from the booth, went out to help his comrades—which proved to be his big mistake according to the state attorney's office. Percy saw the team of five wrestling with the kid and thought that one of them was going to get stabbed. So he kicked the kid in the arm four or five times and once on the side of the head. The camera caught everything. Percy was suspended with pay pending an investigation.

Now, this man who thought he was doing the right thing was brought into court and charged with assault and battery. The district attorney told Percy that he could resign temporarily from the jail and be on probation for a month or two. Well, that was just too much for Percy. He lived for his job and did it well. But losing his career for helping out his fellow officers was just too much for him. He fought the system. The DA kept telling him just to resign and it would all go away. But in a month Sergeant Percy was sentenced to three months in a correctional facility and lost his job. The poor bastard. He went to a facility in the western part of the state designed for cops, politicians and COs. He did not keep in touch with anybody after that. He eventually lost everything. And Greenberg never even called Percy. He never acknowledged Percy again.

CHAPTER TWO
TROUBLE BREWS

I had been there a little over a year and I had pretty much control of the block. It was all routine. You knew what day it was by what activities there were and what was for chow. Having a rotating schedule and mostly weekdays off, you really had to think about what day it was. One fine Thursday morning, the EMT approached me and a couple guys I was working with and asked if he could have an inmate beaten up. It seems that this EMT's estranged wife was banging this drug dealer from a small town. Now I knew that this drug dealer and the estranged wife probably need a good beating, but I couldn't risk my job and I really didn't want any part of it. Especially the way the courts can be, it just wasn't worth the risk.

The other two officers walked out with the EMT. I thought they were just telling him to chill out and let it go, that she wasn't worth it, leaving him for a drug dealer. Well, the following Tuesday I was in the booth running canteen and I saw this inmate named Angel wave to me on his way by my booth and shake hands with Davey on the bottom tier. Wait a minute! Angel was in another block. What the hell was he doing here? I called for him on the PA system and he came back by me a couple of minutes later with a pair of sneakers and headphones on. Angel said, "Thanks, Mike, you're the best! Don't ever change." I kind of just shook my head, thinking someone owed him something for gambling or protection. But

Davey was there and nothing would get by Davey without his consent. And I had an officer there at the beginning of the tier sitting on a chair just keeping the peace. Hmmm…Maybe it wasn't anything after all.

A few minutes later after I had forgotten all about the incident, I saw and started to smell smoke about halfway down the tier and getting very thick. I looked down at Officer Rodas who was just gazing down the hallway, oblivious. Rodas was a temporary officer. It was common practice for the sheriff's department to hire people, give them forty hours of classroom training and let them work at the jail until they went to the academy, which could be years away. Rodas was a policeman in a ritzy town, but his job must have been a political favor as he had no clue what was going on. I banged on the thick semi-bullet proof glass booth window to get his attention. Finally he looked up at me like a deer in headlights and I pointed down towards the smoke. Now he looked at me like I was crazy, so I radioed him to come into the booth to get a fire extinguisher and head down there. The radio may have as well been translating in Greek. I waved him into the booth.

Now the inmates were walking off the tier and into the hallway next to the canteen. One inmate named Bird ran by Rodas, clipping his torso. Rodas paid no attention to him and came into the booth. Getting a fire extinguisher ready, I yelled, "What the fuck? Don't you see or smell the smoke?"

He replied, "Oh, no, I didn't. I was looking at something else." I said on my way out of the booth, "Something else? You can't see anything down the tier!" I told him to man the booth and pay attention to the radio; then I raced around the corner and down the lower tier. Thick billowing smoke was pouring out of the sides and bottom of a solid steel cell door. It was getting worse and into my lungs. My God, what could be burning in a concrete prison? I arrived at the cell and looked in. It was totally black, smoke still is pouring out. I felt the door, and man, it was hot. I shouted out, "Who lives in here?" Nobody seemed to know. So I called for assistance on the radio and for those responding to bring Scott air packs and fire extinguishers with them. I never liked to call for help, but this was really getting out of control and lives could be in danger.

A few officers arrived and they asked what they could do. I asked them to clear the tier of inmates and bring them into the gym so they would not suffer smoke inhalation problems. I was coughing and the smoke was getting to me. I sprayed the door and slowly opened it while blasting the fire extinguisher continuously to avoid the flames shooting out at me. The wall of smoke made me drop to my knees and start gagging. I was praying that no one was in that cell. I was on the ground covered in water and soot spraying H2O like a madman. I should have had a Scott air pack on, but I felt time was crucial if someone was in there.

I radioed for the fire fans and the back exits to be opened once the entire block was evacuated and accounted for. I could start to see through my watery eyes that there was no one in the cell and that the mattress was burning with a dull flame but with enough smoke to fill a large warehouse. Other officers were spraying the walls and mattress with the fire extinguishers as the walls were literally cooking and the paint from numerous coats had melted and assisted in the billowing smoke. They had opened up the back corridor that led into the yard to relieve some of the smoke-filled tier. That burnt smell was embedded in my nose and throat. I dragged the culprit, a mattress out of the cell down the corridor and into the yard. It was totally soaked, but it was still smoldering. The hallway looked like a burnt-out brick building with soot and water on the floor. Some of the inmates had to be treated for smoke inhalation. I was told by another officer that I looked like something out of the movie *Backdraft*. When I was in the yard, I half vomited and half gagged. Nothing but thick black residue was coming out of any hole in my head. I can see how people get hurt or how fatalities occur in fires now. And this was a concrete prison. Imagine if it had been made of wood and more mattresses were involved!

I decided to go get a glass of water, as I was still gagging, when Deputy O'Malley showed up. I had my chest out, although gagging, my head high, expecting a huge "atta-boy, Mikie!" But what I got was quite different.

"Where the heck you going now?" was his first response.

"What? I just put out the fire! I need a drink. Look at me!" I protested.

"Well, hurry up. You've got a lot of work to do."

I knew it was my job, but a little acknowledgement would have been nice. When I returned, the deputy had me come into his office. "Hey, good job, Mikie," he congratulated me in his Joe Pesci voice. "I mean it. You did a great job, so why don't you go to the infirmary, get checked out then go home and relax. We got enough guys to clean this place up."

I really didn't want to go home; then the guys would think that I was sick, hurt or a pussy. But after talking to a few of them, they were praising me and said that I should take the whole week off. So I went, still spitting out black soot from my nose and throat that evening. The next day at work, I had to write a few reports and when I was almost finished, the deputy called the booth looking for me. "Get over to my office." I figured I was going to get a little more praise, but deep down I thought that would have been overkill.

This man was in charge of seventy-five officers, two hundred fifty cons and made eighty five thousand dollars a year and his office was the size of a closet. I walked in and he was finishing up a phone conversation. "Yeah, I'm dealing with him right now. I'll see you in a few, Gaff." Gaff was short for Deputy Gaffney, the number three man at the jail. He could be a real ass most of the time without even thinking about it.

O'Malley looked up at me and said, "What the fuck did you do to that Birdie kid?"

"I didn't do anything sir." I was very confused. But now I remembered him running by Officer Rodas and how the EMT had asked to have him beaten up for sleeping with his estranged wife. *Oh boy*, I thought to myself. *This could get ugly.* But I had told everyone that I wasn't going to get involved at all, and here I was apparently awaiting punishment for that fiasco.

"Well, Birdie came into my office last night with lumps on his head, missing property and his cell was set on fire! Do you think all that is a coincidence? Are you gonna tell me that you guys had nothing to do with that?" O'Malley asked.

"Deputy, I didn't do anything to that kid and I didn't have anything planned," I protested.

"Well, this kid called his lawyer and is now demanding that we do something about it, and the ol' man is pissed." He was referring to Sheriff Smith. "We gotta go out front and see Gaff. You tell him that I chewed your ass off for an hour and everything will be all right. For crying out loud, Mike, this kid was banging the EMT's wife and now this shit happens to him!"

My only response was, "I didn't do anything, sir. But I will go out front to Gaff's office and pay the piper." I figured this was going to be a firing or long-term suspension. Any way I looked at it, I knew after this that I'd never get promoted or land a decent job. And that was even the better scenario in my mind. I know deep down that my two coworkers had Angel do whatever it was to the kid, but I would never rat. Being a rat was just as bad as being a skinner. So I made up my mind that I would just sit there and say *yes sir* or *no sir.* That was it.

On the way to Gaff's office, Deputy O'Malley had his hand on my shoulder for a minute or two just reassuring me that everything would be okay. The walk took forever even though it was only a football field's distance away. O'Malley stopped me at the outer entrance of Deputy Gaffney's office, and I noticed his beautiful secretary. She was half white and half black, a gorgeous lady with great curves that took my mind off of the situation for a couple of minutes. She was looking at me to say something, but I didn't know if I should start flirting or even talking to the number three man's secretary. I mean, she could have been dating him or whatever in this political environment.

She looked at me and whispered, "Hi, Mike," with a knowing smile. She appeared to be on hold from a phone call to someone. My mind was wandering now and I had forgotten, even if just for a minute, that I was in some sort of trouble. Then I heard Deputy O'Malley and Deputy Gaffney talking; Gaff said in a hurry, "Let's get this done." They walked by me as if they were looking for something and then called out for two other deputies to come with them. Then Deputy Gaffney summoned me into the locker room. I thought it would be funny if they tried to stuff me in a locker. But I kept my mouth shut. Gaff brought me to the far end of the three lane locker room and made me sit on a long pine bench that ran along the front of the lockers. The locker room smelled like dirty socks. But I guess that's what it's supposed to smell like. O'Malley stayed at the locker room entrance as if to keep anyone else out who might happen to venture in. I had one deputy's hand on each of my shoulders as if to let me know not to get up. AT first I thought that these guys were going to try and fight me.

Gaff pointed his finger into my chest and said, "You think you're a fuckin' tough guy?

"No sir," I curtly responded.

"You think you're a fuckin' tough guy? Do you know how much bullshit you're bringing down on us? My secretary has been on the phone with Bird's lawyer and now we have to work out a deal with him and the court to release this scumbag. The next time you think that you are a tough guy, you come out here and see me. You got it?"

"Yes sir." That's all I was going to say. I could have told them that they were a bunch of pencil-pushing pansies, but that would probably land me in trouble and now I was done. The incident was behind me and there was no need to bring back the heat. Gaff reached out his hand to shake mine and he said, "No hard feelings? O'Malley said that you were one of the best here."

"No hard feelings, and thank you, sir." Wow…he was just going through the motions with me. Just a little brow beating and then a handshake with a nice compliment. That was okay by me. Back to the block. That had really thrown me for a loop. Maybe I would eventually get a decent job or even a promotion someday.

***

A few more months passed in the medium "C" block. Just mundane routine after mundane routine. One day I overheard something interesting from a friend of mine, RT, an officer who was more into Harleys and women than he was into the job. I related well with RT, but I was still semi-new so I was a little more into my job at the time. RT was a pretty cool dude. Not much seemed to bother him if he could take a ride to the beach and smoke a joint now and then.

He was having some words with an inmate named Brian Grenier. I was familiar with Brian, as he had escaped from the jail by grappling onto the roof from a curiously placed dumpster and the corner of the building. The jail is only two stories high and there was only a little old fashioned barbed wire on the roof. Anyone not on crutches could escape once on the roof unless someone happened to see them from the parking lot. Brian was not alone in his great escape. He was actually talked into escaping by his cellmate, who was having problems with his girlfriend. Brian was caught at his parents' house the day the same day that he escaped. Not too bright to go right back home when you escape from jail. The other kid at least made it a little longer after going to his girlfriend's workplace. He slapped her a few times and called her a cheating whore in front of some terrified accountants. I guess he was just trying to send a message to anyone who was having sex with her. Then he went to a lake, called the police on himself and was arrested again after a leisurely swim. He ended up with six months for the escape and six months for slapping his girlfriend. Needless to say, the jail spent a cool million plus installing Constantia wire around the roof and corners of the buildings.

I walked over to listen in on RT and Brian arguing and Brian was saying that all cops are pussies. Calling us cops is slang. Most of the time we are called COs. RT was retorting that inmates are pussies as they will start a fight and if they lose, they are right on the phone to their lawyers or to one of the many inmates/ rights groups. Brian lost it; he knew RT was right but yelled out, "I'll fight anyone of you fuckin' punk cops right now!"

RT would have given Brian a good fight, but he was probably still buzzed from the morning's drive in. *Don't look at me RT, don't look at me*, I thought. Fuck, he looked right at me and said, "Mike would kiiiillll you in a fight."

Brian responded, "I'd fuck him up in less than a minute." He seemed very confident.

RT said, "Dude, go fuck him up, Mike."

I really didn't want any part of this. I had just gotten called out front a few months ago, and I didn't want to go again—especially not for fighting a planned fight. I explained to RT that I didn't want to get into trouble. RT was explaining to me that no one would find out, but there were a few cons following us down the lower tier. RT was actually guiding Brian and me to Brian's cell. I explained again that I did not want any part of this. Brian responded, "See, I told you that these guys are pussies."

Now what was I supposed to do? Walk away and let the cons think that they'd won this one? Fight Brian and kick his ass, risking punishment from the administration, or possibly lose the fight and all respect in the block? It seemed like a lose-lose situation. I wanted to be professional, but I was in the jungle. How could I save face in this situation?

Brian stepped into his cell and said, "Let's go, pussy!" Now I really couldn't walk away. I took off my brown polyester uniform shirt off and handed it to RT. Then I walked into Brian's solid door cell with the dictionary-sized window that RT was covering with his arms like he was watching a peep show. I honestly had no idea what to expect. Was Brian kidding? Would he back down? Would I get in big trouble?

Still hoping to avoid a fight I turned to Brian, asking, "Why are you calling—ooouuuufff!" Brian hit me with a left hook on the upper part of my right forehead. My adrenaline was skyrocketing and now I had tunnel vision. "You motherfucker!" I was pumped. I grabbed Brian's shirt near his abdomen and by his left shoulder and threw him against the wall above his bunk. Then, without letting my grip go, I threw him into the metal stationary desk and then tossed him onto the bunk, where I knelt on top of him and gave him two quick lefts to the jaw. Nothing earth shattering, but enough to take the fighting spirit and will out of my loudmouth convict. I put my right hand around his neck and squeezed. "You want any more, bitch? Anything to say, bitch?"

Brian could not answer me, but he shook his head from side to side a little. I asked him if he was okay and if he needed to see the nurse. He stated that he was fine. "Just give me a pack of smokes, Mike, and we'll forget about this."

I said, "Fuck you and all your pussy convict friends."

RT was praising me like I was his hero. "Dude, you are one of the toughest dudes I've ever seen. You manhandled him like a sack of dirt." I was just happy it was over and there were only a few cons around. Maybe, just maybe this would be kept quiet. I wanted to go up in the ranks. I guess I was lucky; I never heard another peep about that from anyone.

One weekend I heard a call over the radio in the maximum security block (maxi) that an inmate had wrapped himself up in toilet paper and lit himself on fire. It was Nikos, the large hairy Greek who started the near riot over a year ago. I walked down to maxi just to see what was going on, but the smell of all that burnt thick black hair was so bad that I just couldn't go in there. Phew...that smell is horrendous. If you've ever smelled burnt hair, you know what I'm talking about. I decided to stay out. Besides, the maxi officers didn't like any outside help from other areas unless they absolutely needed it. *Poor Nikos*, I couldn't help thinking, *the giant just doesn't want to stay out of trouble.*

***

One day while punching in for work, I noticed a posting for four sergeant positions. It stated that you only needed to have been on the job for one year. I wondered why they would do that. It seems like you'd want at least five years under your belt just for experience's sake.

Well, needless to say, I applied. There was a formal interview with two deputies and a captain who asked me a multitude of questions. The story around camp was that it didn't matter how well you did or didn't do. It was going to go to the highest bidder. They said that the sheriff always knew whom he was going to promote even before the listings were posted. I guess I was naive to all this political crap. I was told when I first started that job performance, military; college and time in were the factors. Not how much you donated. I studied the policies and tried to memorize what key went to what door, but there were over five hundred keys in that place!

Well, the interview came and went. It was a little nerve-wracking waiting outside the conference room door waiting for my name to be called to come in, but once inside, the atmosphere was semi-formal. They told me to relax and just try to answer the questions, all of which were relatively easy. I did fairly well and answered all but one question correctly. We all shook hands and I left the room thanking them all for not giving me trick questions.

Then it was just a matter of waiting. One day, after eating till my belly was full, I came out of the staff dining hall and saw a captain, my lieutenant, another lieutenant, and one officer corner this really grubby looking kid. The kid was a kitchen worker and a devil worshipper to boot. He had a straggly goatee, cuts all up and down his arms due to his religion, and greasy long hair. I walked over to see what was going on and if anyone needed my assistance. I heard my captain firmly state to the grubby con, "You're going to protective custody for your own protection and will be getting a d-board for spitting into the staff food."

Oh…why did I have to hear that? You always suspect it, but never expect it. There were many inmates complaining and actually refusing to serve the food because of this kid repeatedly spitting in the chop suey. I felt like sticking my finger down my throat and hurling, but tried to be cool. I'd just had two heaping bowls of the stuff. Most people don't like prison food, but I didn't mind, having been in the military. It was a nice perk for us and it was all you could eat. That's probably why you see quite a few "husky" prison guards.

Now I didn't feel so well. But I know it was all in my mind. I guess the state's reasoning is that it saves a few bucks to have the convicts make the food under one or two staff members' supervision. The problem with that is that only one or two kitchen cops are keeping an eye on that large of an operation. Feeding thirteen to fourteen hundred people is no small task. Do you really think all the kitchen workers wash their hands? If they murder, rape, steal, or whatever else they do, are they really going to be sanitary with the food? Anyways, it was always in the back of my mind, but I tried not to think about it. And there were very few incidents of people getting sick from the food.

"You guys ain't that bad to take me to PC!" the dirty devil worshipper bellowed back to Lieutenant Charlie.

Charlie gave the kid three more commands.

"Fuck you! You clowns ain't bad enough to bring me to the movies!" the grubby, stupid, little shit yelled. The staff moved in and kind of semi-cornered him. The sergeant grabbed the punk's arm and I came in from his right shoulder and blind-sided him. I put the kid in a headlock and threw him to the ground with me on top of him. I figured that I would just keep the dirty punk on the ground until my guys hand cuffed him. It was taking a few more seconds than it should have to cuff this creature. To my amazement, the kid kicked Charlie in the stomach and he went backwards, landing on his tailbone. The lieutenant was in a little pain, and the older veteran lieutenant whom I had never seen before tripped over the kid's flailing legs and went into the wall. At that point another officer came around the corner and dove in; it was usually customary to help out, get a few licks in and not have to write reports. But the officer and the other officer who was there from the start looked like neither one had ever put handcuffs on a struggling inmate before.

The sergeant, Dave Callahan, however, was a scrapper and quite a madman. Dave was busy jumping up and down on the punk's torso; then he leaned over and told me to move my arm. I rolled over to the middle of the kid's back with my right hand on his head. Dave wound up and kicked the devil worshipper's head like he was punting a fifty-yard field goal. Well the kid stopped moving and was handcuffed. I was just hoping that he was still alive. His groans were the only sign of life. Now I felt bad for the kid. Just a little bit.

Dave said that he would bring him to maxi. He picked him up and used him like a pinball game along the corridor. "I guess we're not tough enough, huh?" Dave said sarcastically to the kid. You could only imagine how many kids' heads were bounced around like pin balls by the madman. I have to admit it, though: Dave was respected and feared. He never hid behind his badge as so many officers do, using it as a shield. When you crossed him, he would get you. Whether it was spraying you with pepper spray or just plain old kicking your ass, he would get it done. That's why he was the maxi-sergeant. He was quite a cowboy.

Now I wanted to become a sergeant, too. Maybe not quite as wild as Dave, but I did like some of his traits. Having the inner control of the prison. Not wearing his badge on your sleeve. That seemed cool.

So I was heading over to the deputy's office with Lieutenant Charlie, and O'Malley said, "Well, I think we're losing Mikie here. I heard his name being mentioned out front."

I said, "No way! You heard my name out front, sir?"

,"Yup. I hate to lose you kiddo."

My head was getting swollen and I could not contain my smile. My boss said that I was getting promoted. I smiled like a drunk at a pretty lady. Everybody in the office and surrounding areas shook my hand and gave me the customary compliments. But there was no formal announcement from the front office.

A month had passed by and I heard nothing. Having been extremely giddy at first, I slowly began to wonder if they had changed their minds. Was the Birdie incident a factor? Was my short length in service a factor? Was I blamed for the near riot? But no one else was called out to the sheriff's office. Another week passed by and I was told to go out front to the sheriff's office. I wasn't exactly clean-shaven that day, so I grabbed one of our indigent packets for the cons. These packets have soap, shampoo, a razor, toothbrush, toothpaste and a comb in them. We give them to cons that don't have enough money on their books to buy them in canteen, or when we feel like doing them a favor. They were handy to have in cases like this.

My coworkers joked with me and asked me if I'd brought my checkbook. Funny thing, I never donated money to the sheriff, and I said so. Laughs erupted from my coworkers in the booth. "Bullshit, Mike," RT calmly stated. I knew they'd never believe me; they already had their minds made up. They were like a pack of sharks. No need to let them smell any more blood.

When I got out to the lobby, I saw three other guys, two of whom were with me in my academy class. I guess the sheriff wanted some new blood in the ranks. The other guy was known as "Little Hitler." We went into the sheriff's office, which was decorated like the oval office with multitudes of plaques, awards, flags and pictures of Sheriff Smith and other prominent politicians. The warden was standing next to the sheriff. He was like your principal in elementary school—he just had an air about him that was scary. The sheriff, however, was a nice man, just a politician, or at least that was the feeling I had of him. He was pleasant and the warden was his muscle. I guess you can't be the bad guy and still get voted in. When you are a politician and need votes and funding through the state, it pays to have someone else do your dirty work for you. That's where Warden Friese's job and lack of people skills came into play.

There were three medium sized chairs and since I was the last one in I stood. I enjoyed being in the back and standing a few inches taller than Warden Friese. The sheriff was a great big man. He was probably six foot three and around three hundred and twenty five pounds. All the cookouts at his farm on the jail grounds and free food supplied by the state or some person looking to kiss his ass would bring high quality and quantity food to his farmhouse at night. The sheriff was also entitled to free housing on the property, about a third of a mile down in a little valley with barns, livestock and fields of hay and vegetables. It was a nice little perk for someone making a hundred and ten thousand a year plus a brand new loaded Ford Expedition, company credit cards, expense accounts, free gas, and "donations" from the public as well as from cutthroats who would sell out their family and friends to get in good graces with the powerful politician.

The sheriff greeted each one of us as we walked in and asked how we were doing and the general niceties. Then he walked behind his huge oak desk with the US and state flag on it and sat in his oversized black leather chair. He said with an air of comfort, "Boys, we have concluded our interviews, read your evaluations and deemed that you men would make fine leaders."

Warden Friese chimed in," Do you know what we expect of you?"

We all looked at each other and started to just nod and mumble yes sir. Friese continued, "We expect you to do your job. If a fellow employee smells of booze, you send him home. If a subordinate of yours has a problem, write it down and turn it in. You are our eyes and ears. We don't care who you know or how you got here, we just want you to run a tight ship and keep a paper trail. Do you have any questions?"

We replied," No sir."

"Can you men handle that?" he asked.

"Yes sir," was our sheepish reply.

Then the sheriff stood up, extended his hand across the desk and shook each of our hands. "We'll be in touch with you boys."

When we all exited the office I was still a little confused. The sheriff hadn't exactly said that we had been promoted or pinned a badge on us, as I had expected. What was I going to tell the guys or my boss? What was going on? Were they waiting for gratuity?

I saw Deputy Gaffney in the hallway and, since I was had just been in the sheriff's office, I figured he couldn't give me too much shit if I inquired about my status.

"Excuse me, Deputy?"

"What's up, Mike?"

"Sir, I was just in the sheriff's office and he didn't exactly tell me that I was going to be a sergeant."

"Mike, how many officers went in with you?"

"Four of us sir."

"How many sergeant positions are there?"

"Four, Deputy."

"Well then, you do the math and figure it out."

With that, he shook my hand and said congratulations. I went back to the block and was bombarded with questions from my buddies. "Did you get it? Did the check clear? Did you swallow? How long were you under his desk?" One of them even took a tissue, wiped my chin and said, "You spilled a little." That got quite a roar of laughter from the five or six guys belittling me. These were the likes of any group of guys that have been together in tough spots before, and that was certainly us.

***

I went back to work. Another mundane week passed, and then another, and then it was a month. My giddiness was replaced with thoughts that they had decided not to promote anyone. I was seriously wondering if that was the sheriff's way of passively luring officers into giving donations to his campaign fund or slipping cash into an envelope and dropping it off on his desk.

The officers who worked out front in control number one were all too glad to let the rest of us know who went into "the old man's office." Sometimes they embellished the events, saying that they saw an officer pull out his or her wallet as they entered the office. Control Number One controlled who came in or out of the facility. There was a metal detector like the ones at the airports, but not as sophisticated. They also worked a vehicle trap on the back side of the control booth that was used for the transportation department. Every weekday, between eighty and one hundred and twenty inmates went to court or on hospital trips. Sometimes the hospital trips were scheduled, sometimes they were not. The ones that weren't could be very serious. The medical staff at the jail did a wonderful job patching up cons and diagnosing their many ailments, but they didn't always have the most up to date equipment. They were good with helping staff, too. After all, you fight, get attacked, have existing health issues, and it's a comfort knowing that emergency medical help is only a radio transaction away.

CHAPTER THREE
A SERGEANT IS BORN

One evening at home watching "Seinfeld" or "Raymond," I receive a phone call from Pam Antonucci. Pam was a lady in her fifties. She was the secretary for minimum security. Most of the staff, men and women alike, raved about Pam. Not only was she easy on the eyes, she pretty much ran the building, not the captain or the deputy—although she never would cross the deputy. The deputy we'll get to in a bit. But the captain, Captain Heinz, also known as "the Hammer," was an older man with the gout. He was a hard drinker. You know the type. Every night at least a case of beer would pass down his esophagus. We all know people like that. The next day he would come into work still reeking of booze and bark out orders that nobody would listen to. Most people would just "yup" him and he'd go sit in his office, read the paper and have coffee and toast brought to him by the kitchen workers in the building.

This building was its own entity. It used to be a recovery building for the old county hospital. The old brick three story with a large fence around it was nestled among pine trees and looked like a quiet place to be. The top floor housed the new inmates in an open bay type area. The second floor housed all the farmers and outside workers for the garage, and the bottom floor housed kitchen and maintenance workers.

One morning Pam called me and said, "Michael, the captain wants you to come in tomorrow and give you the SOPs (standard operating procedures) and your new schedule." This was a cushy assignment. I was elated, as I knew that this was the only promotion that wasn't slated for second or third shift.

I asked Pam, "Does this mean that I got the promotion?"

She said, "Yeah, silly. Didn't they tell you?"

"Not really."

"Well, congratulations," Pam said, "you are a sergeant and you'll be the relief sergeant up here at Minimum Security Facility. See you in the morning."

Now I was giddy. Relief sergeant at the MSF! I didn't know who to call first. I knew I was definitely not going to call my buddies from work. I didn't want to ruin my giddiness. I was on cloud nine. Thank you, God!

I went to MSF, my new assignment and met my new bosses. The officers are always skeptical of a new boss. They wonder what or who you did to get promoted, especially to a cushy spot like minimum security. My deputy, Lusignan, was a no-nonsense guy. He was in with the administration and well respected by his men. Things ran well with him; even his hot little secretary was in check when he was around. My first day I arrived about an hour early as the newness kept me up half of the night wondering what kind of sergeant I would be. It only took a couple of weeks for me to adjust to the routine, which was simple. I worked two seven to three shifts and then my next two days I worked three to eleven. Then I had two days off. It was easy, as I was just sort of a fill-in for the first and second shift sergeants.

As soon as I walked in past the gate and I smelled marijuana coming from somewhere. I peeked my head around the corner but didn't see or hear any inmates. Then I said hello to the night sergeant and his sidekick, who were giggling. I really hoped that they weren't smoking pot up here on my first day. They gave me a look like they were testing me. Then they both laugh out loud.

"We're just fucking with you, Mike. We found a tiny roach last night in the visiting room and thought we'd give you a surprise."

"Funny guys!" I responded. "Sorry, but I have to write it up anyways." They looked at me in shock, and it was my turn to have the upper hand. "I'm just playing with you now," I reassured them.

The night sergeant showed me my office and how things basically worked. The day shift was busy. The building housed about eighty inmates and most of them went out to work on the jail's property. My job was to see to it that when the departments such as the farm, garage and warehouse came to pick them up, I would call the officer on the floor, he or she would send the cons to me, and I would log them in and out. I would also be called to handle any disciplinary problems. There weren't many problems in minimum. The inmates wanted to be here and to work. Work kept their minds off of their problems and made the time go by. It gave them a feeling of normal living, except that they had to sleep here. These cons were sentenced to only six months or less, doing time up here as opposed to the main jail where recent murderers and crazy cons were housed awaiting trial.

I enjoyed my three to eleven shifts immensely. They were quieter and the brass was gone except for me. On more than one night, my deputy called me up and asked who was there with me. He would have me tell the other officer to cover the desk while I ran an errand for him, usually to pick up Deputy Gaffney, who had lost his license for drunk driving. The deputies would hang out at a local restaurant in the lounge.

This is where I was told they made most of the key decisions about the jail from promotions to new hires to policies to trading staff members. I was told not to say where I was going, but I'm sure the officers had an idea. I was offered many beers, but being in uniform and on the clock made for bad public relations. So I gave Gaffney many rides home and made small chit chat with him along the way.

I had a funny older friend John Berthiaume. He was later nicknamed Lefty because of his lack of marching skills in the academy. You always see it in comedies when the drill inspector yells, "Riiighttt face!" and one of them turns left. That was John. He was assigned to "A" floor, the same floor as my office. There were only fourteen inmates there and most of them were our kitchen workers. Our building had its own kitchen and little supply room. So Lefty had a good gig; although most people don't care for second shift, he did. Lefty liked to cook. And eat. He was a good cook, too. One Sunday afternoon while watching football, Lefty went out to his car and came back in with a bag full of meats, sauces, and rice. Our parking lot was less than one hundred feet from this building and I controlled who came and left. Sundays were almost always very quiet. The hardest part of the day was just showing up. No inmate traffic and no brass on Sundays. Lefty surprised me with his homemade Chinese food. He was going to heat it up in the deputy's office, as right across the hall from mine, where there was a small kitchen and fridge.

Lefty went in to the kitchen and brought out a few appetizers. On his first trip out, he had a tall white chef's hat. I took off my collared shirt and put it on Pam's chair to avoid any duck sauce stains. Unbeknownst to me, Lefty took my sergeant chevrons and put one on his chef's hat and the other on his white t-shirt. I was eating my good friend's Chinese food when I heard the metal gate slam closed about twenty feet from me.

"Oh fuck! It's the deputy!" I tried to call Lefty. But it was too late.

The deputy had just finished a round of golf and many rounds of beer. He looked in at me and questioned, "Everything quiet?"

I said, "Yes sir."

"Where's your uniform shirt?" he asked.

"It's on the chair drying from a stain."

He nodded and walked back in to his office. Within a minute he came walking out behind Lefty and his chef hat with a huge plate of Chinese food. Lefty tried to break the tension with, "Mr. Lusignan doesn't have a reservation, Sarge. Can we seat him anyways?"

The deputy looked at both of us and said, "Let's straighten this mess out and I don't want to see this again." He was noticeably beer buzzed. The good deputy took about half of the food and left. We never heard another word about the food. The following few months were just easy duty followed by easy duty.

Slowly I got to know the cons and the staff began to think of me as a regular Joe. One afternoon one of the workers was mowing the thin swath of lawn around the building inside the fence and through the window I yelled for him to come in for count. The prisoner gave me the finger. "Get the fuck in here!" I yelled. He turned off the mower and came into the office with a shit-eating grin. I warned, "Next time you give me the finger, I'll break it."

He said confidently, "Sarge, you don't have enough men to break my finger."

"Get up to your room for count!" I snapped.

One of the cons on "A" floor came to me and said, "Hey, Sarge, that kid wants to escape. I heard him say that he and his roommate will do anything to get out of here."

I pondered what the informer said and decided to write a report, passing the information along to the next shift and keeping the inmate from going back outside. When I arrived at MSF the next day, there were four cruisers and at least fifty officers there. Usually there are only five officers assigned on any given shift. Immediately upon entering the building I was grilled with questions about the kid that I wrote the report on.

"Did you know he had a gun?" asked the first shift sergeant.

"No fucking way! He had a weapon?"

"Yeah! We received information that he stole a 45-caliber from the deputy's office in special services. One of the inmates on his floor told us. It was locked and loaded to boot!" The inmate apparently had stolen the weapon out of the special services deputy's desk while cleaning the office—another reason not to have them work in sensitive areas. But I thought the deputy would be fired or at least suspended. He wasn't. The incident made the local paper, but the brass told the reporters that it was just a toy gun. I guess the inmate was right that I didn't have enough officers to break his finger if he had fifteen rounds. But my report helped put him away for a little while.

***

Ahhh—the Christmas party. The jail's Christmas party always made for great conversation for the entire next year. It was always held at the local club, usually a dive/function hall. Very few people brought their families as fights and sex were bound to take place. What else would you do at a company Christmas party? If you brought your spouse, you could almost be guaranteed that you would be defending his or her honor by the end of the night. There was a lot of competition and testosterone whenever these people were mixed with alcohol.

I was blowing the frost off a couple of cold ones when I noticed Dee Dee, Deputy Gaffney's secretary—very voluptuous lady who is half white and half black. She reeked sexuality. She knew that she turned heads, but no one ever seemed to speak to her. She was leaning over the crackers and cheese section of the food table. Her voluptuous upper body was encased with a V-neck pink sweater that revealed just enough cleavage to keep a person looking. She had on tight black jeans and black boots. It was a change from always seeing her in a dress or skirt at work. After a few frosted beers, I approached her at the bar with her much older friend Nancy, a secretary for another lower ranked deputy. She was still attractive and dressed like a classy woman in her upper fifties. But Dee was built to attract men. I said Hello.

"Oh, hi, Mike."

"Wow! You remembered my name."

"Of course I remembered your name, and congratulations on the promotion," She said with a smile.

"Thanks, but I'm only a sergeant. You're working for number three."

"I don't like working for him. He's a pig."

I wasn't sure how to take that, but she was opening up to me.

"This is my friend Nancy," Dee introduced. "She works for Deputy Ellen Harvey."

"Hi, Nancy, I've see you typing in Ellen's office. She seems wicked nice."

"Yes. She is the best. She used to be a nun."

"Wow! A nun turned deputy. That would make a great TV. show." I was being a gentleman, but I also wanted to see if I could entice Dee into dancing or going out for dinner sometime. Although Nancy was not bad looking either, it was Dee that I wanted. Nancy and I always made eye contact and smiled, but never spoke. But I kind of had the hots for Dee and was trying to broach the subject of dating, especially now I knew that she wasn't dating the deputy.

"So Gaff's a pig? A lot of the guys are scared to talk to you because they think that you two are an item."

She was outraged. "What? Who? Tell me who! He doesn't tell me who I can and can't date! Who? Tell me who wants to talk to me."

"I can't do that, Dee. They would call me a rat."

"Tell me who, Michael. Is he cute?"

Now I was thinking that if she wanted to find out if he was cute, she was probably interested in flirting or even dating him. Would I be doing my buddies a favor or putting them in the spotlight? Wow! What to do?

"Well, Andrew Anderson thinks that you are smoking." I figured I could find out more about her if I used Anderson's name and besides, he always talked about how hot she is anyways.

"Really?" she inquired. "I always thought that he was stuck up. He never looks at me when he passes by."

"Yeah, Andy's shy. But he always tells me how hot you are." Now I was worried I was helping him out more than myself. I also didn't want to leave Nancy out in the cold so I commented on her dress and hair.

Dee knowingly smiled at me. "Mike, Nancy told me that she wants to dance with you."

"Really? I'll dance with you when a good song comes on." We made some small three-way chit chat and then, sure enough, a slow song came on.

"Get out there and dance, you two!" Dee was forcing us into an awkward moment. I asked Nancy to dance and she accepted. I was looking around at the handful of other people dancing and a few of the officers mocking everyone who was dancing. Maybe they wished they were dancing, but were just as happy making kissing and fake fart noises. Other people were playing cards, some were at the bar discussing politics and some were content with just getting drunk and eating. I don't know if it was me staring at Dee, the beer, or Nancy grinding up against me and breathing on my neck, but I was starting to get that warm fuzzy feeling. I pulled Nancy in closer and started kissing her ear, which she seemed to enjoy. She was holding me tighter and kissed my neck a few times.

After the dance, I said, "Thank you, I'll see you and Dee after I say hello to the boys." I went back to the guys and took a small amount of ribbing for dancing with the MILF. But the guys were not too hard on me; they were scoping out other clerks and secretaries for their own bragging rights. Some of the officers had genuine crushes on certain ladies that worked at the jail. But they had to keep up the macho image by putting their feelings aside and pretending that it was just a score in front of the guys. Certain occupations have this effect on the testosterone level of groups. You couldn't be sensitive or show true feelings here. Heaven forbid that you want to say something genuinely nice about someone else. The rest of the guys would feed on you like a feeding frenzy in a shark pool.

I was sitting back watching the boys play pitch and noticed Deputy Slattery, who we will go into detail about shortly, following Dee and Nancy around. He was a six pack past drunk. Dee was trying to make him sit at the bar, but if his hands weren't trying to wrap around Dee's round glutes, they were sliding up Nancy's just above the knee length dress. Nancy was getting mad and went outside. The drunken deputy followed her. Dee was trying to get one of the higher ups to avert the deputy's route. The other deputies called him, but he was a little incoherent. I didn't want to get involved, being a freshly promoted sergeant, but if I could prevent a deputy from some harassment charges and rescue a damsel in distress, maybe a tactful intervention would be a good move for me.

I went out to the parking lot, and saw Slattery trying to follow Nancy. She was trying to get into her car and the deputy was stumbling close behind. I called out, "Deputy Slattery! Deputy Slattery!! " He looked back and I ran over to him.

"Deputy, the sheriff told me to tell you that your wife is on the phone."

"My wiifffee?" he slurred.

"Yes sir. And he also said that you had better not sneak outside when it's your turn to buy a round."

"Aaahhh, huh, okay, let's go get some, some beers," he mumbled, apparently forgetting about Nancy, who was sitting quietly in her car trying not to be seen.

I later found out that these two had had an affair many years ago and saw each other once in a blue moon for drinks and visit to the cheap motel down the street.

Nancy said, "Thank you, Mike."

Dee came out shortly and said," Let's go downtown to club Cahoots and do some dancing!" I thought that being invited by Dee was awesome and figured the ladies would be more at ease in a club away from company politics. Besides, the rumors that came about were always started by some jealous person. You could just say hi to a person of the opposite sex and by the time that passed three or four peoples' ears, you two were now having sex in the parking lot.

Dee drove us to the club where we sat, drank and danced with each other and a few other people. Sometimes all three of us danced together and others would join in. It was definite booze dancing.

When the club announced last call Dee was dancing with a Middle Eastern guy in his mid to late twenties. The guy, Emil, asked us if we wanted to continue partying up in his suite. I was the first to say," Oh yeah!" Nancy was reluctant but held my hand and said that she'd go wherever I was going. Dee asked if Emil was the only one in the room. He assured us that he was the son of a well to do petroleum businessman and that he rented out a huge suite in the penthouse. When I walked into the room I couldn't believe the view of the city and how nice it looked. Emil handed Nancy and me a beer and we sat on one of the comfy beds. Dee sat on the sofa facing us. Emil had the lights just about off and Nancy was kissing my neck and I started kissing her back. We were pretty hot and heavy and doing a lot of petting when I looked up and saw Dee in the very dim light riding Emil on the couch. She had her pink sweater and socks on; nothing else. I couldn't believe that I was watching Dee on top of this guy she just met an hour ago. She was really into it. Not very noisy, but she was thrusting hard on this guy. She had some cellulite on her butt and upper thighs, but her silhouette was incredible. I was so excited that I hiked up Nancy's dress and we had sex. It was so intense having sex with Nancy while watching Dee. Nancy was kind of boring, but watching Dee fueled my imagination for many months later. I still cannot get the image of her having sex just a few feet away from me out of my mind: nor do I wish to.

Finally we finished. I had lasted longer than Emil, but not by much. He was a lucky dog. We all had another beer, admired the view, and then Dee took Nancy to her home. It was a funny thing, not much was said in Dee's jeep about the night's events. When we arrived at Nancy's house, Dee drove a few houses down and Nancy crouched down as if not to be seen. Was it me? Was it the neighbors who would talk about her coming home at four in the morning? No, it was Nancy's husband! Dee dropped Nancy off and she scurried behind some trees and went to the front door. Dee told me on the way back to my truck that Nancy was married, but she and her husband live on different floors of the house. It was like they were roommates. But still, I felt like an ass now. But I hadn't known she was married. There was no ring, no mention of her husband. I would say that I was used, but I'd had such a good night that I couldn't complain. Dee dropped me off and I gave her a kiss goodnight and thanked her for the ride. We never spoke of the Christmas party again. I was very thankful that I had the next day off.

The months started rolling along and time was flying by. I thought that the state job was very cushy. Up here at MSF the cons were very easy to manage and once you understood the routine, it was a cakewalk. We would from time to time hear about problems arising out of maximum security due to the number of inmates housed there and the deputy, a man who thought that cleanliness was more important than control of the inmates. There were more assaults and fires than you could imagine, even with Sergeant Callahan on the front line. Callahan had to deal with a grumpy captain who never left his chair in the booth and a deputy who was more concerned with curtains for his office and painting or washing the walls of the prison corridors. The deputy was Jack Slattery. He was the deputy chasing Nancy through the parking lot when he was drunk. He was in charge of maximum security, which had three cellblocks. The largest block was called maxi, and it was a zoo, four separate tiers that were independent of each other. If you looked out of the booth, you would have a tier on the upper left side of you, the upper right side, lower right side and the lower left. The lower left was where the severely deranged inmates or suicidal inmates were housed. They stayed in their cells all day except for showers and mental health interviews. The block was the same size as medium "C" but each tier did not have communication with the other tiers. So when a problem arose, it would be confined to twenty-six cells, as there were twenty-six cells and fifty-two inmates per tier—two inmates to a cell, except for the nut jobs on the lower left.

The big problems occurred when you had a mass movement. All the tiers except for the lower left would go to eat or to the gym at the same time. Now mind you, these were prisoners that had not been sentenced yet. The typical maximum security inmate was in for murder, assault and battery with a dangerous weapon, home invasion, and other horrific crimes. They were the more violent criminals. And the maxi block had five officers to watch over the one hundred and eighty-two prisoners. It was not very good planning on the part of the administration. One officer had to man the booth, one had to stay on the high-risk tier or lower left and three had to do the rest of the work. So in all actuality there were three officers watching one hundred and fifty-six prisoners of the worst caliber. More often than not, Deputy Slattery would pull an officer to cover a cleaning detail outside of the block. The officer would stand around and watch murderers paint the hallway or the offices of the higher ups, leaving the other officers in even more danger.

One day while they were having yard (yard was like recess where a hundred plus cons would get to go outside, play basketball, catch some rays, play volleyball and throw horseshoes), an inmate had been digging a small hole to fit into. The inmate was a small Spanish prisoner Julio Fuentes who had been just sitting inconspicuously along the building. His plan was well thought out. Since the deputy had only one, sometimes two officers covering the yard, the fence and large scale fights were their major concern; they weren't paying attention to Julio's spot. Julio sat in the same spot in the yard for three weeks. He was wanted for murder both here and in Puerto Rico. Every day he dug a little bit more and tossed the dirt away from his hole. He had one friend who kept his mouth shut and helped him. Julio made a head out of many bars of soap and stuffed a prisoner's uniform with newspapers to be placed in his bunk with an orange wool cap to cover the top of the head.

The day came for Julio's big break. He waited for evening yard to end. Julio was small and could fit in the tiny, barely noticeable hole. When the announcement came over the loudspeaker that yard was over, Julio curled up into his little hole and his friend put a couple sheets of old newspaper on him with small stones and dirt to prevent the paper from being blown off. The yard ended as usual and the officers checked the fence and looked into the darkening yard, then closed the door. The inmates all went into their cells for a count and Julio's cell had a dummy placed under the blanket. The officers did the count and the dummy passed for the sleeping inmate. Every count, Julio's former cellmate and friend would turn the dummy into another position so as not to raise suspicion.

Julio waited in his hole until dark the first night, climbed up the small gate that had no barbed wire, grabbed onto the drainpipe, and shimmied up and onto the roof. This was not too long after inmate Grenier and his buddy escaped from the roof, and the Constantia wire had not been totally finished. There was only one roll to get across and Julio, being nimble and agile, jumped over it. Julio's dummy worked for three days. Officers are taught in the academy and common sense dictates that when you do a count, you look for living, breathing flesh. But the deputy had these officers doing more cleaning details off the block than doing their actual jobs of watching the tiers. It wasn't until the city police called the jail and asked if we knew a Julio Fuentes that anyone knew he was missing. Apparently, Fuentes was arrested in a convenience store fighting with the clerk over some scratch tickets.

The call was directed to Deputy Slattery, who said, "Yes, I have Inmate Fuentes on a detail right now as we speak."

The police chief said sarcastically, "Have you spoken to him today?"

The deputy replied, "Yes, I have him painting. Is there a problem with him? He didn't tell me that he was having any problems."

The chief finally said, "Hey, Einstein, send a cruiser to our headquarters and pick him up before I let him go. You must be the pride of your department!"

The deputy ran down to the upper right tier followed by a couple of officers. He pulled Fuentes' blanket down and felt the embarrassment of knowing he was going to be the butt of every joke in the large city police department, not to mention the people at the jail making fun of him and his staff. He suspended everyone who worked in that block on a rotating basis to save some face for the impending ass chewing coming from the sheriff. Slattery's emphasis on cleaning instead of security was to blame. The officers, who conducted count after count, had to be blamed also. And they were suspended, but Slattery never was penalized. He was a major campaign contributor and a major ass-kisser. So the sheriff decided to transfer him. His next stop: MSF.

I couldn't believe it. Deputy Lusignan was reassigned to go down and fix Slattery's mess and Slattery was getting the cushy MSF assignment. That wasn't punishment, that was a gift. Now we were stuck with this inept leader who you just knew was going to ruin this good area.

Slattery's first day with me was bizarre. He said, "Sergeant, come with me." We walked around the building while he had his wife come in and put up drapes and lamps in his office. He was pointing out things that he wanted cleaned. "I want this painted yellow, not black. And I want the windowsills scraped and painted gray. I'd like some flowers planted here. Maybe some marigolds would liven up this walkway." He kept making all kinds of silly little changes all the while looking up into the surrounding trees and the roof of the building.

Not wanting to make a bad first sober impression on him I said, "Yes sir. I'll call maintenance and write out a report that you want that done." Those types of projects were for maintenance, not for officers. Could you see state troopers planting shrubs on the highways?

"No, I want you to handle this personally," Slattery replied, "and maybe you could get some paint and get the supply shack painted tonight."

"I'm not working tonight, sir."

Slattery stopped walking and faced me. "Sergeant, I think you should learn from me. If you do, you might go far in this business."

What could I say? "Okay, Deputy. Whatever you want."

I ended up telling the second shift sergeant what Slattery wanted and he more or less told me to "take a bus." I did write a report and some of the projects were completed by maintenance, but the deputy appeared to have forgotten pretty much everything he told me to get done.

One afternoon I was sitting in the office chatting with Pam, the secretary. I asked her if it bothered her when the officers stole her shoes and put them in the freezer and then return them under her desk. She always wore those four-inch patent white or black CFM shoes and either a summer dress, short skirt or tight fitting business suit. She was pleasant to your face, but the administration had made a monster out of her. She pretty much thought that she ran the building. The top officials would ask her about paperwork instead of asking the deputies since they weren't always around. The deputies did not have a time card and there was no accountability for them unless there was a problem. They were mostly a buffer zone for the sheriff and warden, who used them as implementers of discipline and new unpopular policies. Then the sheriff wouldn't look like the bad guy and could still count on votes and donations. Also, when someone was suspended, they could appeal it to the sheriff and the sheriff would knock off a few suspension days, so the officers would be indebted to the sheriff. It was quite a political cycle.

I never flirted with Pam. I looked at her a lot, but I figured she was trouble. Over the year or so that I was up at MSF, I had seen numerous guys come in to pick up their work crews and flirt with her. Some guys would give her a back and shoulder massage while they were waiting for their inmate work crews to come down. At least once a week I would see this one particular guy rubbing her feet for ten minutes or so. Sometimes that was the distraction for others to steal her shoes. I wanted to ask her if she wanted me to tell them to lighten up or stop, but she apparently loved it.

Pam was engaged to a sergeant who worked at another part of the jail. This one particular afternoon while we were alone, I asked her if she wanted me to stop the guys from rubbing her and stealing her shoes and she said, "No! Just don't tell Gary. He would go nuts! He's very jealous. And I like most of the guys here."

I said, "Okay," and that was good enough for me.

She got up from her desk and placed a new memo on the bulletin board. She turned around and noticed me looking at her legs. She asked, "Do you like my new outfit?"

I calmly said, "Oh yes! You look very nice, except the skirt looks like you stole it from a Friendly's waitress." She smiled and asked about my personal life. We exchanged stories, but I knew she was going to be trouble, especially since she thought she was in charge of the area. So I kept my distance from her, but I was very polite, as I was with most people.

The first shift sergeant was quite the character. He ended up going high up in the ranks without kissing any ass. Usually that's not possible, but with Harry it happened. When Harry was off, I would work the first shift as his relief. He had that loud belly laugh and everybody loved him. Harry showed me a trick one day. Captain Heinz, a.k.a. the Hammer, would come into our office and try barking out orders when he was hung over. He was an old, cranky, mean-spirited drunk. The Captain's office was about fifty feet away from ours. Harry would put the handle of our phone on the guideposts so it looked like it was on the hook and when the Hammer came in Harry would dial his phone without him seeing. The Captain had a bad case of the gout so it was hard for him to walk back to his office to answer the phone. After two or three times of this, the captain would stay in his office waiting for the phone to ring again, but nobody ever called him. It was a good tactic to keep the captain out of the way, and I used it frequently.

The captain came up with some bizarre ideas probably given to him by the new deputy and it was starting to bother me. So I decided to play some games with him. One weekend I had moved his office and all of its contents into the social workers' office and put all of the social workers' contents into his office. Most of the furniture looked alike and I was off Monday and Tuesday so I wouldn't hear about it until Wednesday. The captains all had the weekends off back in those days, which was kind of silly as problems in prison arise just as much on weekends as they do on weekdays. I heard the Hammer went berserk when he tried to unlock his desk, screaming for Harry to find out what had happened. Harry never told him who it was, but told me it was an awesome gag. Another day I put a sign over the captain's license plate that said, *Gay and Proud*. I am not knocking gay people; I was just trying to get a little payback on the Hammer for coming into my office barking out orders. He drove around with the cardboard sign on his license plate for two days until Warden Friese, the sheriff and Deputy Gaffney had spotted it. They all roared with laughter and called up MSF to speak with Pam about it. They said the sheriff actually had to change his pants from laughing so hard. The Hammer was furious. He wanted to find out who did it in the worst way. Pam had an idea, but there were quite a few pranksters that worked with us, so it was hard to nail down who would actually have the guts to do that to the Hammer. The top brass just let Pam know to give a pat on the back to whoever thought that idea up.

***

Another couple months went by and my area had been quiet except for Deputy Slattery changing all the paint schemes and planting flowers around the prison building. The mods, however, have been plagued by mini riots and racial tension. There were huge gang fights in the yard, almost always about power, money and drugs—which in prison are one in the same. The Blacks would stand with their backs to one building; the Spanish with their backs against another facing the Blacks; and the Whites would be leaning against another building. When the sheriff's buddy was planning the new modular facility, they never considered that there would be problems with letting six hundred sentenced inmates out into a yard the size of a football field for almost the entire day. Deputy Kelly, who planned the mods, was a wonderful man. But he was hired just because he was a friend and campaign contributor of Sheriff Smith. The sheriff paid him eighty-six thousand a year and expected about five grand back every year in cash.

One Saturday evening the mods called for help. The preliminary call was for an immediate lockdown of the entire prison. The staff at the mods had over four hundred inmates out in the yard that refused to go into their cells. It was the first beautiful night of the year. I was wondering if that was the reason. But no, that wasn't the reason, I would later find out.

Inmate Messier's mother had just passed away. Messier was a regular at the house of correction, always in and out for small drug and parole violations. Monday was to be his mother's wake, and it was customary that he be escorted there by two officers to pay his respects an hour before the family arrived to avoid any bad scenes or escape attempts. The inmate's trip was set in stone on Friday for a Monday trip. Messier was sobbing lightly in his bunk at suppertime under his blanket while Captain Greenberg was making his last round before his last weekend off. The captain told Messier to make his bed—a big fetish for the captain. The grieving inmate wasn't fast enough and Greenberg said, "All right, never mind, you're not going to see your coke-headed mother Monday." That was the catalyst for one of the many Greenberg-inspired riots. He told the officers to shut Messier's cell door, and then Greenberg went about inspecting the rest of the building. The whole while Messier was yelling at Greenberg, but Greenberg pretended not to hear. The rest of the inmate population was growing furious as they were already fueled with the gang fighting and now this little "make your bed" and "your coke-headed mother" gave them all a common denominator. They were just looking for an excuse to cause as much damage as possible and rise up against the institution. The inmates got together, for once sort of on the same page. They felt bad and actually believed that Messier wouldn't be allowed to see his mom at her wake. They thought that Saturday night was the best night to cause a disturbance, as there wasn't as much staff on.

When it was time for the outside yard to be closed, there was an eerie quiet feeling. The call came for the inmates to return to their housing units and into their cells for a count. Messier's cellmate waved his arm pretending to go into the cell, and instead Messier ran out of the cell when it was unlocked. There's another problem with double bunking. At any rate, that was the signal. When two of the officers went to grab Messier eighty plus inmates blocked their path, and one inmate punched the smaller officer in the face. The officers knew that was it. They walked the fallen officer back to the booth. The inmates didn't pursue, but ran back outside to see their comrades.

The mods were set up that you had five separate blocks with no barriers between buildings. You had to go outside to go to the gym building, chow hall, school area and the infirmary. The inmates were busting the doors to get into the school and canteen areas, lighting fires anywhere they could. There wasn't much to steal in the school area, but they were just intent on causing as much damage as possible. A couple more clever inmates went through the ceiling tiles to get into the canteen store. They were carrying goodies out of there by the trash bag full.

When I received the call, the officers me a brief rundown of what was transpiring. I had my area locked down and all the inmates were accounted for, so I was to report to the sheriff with a van and another officer. We only had six officers to begin with, so the operators were calling in people from home to come in. They also called the state and local police departments. We all met at the warehouse at the opposite end of the jail grounds. The officers were coming in and getting organized with batons and pads, and there were attack dogs ready to go. The sheriff told me and Lieutenant Prince to drive in behind the tactical team; they would place the big troublemakers in our vans and we would bring them to another area. There must have been around three hundred officers there. I was anxious to drive in and fight. *Let's get this going*, I thought to myself. There are a lot of officers trapped in that hellhole. But the sheriff waited, and waited, and waited. Wait a minute! Lieutenant Prince? Wasn't he on duty in charge of the mods? Why was he out here? Lieutenant Prince was a friend of a friend of mine; he was a very tall, muscular African American who would have written up his mother if the higher ups told him to. He was petrified of the deputies, but he wrote more officers up and caused more bullshit suspensions than anyone in the jail's history. He was also known to have never owned a vehicle and he bummed rides from his subordinates. If you gave him a ride regularly, you could almost be assured of not being written up for any minor violations—almost.

I asked, "Lieutenant, aren't you working tonight?"

"Yes, Michael, but I had to get out of there or I'd become trapped."

"Trapped? You have twenty-something officers and two of them are female. You didn't want to help them out?"

Prince ignored my last question, and I was really bewildered by his behavior. In the mean time, the sheriff had the kitchen staff make us hot chocolate and sandwiches—but peoples' lives were at stake! Why wasn't anyone taking this seriously? Then I heard a helicopter overhead. It wasn't a news chopper, it was a state police helicopter flying over the mods. Finally! We must have waited three hours in the parking lot next to the warehouse. What the heck was going on here? Finally a radio transaction came over that a lot of the inmates were getting tired and running out of stuff to steal and burn, so they were heading back into their cells. They couldn't escape, as the perimeter of the fence was lined with police cruisers and paddy wagons with eager officers just wanting an excuse to shoot a scumbag in the leg. I was thankful that they were there. The sheriff had us march and drive down to the gate that lets you into the mods. Then he changed his plan. He told me to take a baton and cover the cameraman who was going to videotape the action. I went in directly behind the twelve man tactical team with two police attack dogs at my side. By the time I got to the gate I was wondering why only this small crew was going in when there were at least three hundred other officers out in the parking lot were waiting for action.

I saw my captain at the gate. He was drunk, but they had an officer assigned to watch him. Kind of silly, I think. When we finally went in, the deputy of the special services pushed me and said," Get out of here!"

"The sheriff told me to protect the cameraman, sir!" I protested.

He pushed me again. "You're not qualified to be in here." This was the same deputy who had lost his 45-caliber pistol to the con. I ignored his order and kept walking, feeling a little embarrassed in front of the cameraman and the K-9 units. But curiosity kept me going forward. To my amazement, there were only three inmates left in the yard, and they lay down as soon as the team entered. The team stripped the cons, cuffed and shackled the offenders and carried them into the receiving area. I was told to keep watch on them while the team searched for any stragglers. The inmates who were in my custody were now chatting to me like nothing major had happened. The counts were all confirmed. In all, four officers suffered minor injuries, the lieutenant ran away in the face of danger, the major instigators were given time in maxi, and the mods were repaired while the cons were locked down for two weeks. That was it. Two weeks of lockdown and a few d-boards. But how much did this episode cost the taxpayers? Plenty. What a waste of force.

The inmates later said that they thought the helicopter was going to spray gas or start shooting them and that was one of the reasons that they decided to go in and call it quits. The event made a small blurb on the news and that was the end of that mini riot. Lieutenant Prince was never disciplined for abandoning his post or leaving his subordinates behind, and he continued to write people up for minor things such as not shaving everyday, having their shirts semi-untucked, and having hair touching their ears. What a guy.

***

It was around two thirty one Friday afternoon when Officer Joey Verdini, a casual friend of mine, came down from his floor to buy a soda in the staff locker room. I was feeling a little cocky that day and told him to go buy me a soda, too.

"I'd buy you one if you weren't an ass-kisser," Joey said being cocky back.

This time I said, "Now you're gonna buy Smith one, too."

This guy named Smith was on "A" floor this particular day and he looked exactly like Officer Barbrady from *South Park*. Smith was a small town cop with whom I was friends; I had at numerous times gone out with him and his wife. He was one of those guys who, if he wasn't in the law field, would have been a criminal. As a matter of fact, if you needed something like speakers, auto parts, or computers, he was the go-to guy. You knew the stuff he was selling was hot, but he always pretended he knew a wholesale dealer. Still, the less we knew about that the better. He had the same last name as the sheriff but wasn't related.

Smith heard me say his name, as "A" floor begins at the end of the hallway near our locker room at MSF. He yelled out, "Is this piece of shit giving you a hard time, Sarge?"

"Why yes, he is, Officer Smith," I said playing along.

Smith came over to Joey. "You giving my sergeant a hard time?"

"Fuck you, too, you fat bastard!" Joey responded with a grin.

Smith looked at me. "Woooeeee! Did you hear that, Sarge?"

"Yes and I don't like any cussing, Officer Verdini."

"Then with all due respect: Fuck you, too, Sergeant!"

I said, pretending to be tough, "Buy us a soda, Verdini, and I'll forget about this little incident."

But Joey wasn't having it. "You two aren't man enough to make me buy you fags a soda!"

That was it. I know we were just playing around, but now he was sort of challenging my position and my manhood. Pam was just sitting there with one hand over her mouth semi-laughing. Smith and I followed Verdini into the locker room and while he had his wallet out, I did a controlled tackle on him as not to hurt the kid. Smith just piled on and took his wallet while I held him down. He must have bought six sodas with Verdini's money. Each time a soda would drop, Smith would say, "I guess I'm still not man enough, am I, Verdini?"

The kid was putting up quite a little struggle, but I had him pretty well pinned and his head was in the bottom of the soda machine. He was making quite a racket. When Smith finished with his money, we took the sodas into the office and left Joey with one. Pam drank one, laughing at Joey whose face was red, shirt untucked and his pride a little bent—but he'd recover soon enough.

A couple little details about Joey: he looks like he's a little mentally challenged. One time during visits, an older lady came to visit a convict while Joey was in the office with me. When she saw him, the lady said, "Oh isn't that nice that the sheriff hires the mentally challenged?" I burst out loud laughing; milk shot out of my nose and I wasn't even drinking milk. Another time I was relieving Joey at the hospital covering a female prisoner. (We did not keep female prisoners at our facility, but they were housed at a state facility. When they went to court or the hospital, we had to transport and cover them. This was overtime and done on our days or shifts that we were off.) I could hear the prisoner as soon as I stepped off the elevator. She was a three hundred plus pound African American lady screaming, "Get the fuck outta here, you Down syndrome motherfucker!" Joey was pretty much running out of the room and hospital as soon as he saw me as his relief. The lady never said another word the rest of the night. As for Joey, he became a big city cop and I still consider him a friend. I also want to say that I mean no disrespect for anyone handicapped. I was just repeating a series of funny things that were said about Joey.

My next day at work was a Sunday and I received a call from my inebriated captain. He was slurring his words but I could still get the gist of what he was trying to communicate with me. "Michael, have you been harassing the secretary Pam?"

"No sir. I've never been anything but professional with her."

"Well, she says that you made fun of the way she dressed and didn't want it to lead to more harassment. She also said that you beat up Verdini and took some money from him."

I was shocked. "Wow. She said that I was harassing her? That's bullshit, Captain, but I will apologize to her if you want me to."

"No, Michael, don't do a damn thing. You're on Monday right?"

"Yes sir."

"I'll see what we are going to do and we'll talk then."

I couldn't believe it. I was about the only guy who didn't fondle her or flirt with her. Maybe that was the problem. Maybe she wanted attention from me. I was flabbergasted. She had even told on me for roughhousing with Verdini, even though she'd had a soda from his money.

Monday came and Pam came in an hour after me. I didn't say a word to her. She wouldn't even look at me. Then my phone rang; it was her fiancé.

"Mike, it's Gary. Look, Pam isn't trying to get you into trouble; she's just worried that your antics may get out of control."

Pam could hear our conversation and the phone call almost seemed planned. "That's bullshit, Gary! She lied and cried to the Hammer about me. How can I work with someone like that?"

"Listen, Mike, she's under a lot of stress running that building and has to deal with all the paperwork...so treat her with respect."

That did it for me. I was the only one not rubbing her or hitting on her and I had even asked her if any of the guys were bothering her. I didn't want to tell Gary about her contact with the officers as I know he would think that I was just deflecting the problem. I said, "Gary, I'm the only one up here who treats her like a lady and if you have a problem and want to be a tough guy while she's sitting just a few feet away, come on up and I'll meet you in the yard. No one else will see us. Or if you can't I'll meet you down there in the parking lot. Your choice!"

Gary wisely declined. Gary was a solid and fairly tough sergeant. I was glad that we didn't fight over this woman's quest for attention. For another hour, Pam went about her business and not a word was spoken. Then the deputy and captain came in and went right into the deputy's office.

I received a phone call from the captain a few minutes later requesting my presence. "Well, Sergeant, for the good of the institution, we are placing you on the third shift up here at MSF."

I couldn't stop myself. "That's bullshit, Deputy! You guys are a couple of drunken cowards. You know I never said anything bad to that lady." I'd never spoken like that to an authority figure before. "As a matter of fact, you two are the laughingstock of the whole jail. You can fire me, but I'm not working eleven to seven. I'll even fight you two drunks right now! I'm the best sergeant you have."

The deputy paused, and then said, "Do you want to add threatening a superior officer and insubordination?"

I went home and pondered it. I wanted to quit. But instead I went in during the night shift and tried to get used to it. It sucked. It was the most boring shift. Then I had a friend from the academy show me how to beat the system. The "A" floor officer would normally hang out in the office with the night sergeant. We each took four-hour shifts. One would do the winds and paperwork for four hours while the other would sleep on the couch in the deputy's office for four hours. Then we would switch. It was a pretty good system, but I hated being there at night. I had only called in sick three times in the three years that I was at the jail and thus had a lot of sick time built up. We each received fifteen days a year. So for the next two months, I called in sick seventeen times. The cowardly deputy and captain didn't want to see me for abusing the sick time, so they had Deputy Gaffney talk to me in his office. Gaffney told me that he wasn't going to change the deputy's decision. I told him that I was going to use up the rest of my time and just quit then. I told him he could transfer me anywhere else, even the mods on second shift, which was a hellhole.

Gaffney leaned back in his chair, looked out the window and said, "Listen, don't bang in sick for one month and I'll see what I can do."

"I'm serious, Deputy, I'm not working that shift longer than a month." I left his office thinking that he was just blowing smoke up my ass to get me to ease up on my sick time usage and to get me acclimated to the eleven to seven shift. But I gave him the benefit of the doubt for one month.

CHAPTER FOUR
THE MODS

Well, guess what? A month to the day, a cruiser pulls into my driveway and they brought me my transfer papers. When I asked the female officer who delivered the orders why didn't they just give them to me at work, she told me something to the effect that this was the thirty day mark and the brass didn't want me to do anything crazy. Gaff had kept his word: I was headed for the mods on second shift. It had to be better than *anywhere* on the third shift.

A few years later, I found out that the third shift sergeant Frank Conti, who was a cop in a small yuppie town, was double-dipping. He was on the clock at the jail and would leave to put in some hours at night in his hometown. The officers under his command didn't care for him so they started leaking out info that he was leaving his post. The jail and police department were both onto him, so the jail put him in my spot while I was transferred to his third shift. This put a damper on his double dipping. Maybe they were just trying to put the screws to him, but they got me in the mean time; and I wasn't happy about being ratted on and lied about. My professional attitude was diminishing.

A little side bar about Sergeant Frank Conti: he was always on the third shift, eleven to seven. He was a small man in his early fifties with a thick mustache and slicked back, thick dark brown hair. He worked in special services for many years but he would either not respond to any calls from his fellow officers, or else show up after the problem dissolved. Sometimes an irate person trying to bail someone out would have to be arrested, or someone drunk or high would be trespassing on the jail property behind the fence. The special services unit, as I had mentioned was filled with officers who either wanted to kiss ass or were deathly afraid of inmates. The special services unit was also in charge of investigating officers. When the sheriff was done with someone or they badmouthed him, he would have special services tap the phones, and then have inmates make false accusations against the officer. The inmates would be promised rewards of jobs, smokes and extra good time. So you can see why this type of officer worked in the special services unit.

When Frank came to work at the jail, he had a brief case filled with reports and blank forms. He had every possible known form the jail printed. Since Frank was on the night shift and had almost no contact with the prisoners, I found it odd that he carried a briefcase loaded with inmate request forms and canteen price lists. Maybe he was just being thorough. When he was getting dressed for his part time police job in the small town, he wore his forty-caliber service pistol. He had a small twenty-five strapped to his leg and another strapped with a shoulder holster to his bullet proof vest. He also had two knives on him at all times. And yet this guy never went to a call if he absolutely didn't have to. Even the yuppie town's policemen had told the jail that he sometimes didn't come to aid his fellow officers. Then why did Frank carry all that paraphernalia? Did he just want to play a cop's role in Hollywood? He was definitely overdramatic when giving instructions for the eleven to seven shifts. "Now, men, the deputy wants us to make sure that our paperwork is signed." (Lengthy pause.) "Try to stay awake." (Lengthy pause.) "There are lives at stake here." It was just the stuff a supervisor didn't have to say—unless there had been a problem with basic corrections. It was like a manager telling a clerk to put paper in the copier.

Later in my career Frank was working down the mods on the eleven to seven shift at about six in the morning. The inmates that were going to court for minor offenses while already doing time for another offense would go to eat breakfast before the rest of the population. There were usually only about twenty of them. One of the officers that worked in receiving would escort the bunch over to the chow hall and the inmates would eat. Very rarely would a fight break out before court. The inmates were usually too preoccupied with trying to prepare their cases or wondering whether their girlfriends would show up at the courthouse.

On this day Sergeant Conti was walking down by the chow hall when the receiving officer stuck his head out of the modular chow hall building and yelled, "Frank! I need help in here! There's a fight!"

Frank looked up at the officer and calmly stated, "Okay, hang on; I'll radio you some help."

"No, Frank, I need you now!" the officer responded.

"I can't," Frank replied. "I have my coffee and reports in my hands."

The receiving officer finally got a couple of officers to the chow hall to drag out the combatants, but word spread quickly about Frank's cowardice. Not only was he a coward, he was a sergeant and a part-time law officer on the outside to boot.

This particular episode happened during Sheriff Gobi's term in office. That night Frank and his wife had each written a check for five hundred dollars to Sheriff Gobi's campaign. (This is not counting any cash donations they might have made, as the most a single person can officially donate to the sheriff is five hundred dollars.) Guy Gobi made a small investigation and Frank was transferred to…you guessed it…special services. The officers were so mad at Frank that the event made the paper. And it made the public a little aware of the new sheriff's priorities.

There will be many more stories about the new sheriff's regime later, but I will say this. He only wanted to boost his campaign—his war chest, as he called it—even if it was at the expense of the staff's safety. Nobody really cared about the safety of correctional staff, due to some of the boneheaded actions of a few men or women officials in the field. We all want the murderers, rapists and thieves put away for life, yet when inmates get hurt from acting out in prison, the inmate rights activists want heads to roll.

The system has been funny during my tenure. I've seen men in jail for absolutely nothing. I can't count the amount of times I've had to tell a lady trying to visit her estranged husband or boyfriend that she can't visit because she has a restraining order on him. "I just wanted him out of the house for the night!" one lady sobbed, "He never touched me." I had to reply in disgust, "Ma'am, you should have thought about that before you called the police." If I had a dollar for every story like that, I'd have a yacht by now. But on the other end of the spectrum, I've seen a couple of innocent people get killed because the parole board deemed certain inmates no longer a threat to society. It's a hard line to walk between the lawmakers and the lawbreakers. The police arrest the criminals, the judge or jury arraigns them, the prison system holds them for trial, the prison system brings them back to court for trial, and they either get sentenced or released. If they get sentenced, the correctional staff spends twenty-four hours a day with these thugs, people watching the dregs of society. When they come into a county jail the prisoners are often still drunk, high, crazy and not house broken. The county jails are where they become institutionalized, adjusted to the routine. It's kind of like a cowboy breaking in a horse. After they are house trained, they can go off to bigger and better prisons in the state and federal system.

As for me...I was off to the jungle.

***

Made up of five buildings containing one hundred and twenty inmates each, the mods were white, two story buildings with a yard about the size of a football field. The kitchen and the gym were at the top of the runway, the stretch of asphalt that went from the front gate of the mods to the very last housing unit or cellblock, when you first entered; and the school building was on the right side. All of the buildings had pretty much the same exterior design. I was assigned to the "I and J" buildings. Since I was the second shift sergeant, my job was to keep the buildings quiet. The "J" building was later to be made into the segregation unit, but for the time being it housed regular county inmates.

There was one inmate in the mods that was famous in state and local police departments for being able to break handcuffs while they were on his wrists. Donny Besse was a local city man who was fairly strong and muscular, but nothing special if you saw him with a jean jacket or sweatshirt on. As a matter of fact, he looked like something of a dork when not dressed for combat. The city police had arrested him for a domestic on his girlfriend. The two of them were doing lines and Donny thought that she was always taking the bigger half, so he smacked her and someone close to the couple called the cops. The cops handcuffed Donnie, as they had many times before, and Donny cooperated because he didn't think that he was going to be arrested. But after the police spoke with Donny's girlfriend, they placed Donny under arrest and shoved him into the cruiser.

Well, that just infuriated Donny. The cruiser drove off down the city streets and Donny kicked the door twice, busting the latch holding it shut. That's a lot of leg strength! Donny jumped out and rolled to the curb. The officers stopped the car and got out in shock; they had seen never seen the door get kicked open. Donny was facedown trying to break off the handcuffs over the curb. Blood trickled from the edge of the cuffs digging into his wrists, and the hinge broke off on one side. Recovering from their shock, the officers jumped on Donny and proceeded to try to subdue this pain-loving maniac. They had spray and batons, but Donny was getting in a few shots from the ground. The officers knew they had to keep this fight on the ground or they could be in serious trouble. Luckily another cruiser pulled up with two more officers, and Donny was finally subdued and restrained. Thus the legend grew about Donny.

Now during my first week in the mods, I was told by the lieutenant and another sergeant that Donny was handing off his psyche meds to other inmates that would pay top dollar, or I should say top canteen, for the powerful medication. They asked me what I was going to do about it.

I said, "You saw the transaction, so you have to write the report."

"Yes, Mike, we will, but you have to go tell Donny that he's locked in. He's in your block."

I grabbed one of the more seasoned officers and told him what we had to do. He wasn't happy that he was going with me to lock in Donny. Would Donny fight us or would he cooperate? There was no way to tell. We walked along the second tier's horseshoe shaped catwalk, which housed half of the inmates in the "I" building. When we arrived at Donny's cell, I figured that I would befriend him and use brains instead of brawn.

"Donny! What the fuck did you do? The lieutenant saw you give out your medicine. He yelled at me, too. I stuck my neck out for you and told him that it wouldn't happen again and that you'd do your time quietly in your cell."

Donny was caught off guard. "I'm sorry that you took the heat for me, Sarge," he said. "How long will I be locked in for?"

"I'm not sure, Donny, but we'll get it as low as possible from the d-board people."

So the brute was conned, and he now respected me. I was bringing him a feed-in tray one evening (like jail room service), and Donny was trying to play wrestle me in his cell—just like a teenager trying to bump another teenager out of the way in school. I made the mistake of pushing him over on his bunk, and he started to get that rage look in his eyes. Quickly, I said, "Loser has to eat this meal." He laughed but still grabbed hold of me; so I pushed him backwards over his bunk again while he was getting up. I had him pinned, my knee buried into his solar plexus, but I saw him grinning. I was trying to keep his arms from getting hold of me. I bounced my entire body weight up and down on his solar plexus. That should have made almost anyone stop in their tracks. But he was just grunting with a crazy smirk on his face. Then he landed a left hook into my kidney that knocked the breath out of me. I told him that they were calling for me on the radio and I'd be back later to finish the match. I hobbled to the booth and lay down on the floor trying to catch my breath.

The other two officers asked me if I was all right. I said, "Yeah, I just wanted to manhandle Besse." They couldn't believe I had wrestled him by myself. But I never went back the following week to deliver his food. A month or two later he was brought up to maxi because he was trying to take on the Latin Kings. They were one of the most powerful gangs in the jail and ran a good percentage of the drug business.

The drug business was big at the jail. During contact visits and some of the cons' girlfriends or wives would bring heroin or coke into the facility, packed in small double wrapped balloons inside their mouths. They would kiss their husband or boyfriend, and the con in turn would swallow the balloon and dish it out, or tuck it into an orifice when the visiting officer wasn't looking. The danger of swallowing it was that it could rupture and the convict would overdose. That occasionally happened. If they did swallow it, as so many drug smugglers do, they would have to retrieve it when it passed through their system. The upside on the cons' end was that a ten dollar bag of heroin on the streets costs thirty dollars on the inside. The money would be delivered by the junkie's friend on the outside to a third party contact of the dealer on the inside. The third party got a cut and the woman dropping off the package got a cut, the dealer made a profit and the junky got high.

Some of the prettiest women would come up and visit these guys. It was hard to believe, but I guess they were just junkies, too. It's a shame and what a waste. One time when I was at MSF, one of my garage workers came to me with holes in his shoes and asked if his wife could drop off a pair of shoes for work. I told him no problem and the captain concurred.

The lady brought them up and Lefty met her at the gate. She said, "Can you deliver these to Sergeant Mike, please?" Lefty brought the shoes inside and threw them on the desk. I had another officer check them out for contraband.

After a minute, he said, "Hey, Sarge, feel this."

"Feel this," I replied back.

"No really, Sarge, something feels funny in the tongue of the boot."

I felt something a little lumpy and crunchy. "Cut it open!" I commanded. The officer did, and behold, it was five packs of heroin individually packed with the word *Scarface* on each packet. We called the necessary authorities and the lady was arrested. When Lefty and the other officer went to court to testify, Lefty told the judge that the lady said explicitly to give it to Sergeant Mike. I could only imagine what the judge was thinking. The worker received three months concurrent and I fired him from his job. His girlfriend only received probation. It kind of sours you that you get a good bust like that and nothing is done to the drug smugglers. You hate to punish anyone for doing drugs, but they plotted and planned to beat us with my kindness.

The drug business was also divided up by gangs, and the day shift was having problems with crazy Donny Besse extorting the Spanish gang's drug network. For some reason Captain Greenberg was siding with the Latin Kings and decided to remove Donny rather than break up the gang's drug cartel. Donny went to maxi peacefully only after Greenberg promised to get him back down and make him a worker in a week's time. A week came and went, then another; and Donny soon realized that he wasn't going anywhere. He started threatening any officer who walked by his cell. He told them that he was going to snap the neck of the first officer he got a hold of. Donny was not to be taken lightly. It wasn't as though he was tougher or stronger than most officers, it was that he was a little crazy and had a high tolerance for pain. He was a hard man to subdue. The officers in maxi decided to call the tactical team and have Donny strapped down to his bed for everyone's safety.

When the tactical team arrived, Donny had broken a piece of metal tubing off of the desk support. Each cell had a built in metal desk, and the support was a couple of metal tubes. Donny was brandishing the tubing, pumped to fight. There were usually five guys on the tactical team. With Donny they were using seven. Even so, the team was apprehensive and saying things like, "Let's get him, fuck him up!"—all of which was recorded on the move team's camera. Donny just wanted to fight, even if it meant an extra six months for assaulting a member of the move team.

The cell door opened and the team pushed in hard and fast. The shield man was six foot five and two hundred and thirty pounds. Donny stepped to the side in a low karate position and tripped him, sending him sailing into the metal bunk. Donny punched the next two guys hard enough to create a bottleneck at the entrance of his cell. They scrapped and fought for a good four to five minutes before they finally wore Donny down—and he had never even used the metal pipe on anyone. Thank God he didn't. They handcuffed him and strapped him down to the bed. Donny seemed unaffected by the event. The team was hi-fiving each other and were yelling things like, "Yeah! We fucked him up!" while still being recorded. I could understand their enthusiasm, but you have to do that stuff off camera.

Not five minutes after they had left the cell, they received another radio transaction that Donny had broken the restraints and was acting up again. The team's spirits were down now. They had to wrestle with this creature and restrain him all over again. This time they spared no force. Donny was hit hard with the shield—the shield man wasn't going to be made a fool of again. Donny went into the toilet and all seven of the officers showed Donny that he wasn't in charge; they were. Like I mentioned earlier, Donny wasn't the strongest or toughest guy in the jail by any means. He could just tolerate a lot of pain. Those types are tough to beat. He may not have been even in the top ten, but he was a force to be reckoned with.

***

Meanwhile, I was becoming a little dissatisfied with the captain and his cronies. They were almost giving a blind eye to the drug trafficking as long as the blocks were clean and the beds were made. I had found out later why Captain Greenberg had such a fetish for making the beds. If the beds weren't made, he would lose his mind. I found that rather odd. I would much rather have control and leverage over the inner workings of the prison. Greenberg had left his wife of almost thirty years for a twenty-two year old buxom, blonde female officer under his command. The buxom blonde was a friend of a dispatcher that I had dated for a short while. The dispatcher told me the when the blonde and Greenberg first hooked up, she'd had some intimacy problems. She was fearful of men sleeping in her room, so she made Greenberg sleep on the floor. This man was older than her father! The blonde was also a sloppy housekeeper, so Greenberg did the household chores. Hence, he had to make the bed where he wasn't allowed to sleep or even touch her. When they had sex, it was on the sofa or in the shower. He wasn't allowed on the bed. But he still made the bed every morning before work. This was, apparently, where his fetish and/or hatred of the beds not being made began

So as long as the captain's obsession was taken care of, nothing was done about the rumors concerning some officers bringing in drugs. I didn't want to believe that an academy trained officer would bring in drugs, but I knew it wasn't outside the realm of possibilities.

One evening I walked in the block from the outside yard and went right over to a cell where some white dudes that I had become familiar with were hanging out. There were three guys in there with a supermarket brown paper bag overflowing with weed. The lookout came running in and said, "I'm sorry guys, I missed him." I couldn't believe the amount of marijuana that was coming out of the top of the bag. The street value of this must have been phenomenal. There was no way that these guys got this in from a visit or tucked up someone's ass. A staff member must have brought it in. It was just way too much.

I wondered who delivered it. I didn't even think that most staff members could afford this much. I mean, it was literally a shopping bag full. Over full. I decided to flush it. I grabbed the bag and started pouring it in the toilet. They pleaded with me not to, but I told them to shut up or they were all going down. The three inmates in the room were yelling at the lookout, who had been distracted by the ball game on TV. I told them to keep it down and locked them in for a couple of days for disorderly conduct. Later on they thanked me when they realized how much trouble they could have gotten in.

***

I got into the routine down at the modular complex pretty easily, thankful that I was off the night shift. I heard an enlightening story about my former captain, the Hammer, that ended up in all the newspapers. There was a miscommunication between the second and third shifts at MSF about an inmate released to parole. Someone had screwed up the logbook, and his release was reported as an escape by the night shift. The deputies were all notified and the jail went into lockdown mode. Captain Heinz, the Hammer, was drinking with the boys at a local watering hole when he heard the news. Instead of realizing that he was too drunk to drive or to solve the problem, he drove around the MSF area looking for an escaped criminal.

The county hospital was only a couple hundred feet away from MSF. The hospital was closed, but the boiler room was still open and manned to keep the pipes working until the state decided what to do with it. The captain noticed a man standing in the doorway of the boiler room with a tool belt on, pulled out his gun and told the boiler man to get into his car. The man tried to explain who he was, but the Hammer brought him to MSF at gunpoint.

"I got your escaped convict right here," he said. "Don't you clowns have any idea how to run a prison? Do I have to do everything around here?" the captain was really proud of himself. The man pleaded with the sergeant on the desk and asked for a phone call. The captain, still proud from his bust, yelled comically, "A phone call? You've been watching too much TV, kid!"

It should be noted that the captain had no arrest powers, so this incident would be considered kidnapping in most states. He had also brought the man into a correctional facility without any rights being read—and he was drunk. The sheriff tried to get him into a program to control his drinking, but it was actually just a political ploy for the media. And you can be sure that the next day, the news stories were buzzing. The warden said that Heinz was a "special captain" with arrest powers, was another media ploy. They offered the boiler room man a job at sixty thousand a year, but he refused and sued the jail. I'm not sure how much the captain's actions cost the taxpayers, but I'm sure it was plenty. The captain never went for help or even apologized to his victim. Eventually he retired so he could drink uninterrupted by work. Oh, and just for the record, Sergeant Conti was on the desk and let the drunken captain bring the hospital boiler room man into the facility without the proper paperwork.

Being on second shift, I had Lieutenant Prince as an immediate supervisor. He was a puppet for any regime that ruled the jail. The administration would tell him to write up officers that they didn't like or that didn't participate in fundraisers for the sheriff. Prince didn't mind not being liked by anyone. I actually think that he thrived on it. He never bothered me, partly because I never gave him the satisfaction of pissing anyone off in my new assignment. I also gave him the occasional ride home, as I had to drive by his apartment in the city to get to my house. The rides were usually quiet; we just talked about people we knew or football.

One night he had to write a bunch of reports at work about the racial breakdown in each cellblock. He wasn't the brightest, and when you threw math into the equation, forget it. It was good that the deputy gave him that much work since it kept him from nitpicking the officers so much they couldn't do their jobs. That night on the way home, he reached into the sweatband of his hat and pulled out a joint. He calmly questioned, "Mikey, you mind if I smoke this in your truck?"

"No, it's all you," I replied back. I couldn't believe that my lieutenant would smoke in front of me. Was it a test? This should negate any reports that he would ever write about me. I know it was only a joint, but he was a lieutenant and in uniform. I personally could care less, but I was just amazed. The next few months I barely had contact with him other than just having him sign reports.

One particular evening, "Little Hitler," one of the guys who was promoted with me to sergeant, was walking down the runway. Little Hitler got his reputation as being a tough guy from a distance, especially when he was in the security of the booth and could yell at people without fear of repercussion. He was having a loud verbal interaction with a con walking back to the housing unit after leaving the modular chow hall. The chow hall was at the top of the runway near the pedestrian entry gate. I saw streaks like fireflies around the little Sergeant Hitler and wiped my eyes thinking that I was seeing things. When I got closer, I noticed that they weren't fireflies, but matches. The con was flinging lighted matches at little Hitler. I grabbed the inmate by the arm, walked him down into his cell and tossed him in. The whole time the inmate was calling Little Hitler a pussy and a little bitch. I guess he was right. The sergeant was not responsive to anything going on around him, including my inquiring if he was okay.

A few months later little Hitler passed the test for the state police, a job he had been drooling over for years. He definitely had the little man's disease. That came back to haunt him. One of the rookies he had yelled at for sitting down in the control booth after his turn on the housing unit floor was a nephew of the major in charge of the state police training unit. Little Hitler was used to yelling at people but wasn't prepared for the verbal abuse at the state police training center. It was tough enough, especially for a person without a military background; but now he had a major adding a little zest to the training. He got a taste of his own medicine and quit during the second week of the state police academy. He went to work for a small town's police department. We never heard from him again. I guess he knew we'd figured him out.

***

The months rolled into a year, and the racial problems were fairly quiet. I mingled with all the groups of cons, acting like a big brother when trying to settle the little problems that become magnified in prison. Small things like toothpaste and shower shoes almost become big ticket items. I made sure that each gang leader had enough toiletries for their indigent members so no one had to steal, and that way my blocks stayed fairly quiet. The bikers were granted control of one area, and the Latin Kings would ask me to move someone closer who needed protection. The Vice Lords and Killer Bees members would usually ask for the leftover feed-in trays, and I would help them out if possible. They would come to me when there was a problem, and instead of telling them to shut the fuck up, I would find a resolution that everyone could live with. So now, if one of my officers had a problem with a con in either of my two housing units, I would have the gang leaders "speak" to the troubled individual, who usually came up and apologized.

During the holidays, while other cellblocks were putting out fires or breaking up fights, I usually put on a *Girls Gone Wild* or female wrestling video so my inmates could pleasure themselves and fall asleep before lights out. Sometimes the holiday season is worse in prison. It's a funny thing: when the cons are on the outside, they don't give a rat's ass about their families; but once they come into jail, all of a sudden they're Mr. Daddy. It's the same with the Bible. I'm glad these guys find God, but why don't they stay with the Bible on the outside?

The maintenance department had been taking measurements and welding things in one of my housing units to convert it into a segregation unit or the hole. The administration has finally realized that it needed a place to put prisoners who refused to follow the rules of the institution. For some strange reason, they had picked the "J" building—my block. It was going to be a shit hole working there once it was converted into a disciplinary unit. These housing units were like big gymnasiums with cells on the perimeter. The middle was wide open and there were showers on the end beneath the booth. The building hadn't been designed to keep problems in a confined area, and when you had one hundred of the worst of the worst, it was a recipe for hell.

Meanwhile up in maximum security, Deputy Lusignan who took over the three cellblocks from the incompetent Slattery conducted a three a.m. raid on his sleeping officers. He wanted to shake things up and rid the area of the Slattery stench that made maxi less than a well run housing unit. The deputy had one of the special services officers walk down into the central control area at three a.m. for a seemingly harmless cup of coffee. She was to quietly hit the back exit control button to let the deputy and his brass in without anyone seeing them. Lusignan and his posse would use keys to get through the fence gates and then when the emergency exit door was opened they would all split up and nab the sleeping officers. The third shift was famous for sleeping—and who could blame them? It was a boring shift, but they did have some troubled inmates and some were on suicide watch. Based on reports, I believed that a lot of incidents would have been preventable if the officers hadn't been sleeping. Only the deputy could say for sure.

The female officer went in for coffee as she normally did, and as usual, most of the gates were open in the inner part of the jail. That way the officers could get around without making noise via the radio, and nobody was wakened by the rumbling of the gates. The officers still had fire winds to do: every hour an officer would have to go through all three cellblocks and use a magnetic recording device, called a wind gun, touching it to strips on various places in the cellblock. The next day, the deputy would print out the readings to ensure that the blocks were being monitored and someone was awake to make the rounds. If a wind was missed, reports had to be written. If a wind was missed and something had happened, well, let's just say there would be heck to pay.

The deputy made it to the back emergency exit and the special services lady quietly popped open the control knob. The night shift had about twelve officers in maxi. The deputy and his henchmen caught seven of them sleeping, and three of those men were out of uniform. One of the victims, or culprits, depending on how you view it, was my buddy Sergeant Dave Callahan. He was on an easy overtime shift and was in shorts and a sweatshirt. There was a brief moment of chaos until the officers realized that they had been duped. Big suspensions were given out and two people loss their rank, including Callahan. Poor Dave. He was just trying to make a few extra bucks, and he ended up losing his rank and ended up with a six-month suspension. Lusignan didn't want to get rid of Dave, but he was the sergeant in charge; so if he wanted to start house cleaning, Dave had to fall, too. But I always thought Lusignan was fair. If you screwed up, he would yell at you and that was it. There were no holding grudges with him. The next day it was forgotten. We later found out that Lusignan was a Vietnam vet who specialized in interrogations. The top brass knew that if they wanted to win back maxi, he was their man.

There was another little incentive for Lusignan to clean up maximum security. He could take any ten officers that he wanted. My phone rang the next day. It was my deputy from the mods.

"Hello, Deputy, what did I do wrong?"

"Nothing. Lusignan wants you to go work maxi."

"Really?"

"Well, actually, you were his second choice. Sergeant Lau declined going to first shift."

I was still thrilled. "Wow! First shift, too?"

"I'll take that as a yes then, Mike?"

"I'd love to work first shift, boss." That's something you should never do—ell the bosses that you love or dislike something. They can always use that to punish you in the future. If they know you hate third shift, as a lot of us do, they'll move you there just to mess with you or get back at you for something. It might not happen right away, but they remember that stuff.

My deputy said, "Mike, I just want you to know that you did a good job down here and we'll miss you."

"Thanks, Deputy, and when Lusignan gets sick of me, I'll see you again."

"Good luck, Mike."

The two years that I had spent down at the modular complex, I only spoke to the deputy once. And that was the conversation. Now I had a total of five years on the job, was a sergeant going on day shift, had never ratted anyone out, and had never bribed or donated money to a politician. I felt pretty darn good about myself right about now. Even though I had worked in two different areas, I wasn't quite sure about what to expect from maximum security. I was replacing Sergeant Callahan, and I was sure the troops would be suspect of me. But, I reasoned, if I gave them the time to get to know me, they'd like me. I might not be able to live up to Dave's craziness, but nobody could say I didn't go to bat for my officers.

CHAPTER FIVE
MAXIMUM SECURITY

My first day in maxi was quite memorable. I walked down the lower tier, the inmates not knowing what to make of me. *Is he cool? Is he a punk? What's he doing here?* and the like were probably going through their minds. The officers were probably thinking the same thing. I'd bet that was why I was patrolling the tiers by myself. The other officers weren't really speaking to me yet, but they were keeping an eye on me. I didn't even have to call for the gates. Which was a good thing, since I wasn't one hundred percent sure what each gate was called anyways.

I walked from the lower right tier to the upper left tier quietly as to take in all the activity and try to figure out who the gang members and the heavies, or the muscle of the block, were. There were two flights of stairs right out of a horror movie that you had to walk up in the back of the block to get to the top tier. Inmates were never allowed back there, so the stairs were partitioned off by more steel gates and solid steel doors. If you screamed, no staff member would ever hear you; and the noise would be absorbed by the noise of the fifty-two inmates on each tier. That was why it was important to have your radio on and a fresh battery in it. If you couldn't communicate with the booth, you were screwed.

When I made the corner around the gate, I saw one of the most bizarre sights that I've ever seen. There was this pale little white kid on his bunk getting plowed in the ass doggie style by an older black inmate with a straggly beard. The inmate who was doing the driving was sweating profusely. There were two other black kids in the cell waiting their turn, and one Spanish inmate holding a shank to the crying white kid's neck. The Spanish inmate turned and looked at me, holding the shank. I was worried about the shank and where it was headed, but he dropped it in the toilet and hit the flush button. I radioed for an officer to assist me and I believe about ten showed up. That's the good thing about working in a prison. When you call for help, a lot of officers show up with a lot of energy.

Although I tried to block the cell door, two of the assailants got past me. The older inmate doing the banging put his hands up and said, "All right, Sarge, you got me. I'll give you that." I really didn't want to look, but I noticed a little blood and feces on the mattress sheet. We locked down the tier and thankfully the other assailants didn't attack me. The two that pushed by my legs were grabbed afterwards and brought down to the lower left where the disciplinary problems went until the seg. Block was finished.

The inmate who was doing the anal penetrating was still inside the kid when my help arrived. It was a freaky sight. The white kid was brought to the hospital and treated as a rape victim. The investigation concluded that this kid promised some cons sexual favors in exchange for a couple bags of heroin. Then the kid reneged on his deal, so they took it from him. I felt bad for him at first, but then, he was a heroin junky and had promised something that he had no intention delivering. Regardless, both of these activities were wrong and called for disciplinary measures. The reports absolutely sucked to write. Who wants to write about a junky taking it in the ass and five other dudes watching it and waiting their turn? Even more troubling was that if I had walked into this mess on my first day, what the heck else was going on?

Lusignan called me into his office. "Welcome to the real jail."

"Can I go back to the mods?" I joked back.

He told me that a few of the better officers would be back after their two days off and we'd start tier by tier. Gang members would be warned, and we would do a huge shakedown of the entire block. He promised me that we'd have fifty officers to tear through the cells and remove all contraband. Lusignan came through on his promise; the sheriff gave him fifty something officers who tore through the block and removed fifteen shanks, some drugs and a lot of contraband. I was off that day, but now there were two of us sergeants during the daytime in maxi. Scooter was the other sergeant. He was small and wiry and had a knack for finding hiding places and contraband, while I was into befriending the gang leaders and making sure the officers had respect. It was a good combination. The inmates understood that the deputy wasn't going to put up with any bullshit. He would be fair as long as the block behaved themselves. The cons would get two gym periods a day instead of one, and bigger dayroom televisions. They enjoyed these small perks.

The routine took a little longer, as we had three cellblocks for maximum security. Occasionally, the captain and/or lieutenant would swap our housing duties around the three maxi blocks. The big block was maxi. Then there was maxi A-1 and maxi A-2. These were all pretrial inmates with varying degrees of crimes and needs. Maxi A-1 and maxi A-2 were fairly good assignments. The A-2 block was really quiet and housed mostly protective custody inmates who were afraid of anyone over twelve years old. Hence their crimes were mostly against little kids. These were the predators. But they were afraid of jail and rightfully so. If a regular con could get to one of them, they would beat or stab the skinners. The skinners were also the ones who attacked on senior citizens.

When I talked to the inmates, they'd complain about the courts being too harsh. There was this one scumbag who attacked a senior citizen with a hammer at an ATM machine, robbed the man and then complained that he received a year in county. *A year* for assaulting a senior citizen with a hammer? He should have received more.

Every day Scooter would check all the tiers for weapons. It was a rare day that he didn't find one. Sometimes the weapons were crude, and other times they were creative. Scooter would go down one tier and up another by himself. The inmates would playfully make fun of him for being small. He was around five feet seven inches and two hundred pounds. When I thought about that, he didn't seem that small in real life. But in terms of the maxi officers, it wasn't that big. Most of the officers I worked with were built like professional football players.

Scooter found shanks made from everything from the dayroom ceiling tile frames to toothbrush handles with razor blades melted into the ends. Sometimes the cons would find a metal screw and melt a plastic pen or toothbrush handle around its head. Then they would tear strips off of a bed sheet and wrap it around the connecting parts for reinforcement should the need arise to actually use it. I started separating problem inmates from their bad influences. Since nobody had been sentenced for their alleged crimes yet, I might have a murderer living in a cell next to a chronic shoplifter or even in the same cell with him. I tried to keep inmates in the same cell that got along with each other. If I found that there were too many of one gang together on a tier, I would move a few out to another tier. They would still see each other during chow time or gym. I got into a few verbal exchanges, but usually they moved without incident.

The area in maxi that usually had some action was the lower left tier. I mentioned before that as you looked out of the booth, there were four tiers. Looking at them clockwise from the booth window, there were the upper left, the upper right, the lower right and the lower left. The tiers were separated by a pipespace that contained all the wiring and plumbing to the cells. The pipespace ran the length of the block, and the inmates couldn't go in there unless they were supervised, and then only to clean. The pipespace had small grills that looked into all the cells. They were very finely meshed and many an officer walking down the pipespace would overhear or see, unbeknownst to the con, some sort of bad behavior going on in the cells. We didn't hang in the pipespace long, as it stunk due to the waste from the inmate toilets being piped through there; but it was a valuable source of information.

I made a few good friends in maxi. Carl Sampson was one of them. He was six foot one and three hundred and fifteen pounds. Combined with his thick brown beard, he had the look of a mountain man wit his head shaved to stubble whenever the inmates received new clippers for their hair, which was about once a month. Despite Carl's size, he was strong and fast. I pictured him in overalls, no shoes, in the Ozark Mountains. He was a hunter and fisherman. Carl was also the go-to guy when trouble occurred. He almost always had a cigarette going and when he didn't have a cigarette going, he had a coffee. Many times Carl had both going, and still the inmates never messed with him.

Carl, the senior officer, Pete McCormick, and I were standing in the inmates' chow hall with about one hundred and fifty inmates eating, and we were picking on the kitchen officers. When Carl spoke it was always loud, and when he was loud, he sounded like Yosemite Sam from the Bugs Bunny cartoons. Carl bellowed out like a hillbilly, "Where's my God damn pot pie, woman?" The two officers threw a couple of rotten apples our way, hit the wall and made applesauce. Carl and Pete threw stuff back at the kitchen cops. I could see this getting ugly, but I thought that Carl and Pete did this regularly and knew what they were doing. I didn't want to be a party pooper either. Then I saw one of the kitchen officers grab a ladle of oatmeal after the line of inmates had gone down, and make like he was going to fling it at us. I yelled, "Hey, look out!" Before I could get another word out, Carl, Pete and about one hundred cons were throwing apples, open cartons of milk and spoonfuls of oatmeal at the kitchen officers and inmate workers. The kitchen staff lowered the two thousand pound steel window that separated the chow line from the inmate dining area. Even so, they were covered with food and milk. It was a scene from Animal House. Apparently this was a regular event. I hope it wasn't every day, or even just on oatmeal days, as oatmeal was served three times a week.

Carl normally spent the morning on the lower left tier with the special needs inmates. He sat at a metal desk bolted into the concrete floor about four feet from the very last cell in the corridor. There was always a nice comfy chair there, though. Inmates delivered from the streets on detox were housed there, as well as inmates on suicide watch, disciplinary problems and inmates that needed to be monitored for minor medical problems. Each officer had to spend two to three hours on watch, which was usually a job that no one wanted—stuck there with the whiners and the crazies. You spent two hours making sure that they were alive and behaving, and three times a week they were given showers. Carl liked to get his watch duty hours over with first, and since he was senior and the strongest, he usually got his way.

Occasionally you would get a high profile/front page type inmate, often a high profile Mafia member or some politician or policeman from another county who had snapped or gotten caught up in something stupid. We held this one big Mafia figure from the biggest city in the state, and he let Carl and me read some of the court transcripts. There it hit me as to how real some of these crimes were. Giggling, Carl showed me this one page where the defendant had disposed of a body but was waiting to get rid of the head. I guess it was because of the teeth that could identify the body. When the SWAT team raided the Mafia big's house, they found the head of his alleged victim in the back of his toilet tank. I was reading this court transaction just a few feet from the guy who did the act. It was a pretty sobering feeling.

One Friday morning and a payday to boot, I was punching in at the time clock when I heard this awful deep yelling. It was the deepest voice I think I've ever heard, and it was coming from my block about one hundred yards away. I was wondering what the third shift people were doing and why they would let this much noise come out of the block at six forty-five a.m.

I decided to walk down to my block a little early and see what all the commotion was. The gates were opened for me, and the voice got louder as I entered the housing unit and turned down the lower left. As I was walking down the tier, the other inmates were saying things like, "What's wrong with that dude? Can you shut him up? Kick his ass for me, Sarge!" I heard verses from the Bible being quoted in an almost demonic voice. "Pray for your enemies, do good unto those who wish you harm!" When I got to the cell, which was open, I saw a man roughly five foot ten inches, naked with huge rippling muscles and standing on his bed. The night sergeant was lecturing him to be quiet, but he couldn't hear her. His voice was terrifying. He didn't appear to be yelling and yet it was shaking the concrete walls and floor.

I saw Carl and Scooter in there along with two other officers. Scooter was trying to hook up the leg shackles on the inmate so that he could be restrained until a mental health professional could speak to or get him the proper medication. Two of the officers were standing back just asking him to cooperate and lie down on the bunk. Scooter got the leg irons on his thick, muscular ankles, and Carl went to grab him by the arm; the guy grabbed Carl by the throat with both hands and lifted him off of the ground, all three hundred and fifteen pounds. The guy lifted his head near the ceiling like a priest holds a chalice and said, "I'm going to bless you!"

I have to admit that this was the scariest moment of my prison career. My body was telling me to run, but my sense of duty to others was trying to overcome the fear. This man's voice alone was scary. Plus he looked like an unnatural bodybuilder on steroids for years. Now he had Carl up off the ground, and Carl's legs were dangling around the height of the bunk. I saw everyone freeze except Scooter, who was reaching for more restraints from one of the officers. Everything was in slow motion and I had tunnel vision. Scooter reaching for more restraints made me think. I grabbed the chains on the leg irons that Scooter had just placed on this guy's ankles and pulled them towards me. He fell! Thank you, God! When he fell on his bunk, he let go of Carl and I dove on top of him.

Carl gasped, coughed and yelled forcefully, "You motherfucker!" Then he dove on top of the naked dude, too. I had both of my hands trying to hold the inmate's left arm from grabbing me or anyone else. Now the adrenaline was pumping.

"Keep him down!" Scooter yelled. The guy's legs were trying to either kick me or get around me and Carl. I knelt on his solar plexus and heard some ribs cracking . The crazy man just kept looking at me with a smirk and harshly said, "I forgive you, my brother. I forgive you!"

Scooter and Carl were still attempting to handcuff the guy, and two other night shift officers finally got into the battle and chained the leg irons to the bolts in the concrete floor. The guy actually started to turn and get off the bed with Carl and me on top of him. I thought, *if he gets up we'll never get him back down and he'll hurt some people.* He looked at me and gave an unearthly growl. I was frightened. So I wound up and punched him. Then I punched him again, even harder. Blood was coming out of his nose and mouth, but he looked up at me and said calmly but deeply, "I forgive you, my brother. I forgive you."

I hollered at him wordlessly, and, since my right hand was still holding his left wrist, punched him with my left hand so many times that my knuckles were swollen. Blood was all over his face and neck. I never did find out what his story was. Why was he preaching? Why was he fighting us? What had happened to make this obviously competitive body builder snap like that? Was it steroids? Was he possessed? Was he on PCP? He definitely had some super human powers about him. I will never forget that face looking up at me and saying, "I forgive you, my brother! I forgive you." He didn't feel like my enemy. He didn't exactly feel like an inmate to me, either.

After I hit him, we finally got him back down and got his hands cuffed and shackled over the end of the bed to the bolts in the floor. There were round bolts in the concrete floor in half of the cells on the lower left tier just in case you had to subdue someone who was trying to hurt himself or the staff.

When Carl and I got off him, we both noticed that this crazy man, or beast, was fully aroused. Yes, that's what I said. He was erect. I couldn't get out of there fast enough and wanted to catch my breath. But no sooner did Scooter and I round the corner and get out of the block did my lieutenant, Ricky Rafferty (God rest his soul) say to us, "Get that guy up, showered and ready to go to the state hospital for mental evaluation."

Scooter and I just looked at each other. No way was that a safe thing to do now. "Lieutenant, we just wrestled with that monster and it took five of us. Maybe have the psychiatrist come here," I pleaded.

"Never mind, I'll do it," Rafferty said. "You two go do your reports. I'll do it myself. Let the old guy do it," he playfully belittled us. As he walked down, we walked a few paces behind him, figuring he would come to his senses and not release the crazed, jacked guy. If he did, at least we'd be there to wrestle the guy again and be able to say I told you so!

Standing a few cells away, I heard the lieutenant say that we had restrained the inmate incorrectly.

"I know, Lieutenant, that's the only way we could get him under control."

At that time inmates who were four point restrained, meaning the two arms and two legs had to be facedown. This was due to the courts and inmate rights advocates. Later in my career, they would change their minds three times. There was a case in the city in which the police responded to a crazy man threatening people with a knife. The police tried and tried to convince the deranged man to drop the knife, but he waved it at them, too. The officers responded professionally and pepper sprayed the would-be assailant. When man went down the officers got on top of the assailant while he was face up, and the poor bastard asphyxiated. As you could imagine, there was a huge outcry.

Well, the lieutenant released the crazed man and walked with him like they were old skiing buddies down to the van taking him to the state hospital. I couldn't grasp how the guy went from crazed preacher to the lieutenant's buddy in a matter of minutes. Was it all an act? No way! I still don't get it, but we never saw the guy again.

Lieutenant Rafferty was around sixty years old. He was stocky and had a pot belly. He loved life, his family and the sheriff. He also had a speech impediment. His *r*'s and *l*'s came out like *w*'s. He sounded like, "Hewwo, fewwas, I'm Wieutenant Waffety." It's horrible to make fun of people with these problems, but when you work in an all testosterone environment and try bossing people around, you have to expect some good, hearty ribbing.

***

The A-1 unit was manned by three officers. One officer would be downstairs on the watch, another officer would control the booth and the other would patrol the short tiers. The upstairs had sixteen cells, and the downstairs had sixteen cells. We had to keep the inmates upstairs separated from the lower tier inmates, as most of the ones on the lower tier were sex offenders. This is where I was first introduced into the legal system as the defendant. Christopher Jacques was awaiting trial for stabbing his girlfriend with a pair of scissors while she slept. He was a six foot four man from Cape Verde. He wanted to be called C.J., but no one liked the guy and most refused to talk to him. He would use the system to his advantage, borrowing things and never paying the cons back, just checking into protective custody. Then when the cons that he borrowed from left, he would go back and repeat the cycle.

He would also do that with us. He would stay in A-1 and when the PC inmates had gym or canteen, he would go with them. When the upstairs inmates would have canteen or other privileges, he would sign off on a release form and we would have to move him away from the protective custody inmates, but not into a block where he stole or borrowed items. Jacques would do this at least three times a week. When I put my foot down and told classification to stop catering to this kid, they "yupped" me and I later received a phone call from my deputy to let the kid sign off. So I bit my tongue for a couple of weeks.

One morning the deputy called me and told me to tell Jacques that he has made too many enemies and would remain in PC for the rest of his time with us. No sooner did I hang the phone up in the A-1 booth did Pete McCormick, the senior officer in maxi receive a radio transaction to send the regular A-1 inmates to the gym. Pete announced it over the PA system and opened the steel trap gates. Jacques had already been let out of the trap, and I had to put him back into the block and explain that he wouldn't be able to play the system anymore. I stopped Jacques behind the booth and said, "Christopher, the deputy called and said that you are all done going back and forth to suit your needs. You have too many enemies and are to remain with the special needs inmates."

"Fuck you, CO!" he shot back. "You don't tell me where I can go!"

"Oh, yes I can, Jacques. You are in jail, not the Marriott."

Jacques then took his long index finger and pointed it into my chest. "Fuck you, motherfucker; I'm going to gym!"

I put my body in front of him. He tried to get by but I blocked him with my out stretched arms. "Jacques! Go back into your cell or you're going to be locked in!"

"Fuck you, pig!"

I really didn't want to write more reports so I asked him two more times, and I received the standard two word response followed or led by *pig*. Scooter heard the commotion and thankfully he came by. I explained the scenario quickly, and when Scooter told him to go into his cell he received the same response: "Get the fuck out of my business and go look at my dirty shorts, pigs!"

Jacques wound up from way back like he was going to hit me. He started to swing this ridiculous overhand punch, so I lunged in and grabbed his collar with one hand and the waistband of his pants with the other, half crouched as to avoid a punch if it ever came. I kicked his feet out from under him and was kneeling over him when he gave me a half-assed punch on the left side of my face. So I gave him a left cross that was only about a six on the Richter scale. His head went back and bounced off the tile over concrete floor. His lip was split but only a little blood came out. I turned his stunned body over and handcuffed him. Scooter and Pete dragged him down the stairs while the councilors manned the booth for Pete.

A year later I received a summons to go to court, as Jacques was suing me for back injuries. The jail represented me, and they were just going to give him a meager one hundred dollars to make the case go away even though he was clearly in the wrong. I told the lawyer, "Don't even give this punk a candy bar." My report and the reports from the mental health and substance abuse worker stated that I asked and practically begged the con to go into his cell numerous times, and still I was assaulted. The court advised Jacques to drop this and any frivolous lawsuits in the future.

***

The substance abuse people held regular group meetings with the cons, and one of the councilors would visit A-1 twice a day looking for new program volunteers. The lady that came to A-1 was Maria. She was pretty faced with long, straight black hair. She wore nice clothes for work, but dressed down to conceal her curvy but thick figure. Maria was thirteen years younger than me and had only been out of college for two years. Pete and I would razz her, and she was frequently the victim of Pete putting toothpaste on the inside of the door handle leading into the booth. Pete was famous for pranks putting toothpaste on door handles or super gluing a nickel on the faucet, so that when an unsuspecting person washed their hands, the water would shoot out and splash them making it look like they just peed their pants. A-1 and A-2 were the only control booth doors that were key operated by the officer inside. The officer inside would unlock it and the person outside would pull the heavy solid steel door open. Pete more often than not would giggle at his victims after the harmless prank, and Maria almost seemed to enjoy the attention. The three of us became friends and I always thought that Maria and Pete would make a good couple, as they were both timid regarding the opposite sex. Pete was good natured and enjoyed a few beers. Okay, a lot of beers, but it never interfered with his job.

I always made fun of Maria dressing like an old maid. She dressed classy, but it was very conservative and outdated. She was one of the few twenty-something-year-olds that would wear a girdle and two slips. I realize that I almost got into trouble from Pam for telling her she looked like a waitress. But Maria wasn't Pam, and Maria enjoyed it when an officer or sergeant was nice to her. A lot of the correctional staff looked at civilians like they were second-class citizens. You know, the attitude you get from a small town cop with nothing to do but look for expired stickers or someone with a light out. Plus the staff knew that the civilians always wanted to talk to inmates, believing that they could save them from a life of crime. In all actuality, the inmates usually went to drug and alcohol programs just for the good time credits applied to their release date. The administration and the state used scare tactics by crying about the lack of funding for drug programs. The fact was that the administration and state just wanted money to get raises and hire friends and family under the guise of drug programs. When a new sheriff came in and demanded more money for more cells, you could bet that he or she was looking for some kickbacks, too.

I was always joking about Maria and Pete going out. They were both too scared to ask each other, so one day I said, "Pete, you go to Barber's Crossing restaurant tonight at eight. Maria, you go there at eight o' five. Okay?" They both looked like shocked little kids, but they agreed. It was a good matchmaking job on my part. Two people, single, both good looking and both a little thick, set up by my good deed. I felt good about it.

One morning I was sitting in the booth starting my paperwork with my other officer. It was so far a quiet morning in A-1. Pete was on the watch on the high-risk tier, suicide watch, and he radioed for me to come down and check something out. I was puzzled as to why he would be calling me first thing in the morning. It had to be an emergency. I walked down the few stairs to the lower tier to the very last cell, which housed an inmate named John Hayes. Pete was pointing at Hayes, who was laying face up and motionless. Hayes was a habitual criminal who looked like a tall, skinny biker without a bike. I looked into the small window of the solid steel door, and agreed with Pete: things just didn't look right. It was one of the few cells on the lower A-1 tier that had a solid steel door. Hayes wasn't on any kind of watch; he was just in protective custody due to his borrowing things from other inmates and not paying it back. He acted like a tough guy around other cons but cried for attention in many different ways.

Hayes had his TV on top of his footlocker next to the door, semi-blocking the view, which is a no-no. I radioed the booth to open his cell, and when I moved the TV and footlocker to the back of the cell I noticed some blood underneath the bunk. Hayes was unresponsive when I shook him. I pulled the covers off and saw a plastic garbage bag covering him, which I removed as well. That's when I noticed blood all over his arms, legs, and the bed sheets. I shook him again frantically and yelled, "Hayes! Hayes! Wake up, stupid!" I rolled him to the side and noticed that he had cut the major arteries in his arms and legs. Blood was pooled all over his bed. He had also put a plastic garbage bag under his mattress so as to stop the blood from leaking out of the bottom of the mattress.

I later learned that Hayes was intent on concealing his suicide, milking the blood out of his system by squeezing it out of the deep cuts he self inflicted and dabbing it up with toilet paper. He had lost an awful lot of blood. Pete fell to his knees, then to the ground. He had fainted. Apparently he could not stand the sight of blood. I radioed the infirmary and told them that we'd probably need an ambulance. The lieutenant was supposed to get the officers and paperwork ready for the emergency hospital trip, but he must have delegated the assignment, as he was one of the first ones to arrive to help the nursing staff. I wrapped up Hayes' deep razor blade cuts with pillowcases, shirts, pants and socks while the lieutenant was busy getting Pete back into coherence. A couple of other officers helped me lift Hayes onto the stretcher and then rolled it to meet the ambulance. I had to write a bunch of reports to the effect that the night shift must not have seen Hayes' cleverly disguised cover.

The hospital informed the jail that Hayes had been very close to completing his task. The funny thing about Hayes and inmates like him was that they only tried to harm themselves when they were in jail. Hayes had been in more times than I could count on both hands and feet, and he had always tried to harm himself in jail. The reason usually was for a wife's or girlfriend's sympathy and a lot of cons manipulated their loved ones this way. It was a control issue. They had no physical power over their loved ones while they were incarcerated, so they played the extreme guilt/sympathy card. Some said that the guards beat them up or that they were sick and couldn't get the help they need. (If you hear this, remember that they are called cons for a reason.)

Hayes tried no less than fifteen times to hurt himself in the jail, but not once has he tried it on the street. We had classes on this every year, and this was a subject that was very dear to me. My best friend in high school hung himself, and I wish I could have seen the signs; but we drifted apart and each had families after high school. The sheriff's department had also had two horrific officer suicides. One had shot himself and let his family find him on the living room couch. The other officer I had been friendly with until he ratted Carl and me out for throwing apples at the wall above his head. But I had forgiven him for that later on. The officer had checked out a weapon and gone to the beach intoxicated. When a rookie policeman approached his truck for parking in a no parking zone, the officer shot himself.

You have to feel bad for the rookie policeman and the officer, and the families. I keep them all in my prayers. This is a very important issue, so as an aside, keep a keen eye out for the telltale signs of depression. As for the Hayes incident, Peter, the lieutenant, and myself all received a nice letter from the sheriff and eight hours off placed on our time sheet to be used at will. I felt like I actually did something worthwhile.

CHAPTER SIX
THREE M'S: MARIA, MAXI, & MORE

I was on the computer one night and noticed that Maria was on instant messenger. She was on my buddy list. I kidded her about becoming pregnant with Pete's baby after their first date. She had told me that they had a nice time, but that there was no chemistry between them. I said that they were both probably scared and shy, and to give it some time. That's when she typed, "Mike, I have a problem and I don't know what to do about it."

I was wondering all sorts of things. Had she brought in drugs? Had sex with a con? Was it a problem outside of the jail?

She then typed, "Oh forget it. You'll just laugh at me." Now I knew it was nothing serious, but my curiosity was going.

"What's wrong Maria? You can tell me anything. I'm Sergeant Mike—LOL."

"Well, I'm in love with someone else."

"Oh no! What about Pete?" I couldn't believe it. She wasn't into Pete like I had been hoping. I thought that they were the perfect couple.

Then she typed, "I'm in love with you, Sergeant Mike."

I thought she was joking, as I had never given her the slightest indication that I was interested in her like that. But then again, I'd never given Pam the attention she apparently wanted either, and look what had happened.

"Are you kidding me, Maria?"

"No! I really love you. Can't you tell? I'm always staring at you, I can't speak like a normal person around you and I come to wherever you are working at least four times a day."

I had noticed that she came to whatever block I was in frequently, but I just figured that it was because I treated her decently, like any other civilian.

"I don't know what to say, Maria. I can't hurt my buddy Pete."

"I know, but Pete knows that we don't have the chemistry and that we are only going to be friends."

I wasn't sure what to do. "Maria, I'm flattered that such a beautiful woman like you likes me, but this is a lot to grasp right now. Let me think about this and I'll talk to you later."

Click…my head was spinning. On the one hand I had my friend Pete, whom I set up with this girl. On the other hand, I had this beautiful young woman who was in love with me. In love with me? How could she be in love with me? She didn't even know me. She just knew Sergeant Mike from work. How about plain old Mike who sat in front of the television and watched sitcoms? Would she love the Mike the biker? Would I ever love her? I wasn't sure. I decided that, regardless, I couldn't do it to Pete. Even if they had become just friends, it would be too awkward.

The next day at work Maria didn't come to the block. But when I came home there was an e-mail from her, and it said she wanted to talk to me. I called her and told her about my positions. No, not the missionary, doggy, reverse cowgirl, or filthy Sanchez; but how I felt about hurting Pete, and questioning how she could love me without even knowing me.

She was very sweet but persuasive and persistent. She said, "Just meet me by the reservoir and hear me out for five minutes. After five minutes, if you are not totally happy with what I have to say, then you can leave and I'll never bother you again. Please!" Against my better judgment I went to the reservoir, and there she was with her sunglasses on and a tight fitting shirt and jeans that she probably needed help getting into. She was a thirty-six D, and this was the first time I've seen her dress so provocatively. But I wasn't going to let that affect my status with Pete.

She got out of her car, grabbed my hand, squeezed it, pushed her sunglasses up on her forehead and kissed me. I have to admit, I didn't push away like I should have. She pushed me up against my truck and cuddled up to me. "Mike, you are funny, smart and a big manly man. You are everything I want. I actually wanted Carl first, but he's married. " She told me a quick little blurb about Carl. The first time she had gone down to maxi, big Carl was escorting a dope sick inmate wearing leg irons and handcuffs on which restricted his walking. Carl was smoking a butt and had a coffee in the other hand. The inmate fell back and to the side from being so weak, and his head hit Carl's styrofoam cup of coffee. Carl bellowed out like a hillbilly and Yosemite Sam combo, "what the hell ya doin', boy? Get on your God damn feet, and you better hope they got coffee in the infirmary!" Then he picked the kid up by the nape of his shirt and proceeded to escort him down to the infirmary. "God damn junky. Ruining my java."

Maria wasn't used to the Carl method yet, as she had come from a hospital environment that treated the junkies a little more nicely. We chuckled over some Carl stories, and then I remembered why we were there.

"Maria, you don't know me. I could be a couch potato, a perv or whatever."

She wasn't going to be dissuaded. "Mike, I want you and I'll take whatever you are." She had me up against my truck and was now feverishly kissing me. She was a strong woman. I started feeling like a high school kid again. I wondered if this was wrong. She was thirteen years younger than me, my friend liked her and she worked with me. I had to break the silence. She was really getting to me. I had not been held or kissed like that in a while. I had had a lot of girlfriends and an ex or two, but she was so into me that it was flattering and I didn't want to be this vulnerable so quickly. Was I already falling for this girl?

"You need some work on your kissing, Maria," I said jokingly so as to break the moment. I didn't want to say anything embarrassing. I heard a horn beep, then another. "Oh shit!" It was the classification department. They were just getting out of the jail, which was quite a few miles away, but this road is a shortcut for the few people who live in North County. Now word was going to get out. I had to tell Pete somehow. We were both off the next two days, thank goodness. During that time, I wondered if stories about Maria and I had made it around camp. A story would get so twisted and turned and by the time they get back to you it has become so tangled; you wouldn't even know it was about you.

I was torn between wanting Saturday to come and not wanting it to come. I would have to tell him, even if nothing transpired between Maria and me. Otherwise it wouldn't be fair to anyone. I was working maxi and Pete, as usual, was working A-1. I called him and asked him to meet me outside in the parking lot, and then I told the lieutenant that Pete and I had to look at a screw in his tire. Being a weekend, the lieutenant didn't care and let us go outside.

Pete was perplexed as to why I was calling him out to the parking lot. The only reason you would normally go out to the parking lot was to fight. Pete wasn't a fighter. He was a good sized man at around two hundred forty pounds and five foot eleven. But he definitely would not want to fight, I thought—unless it was about his potential girlfriend.

We walked over to my truck and he said, "What's going on?"

"Oh Pete, you're going to wanna hit me, and I'm going to let you."

He was taken aback. "What? Why would I hit you Mike?" "Pete, your girlfriend, Maria, told me that she loves me, but I don't think I feel the same about her. But I wanted to let you know that she said that to me and that she wants to be friends with you."

Pete stood quietly for a moment and leaned against my tailgate.

"I'm sorry, Pete, I feel like shit and I told her that my loyalty is to you. But we did kiss. So if you want to hit me, go ahead. I won't stop you." I actually closed my eyes, bowed my head and braced for a few punches. Ah yes, I did cover my private parts.

But Pete didn't hit me. "Wow. I'm glad you told me, Mike. That fuckin' bitch! I thought we had a good time. Well, I'm glad you told me so I won't look like a fool chasing after her."

I repeated how sorry I was and a somber Pete and Sergeant Mike walked back into the jail. Pete and I stayed friends. Maria and I stayed together for a couple of weeks; we would sneak in an occasional heavy makeout session in her office or in the booth when no one was around. She would never come to my house; I would always have to go to her apartment and watch crappy reality shows. We had very opposite tastes, and she wasn't the ideal lover for a man like me. Finally, I pieced together why she liked me in the first place: I reminded her of her daddy. She was a daddy's girl. I was flattered, but we were just too different. She was country living in the hood and I was rock 'n roll living in the suburbs. When I told her that it just wasn't working out, she cried in the hallway near central control and stormed out of the jail. She was later moved to a different part of the jail. She was a sweet, wonderful woman, but we were just too different.

She later took in a foster child that belonged to a junkie. The junkie wasn't happy about her being the foster parent of his child. As one would guess, the junkie eventually made it to jail and told his cellmate JB about the drug counselor's house and everything else he could remember about her life. They had plotted and planned how to get her into trouble. The junkie had no regard for the well being of his kid; he was just jealous. JB started befriending Maria and eventually asked her to bring in a bag of weed. Maria wrote the incident up, but the con explained that they had been dating and that he even lived with her. He also said that she had brought in a lot of drugs in the past, but now she was having him locked in facing disciplinary charges because he was breaking up with her. He told the special service investigators all about her house and family. They fell for JB's story, even though he was a well-known gay male prostitute. Maria, who truly loved her job, was escorted off of the property in tears. No one heard from her ever again.

Time went on. The days turned into weeks and the weeks into months. I was sitting in the A-1 booth with Brody. Brody was extremely funny and we would recite lines from sitcoms word for word. Brody and I were talking about foods that we liked when Jimmy Boutilette walked in. Jimmy was a chunky officer who liked his ice cream as well as his gossip. He was a good kid and he used to be called Boots. But he was so chunky that Boots soon became Butter. I told Brody that I put butter and pepper on my corn on the cob. Boots chimed in and said that he didn't eat butter. Brody looked at Boots in a puzzled/ sarcastic way and said, "You don't like butter? Kid, you look like you eat sticks of butter." The name stuck.

Butter asked me to move over so he could show me some inside payroll department secrets. He claimed that there were some civilians making lieutenants' pay. He also claimed that some officers were making higher pay than the captains. It turned out he was right about some people getting a higher rate than the contracts allowed. It wasn't anything too big, but if this was just the beginning of what I was seeing, I could only imagine what deeper secrets there were.

The next day I was called into special services. This was my first time being investigated by them, and it was in front of the one-way glass where an observer would be spying on me and recording my answers. The captain in charge of the investigation was the sheriff's son, and the lieutenant who was his best friend was there also. They alleged that I had not only breached security but was going to be charged with impersonating someone and using their password.

I explained that I hadn't done anything, and they said, "Who did it, then? And remember, Sergeant, you are being monitored. You don't want to lie."

"I didn't do it," I said firmly. "Someone came into my block and showed me. I can't rat anyone out. And I won't."

"Sergeant, you are responsible for what is on your computer. That is secret personnel information."

I could see that they were just trying to get me to rat out whoever was responsible for finding a way into their personnel files. Thinking about this for a moment, I said, "Sir, the monetary figures on the computer are public information. You know it, I know it and the sheriff knows it."

He insisted, "But you impersonated someone else, and that's a crime."

"I didn't impersonate anyone. Someone else did."

"Then we are going to order you to write a report, Sergeant. We can do that; and if you refuse, you've disobeyed an order."

I knew they could make me write a report, but they were not allowed to tell you what to say. So I wrote the report exactly as it happened, except that I left a big blank where the officer's name went. The two investigators weren't happy about that. I got up to leave, which they said I couldn't do, but I told then I didn't remember who it was. "I'll call you when I remember." That really pissed them off.

I headed right for my deputy's office. He had already been apprised of the situation, and when I had arrived, he inquired, "Why didn't you put Boutilette's name in the report?"

I was shocked to hear that the deputy knew who it was. "I didn't remember who it was."

He laughed and said, "You hot shit. I know you don't want to rat on anyone, but he put you out there."

"I would rather be fired than become a rat, boss."

"Okay, I'll see what I can do."

He must have done some sweet manipulating, as Butter admitted to the whole thing but never got in trouble for hacking into the jail's payroll. Thank goodness. I called the silly event "Computergate."

***

I was on the lower right tier watching some cons arguing about chess when I received a radio transaction from the lower left suicide/high-risk tier. It was John McKinnon, Mickey, as we called him, a good officer from my hometown despite being known for a few DUIs. He said," Sergeant Mike, you'd better get over here now!" Freebie opened the gates for me and I jogged over to see Mickey calling for a cell to be opened.

When I got to the cell I looked in and saw an inmate hanging from the tiny ventilation grate with a shoelace wrapped around his neck. He was out. "Oh fuck!" I lifted the junky up to release the tension on his neck and Mickey got the shoelace untied from the grate so I could drop the kid on his bunk. Then I tried frantically to untie the shoelace embedded in his neck, but I couldn't even get my fingers underneath it.

By this time there were about ten officers standing outside the cell, watching us try to save this junkie's life. I'm usually fairly cool, but the guys watching were making me fumble. "Does anyone have a blade or a knife?" I inquired desperately. Nobody said a word, just a few heads shaking from left to right. Thankfully an inmate in the next cell handed a pair of nail clippers to an officer, who in turn handed them to me. I dug them in to the junkie's neck trying to get the sunken shoelace without cutting his throat. Finally, I cut through the shoelace and the kid coughed and gasped. He looked up at me, not understanding where he was. I stood him up and dragged him down to the infirmary, wondering why I was the only one carrying/dragging this kid. Well, there were feces down his pant leg and onto the floor. There was a lot of it, too. This kid must have died or almost died. I asked him if he had seen anything while being unconscious, but he was still incoherent. The nurse checked his vitals. Turned out he had been detoxing and had some issues with his girlfriend.

Deputy Lusignan called me into his office an hour or so later and asked me about the incident. On the way to his office I saw Nancy, the woman I went out with the night of the Christmas party.

"Why haven't you stopped by my office?" she asked.

"Well, Nancy, you are married and I'm no home wrecker."

She pouted. "Still you can swing by and say hello once in a while."

I just wanted to get out so I took the easy way out. "Okay, I will stop by sometime."

When I told the deputy what had happened, he said, "Nice job. I knew you were the man I needed."

I explained, "Mickey is the one who deserves most of the credit. He found the kid and untied him. I think he should get a letter in his file. Does that sound okay, boss?"

"Yeah, I'll take care of it. Now go write some nice reports."

I went back to the block and told Mickey that I had recommended him for a letter to be put in his file. He was embarrassed, but thanked me for acknowledging his work.

A week later the sheriff, being the politician that he is, had a ceremony for the new recruits graduating from the academy. There were a dozen or so local politicians there, family members and a few state officials. This was a good paying state job for relatives and friends of politicians, so they were always schmoozing up to the sheriff. Anytime a politician or ranking official had to return a favor, they could get someone a job at the county jail. If nothing else, it looked good on a resume. A lot of times, people who wanted to work for a civil service job and weren't smart enough to pass the test would work at the jail until they took the test enough times to know it by heart and finally pass it. These were what we called "dreamboats"— people who wanted to be in law enforcement but could only dream about being smart enough to pass the test. Sometimes these people were more dangerous than the cons on steroids.

The morning of the graduation, Deputy Lusignan told me to make sure that Mickey and I were shaved and looked sharp. I had a sneaking suspicion that he was up to something, but I figured that maybe we would both be sent out to the sheriff's office for another nice letter in our personnel files.

Lusignan called Mickey and me into his. I hadn't bothered shaving that morning, only the day before. "I thought I told you to shave, Szaban!" the deputy said. "Get your ass shaved, and now! I told you this was important!"

"Shave my ass, Deputy?"

"Do you want me to do it, smartass?" he threatened.

I almost ran down to the booth to get one of those indigent kits. When I went into the bathroom, I heard some minor wisecracks from my coworkers as I cleaned up. Just one cut drew some blood.

The deputy had us stand outside with some other officers. They wanted to make the crowd look bigger. I thought the obvious: that we were getting an award in front of all these important people and the new graduating class. But the ceremony went on and on, and politician after politician spoke and posed for the press. Then it came. The sheriff, the most powerful and influential sheriff in the commonwealth, spoke.

"I have here with us today, two men who are heroes. They have gone above and beyond, saving a life just the other day. I want you to take a good look at these heroes. I want you to emulate them. Follow in their footsteps. I present to you Sergeant Szaban and Officer McKinnon."

I felt like such a ham. What a speech loaded with horse manure. We weren't heroes. We were just unhooking some junky. Okay, maybe I felt a little proud. But we were just doing our jobs. When we went back inside, the guys going to bust our chops relentlessly.

The sheriff and some bigwigs shook our hands, handed us a nice letter and told us that we would be given eight hours on our books to be used at our discretion. A few of the local politicians shook our hands, and then we mingled with the graduating class. A couple of the new officers were calling us "ass-kissers" and "brownnosers" and the like. I tried to explain that I had only wanted Mickey to get some recognition, but the boys already had their minds made up.

We left after some good-natured ribbing and some not so good-natured ribbing. When I got to the top of the steps heading into the glass double doors, Deputy Gaffney and Deputy Lusignan looked at me with an evil smirk. Gaff said, "I got ya. How does it feel to be a 'hero' in front of hundreds of people?"

"Very funny, boss; but thank you. It's all a reflection on you," I humbly stated back. What the heck did he mean, "I got ya?" Did he actually think putting me in front of all those bigwigs was a practical joke? Maybe it was. I did feel like a ham—but what the heck, eight hours off for just doing my job.

Mickey and I went back into the block and the boys had a mock ceremony. Carl was waving the flag, and Freitag, the booth master, put medallions made out of soap and shoestrings around our necks pretending to be the president. The word *hero* was carved into the soap.

Soap carvings were an interesting hobby for the inmates. We would pass out generic soap for the cons to wash with. The soap was soft and pliable, so some creative cons would take a razor out of their disposable shaver and sculpt objects. They made jewelry boxes and cartoon characters, just to name a few, for their families. Sometimes the really good ones would charge smokes or food products for their services. I had seen ships made and some nice chess pieces.

That same day Scooter called frantically on the radio from A-2: "Sergeant Mike? I need you ASAP!"

I ran over, as Scooter wasn't the type to call for help that often. He was standing down on the lower tier of A-2. That block is usually very quiet. I saw him standing outside of the solid steel door looking in, and when I looked through the narrow window standing against the back wall of the cell was a chubby Mexican inmate. He was a worker and usually very pleasant to be around. He had sliced X's in his chest where the meat of his pectoral muscle was flopping over, and he was sweating and crying hysterically. He had a few other cuts on his torso that were bleeding, but the meat of his pec looked like it was being filleted. The other X's were bleeding a lot, too. We were freaked out, but Scooter waived for his door to be opened. Then my Mexican friend put the razor up to his throat. I put my hands up at shoulder level.

"Papi, we just want to talk to you and make you better."

There was no response from him, except that he sat down on the edge of his bunk with the blade held to his jugular vein by a shaky hand. He was crying, and we moved closer, not wanting to make any sudden movements that would startle him and slice his neck open. But he was bleeding and we still needed to move quickly. As I sat carefully close to him, I could almost sense that he wanted help.

"What's the matter, Papi? Can I help you? Is it your wife?"

He just continued to shake and cried more. I got within an arms' length and asked for the blade. Scooter was making his way in front of him. As soon as I noticed that Papi had moved the blade a couple of inches away from his neck, I grabbed his wrist as fast as I could and pulled it down to the mattress that we were sitting on. I didn't try to hurt the Papi's arm, as he needed help. Scooter wrapped his pectoral muscle up with a pillowcase as I pried the razor out of his hand. I had a brief thought of this guy slicing me or Scooter. But my duty to help him superseded my fear.

The next day we had a copycat do the same thing in A-2, but this kid was a serious punk who just wanted attention. He had made small cat scratches on his arms. When we opened the door we both dove onto the kid's razor-wielding arm and twisted the blade out to the tune of a few high-pitched girlish cries from the young con. Sometimes cons just wanted attention. Well, we gave it to him.

We had a new addition to the maximum security area. Sergeant Ray Prunier was always at the forefront of some kind of controversy. He was by the book. Well, he was more than by the book with the cons. He was a good addition for playing good cop and bad cop. During one near riot in the mods, Ray let all the cons know that he was a sergeant and they had better listen up. Later that afternoon, the cons had him hanging over the railing edge of the second tier, dangling him by his ankles upside down. The rest of the officers were busy trying to quell a gang fight that almost turned into another riot. The cons didn't drop him, but they held him there for quite a few minutes until he pleaded for his release.

Ray was the administration's wet dream. He was like Lieutenant Prince, except that he wouldn't write up his officers during Sheriff Smith's tenure. Ray had a lot of drive in him. When I first knew him, his drive and anger was directed at the inmates, and the administration loved it. They used him like a tool. Later on in our careers, when Sheriff Smith started blatantly promoting all of his family (some of whom even had criminal records), Ray's animosity was redirected towards the administration. The papers actually used the word *nepotism* to describe Smith and his family.

Ray mostly worked A-1 with Pete. Pete wasn't thrilled about the idea, but hey, it was a new victim for some of his old tricks. I believe on Ray's first day Pete put Vaseline around the receiver of the phone in the booth. He had a signal worked out with another officer via the radio, so that when Ray entered the booth the other officer would dial the A-1 phone and Pete would say that someone just a few minutes earlier called looking for him. When this happened, Ray unknowingly picked up the ringing phone and said, "A-1 booth, Sergeant Prunier, what the...you fucks!" Pete couldn't control his laughter, and Ray made him and his buddy stay out on the tier all day; but it was worth it for Pete. He giggled all day long and told everyone he could that Ray had Vaseline all in his ear. Ray not only learned a lesson about working with Pete, but he also learned that making the other two officers stay out on the tier was a mistake because he had all the paperwork and phones to contend with.

About a month in on Ray's maxi tour, Pete called him for assistance down on the lower A-1 tier. I went over along with a few other officers to see if they needed a hand. When we arrived, inmate Fiske, who was another piece of shit repeat offender, was spitting into Ray's face through the bars. Fiske was supposed to be transferred to another facility to give him the change of scenery he needed to improve his behavioral status. Fiske was refusing to pack up his belongings and trying to make it clear that he wasn't going. Ray stood firmly and directly in front of the cell barking out orders like he was still in the Marines.

"Mr. Fiske, I am ordering you to turn around and face the bars to be handcuffed and escorted...."

Another wad of spit flew into Ray's face. Like the good Marine that he was, Ray didn't flinch.

"Mr. Fiske, are you refusing my direct order?" His face was soaked with spit. Pete was laughing quietly and making faces at me and Carl. I couldn't believe that Ray would be letting a dirty con spit on him like that. They were both about the same size, six foot and two hundred twenty pounds each; but based on his military background, Ray could probably flatten this punk.

I tried to step in. "Ray, what the fuck are you waiting for?"

Carl said, "Open the cell door now!" He waived to the booth and motioned for the cell door to open, and open it did. Carl and I both dove on Fiske, who was seemingly trying to put his hands up. I said, "Hey, scumbag, the command was to put your hands behind your back, not up in the air!" Between Carl's sheer weight and my twisting the con's arm to get control and cuff him, the spitter made some pretty feminine sounds. Carl offered to "escort" him down to the awaiting transportation vehicle. The poor kid.

Ray spent a full day writing reports and Carl and I spent about twenty minutes.

I believe that Fiske received an extra two months for his assault on Ray. But he was out of our facility for now, though I was sure he'd be back within a year or two.

Later that day, Freebie came down to the high-risk tier where Carl and I were and inquired about the incident with Ray. Carl was doing the crossword, which was an oxymoron to begin with. One of the clues was "sign of the zodiac." Carl asked, "Is that like a yield sign?" Freebie got punched for his laughter and loud "duh!" Other Carlisms included: "Carl did you consummate your marriage?" "No. Fuck that! We didn't want our picture in the paper."

"I was hunting this raccoon and it went into a tree about ninety feet up." "What's that, about forty yards?"

"Carl, do you live on a cul-de-sac?" "No, we have town water."

And after the jail implemented a no smoking policy, if the cons could smuggle in a cigarette, it would go for five to ten bucks depending on the area. Carl was doing his "guzinta's" (goes into to's—or math) and said in front of us, "So if I sell a pack of smokes with twenty cigarettes at ten bucks a piece, that's ah…ah, wow. That's a thousand bucks. No wait. What was I thinking? That's five hundred." You can imagine the roars of laughter.

The next night I took an overtime shift on the three to eleven. During Smith's reign, the brass was all gone by six p.m. except for a couple of lieutenants. The maximum security's second shift lieutenant was Lieutenant Meservey, an avid hunter and fisherman. But for some reason the staff always made jokes about him being afraid of inmates. I thought this was just scuttlebutt, as I knew how stories traveled through camp.

I was covering the chow hall during supper with Danny Kelly, the nephew of the deputy who had designed the modular compound. Danny wasn't a political hack like so many other people who had high ranking relatives working at the jail. He just liked to eat and lift weights. He was cut and strong with the typical slim bodybuilders' physique at six foot one and one hundred ninety pounds. The A-2 inmates were making their way into the chow hall. Remember, these inmates were mostly sex offenders and rats. One of the first inmates through stopped and whispered to the lieutenant that Jones and Reyes were going to fight in the chow hall. Jones was a fairly muscular African American and Reyes was a tall, wiry Spanish inmate. They'd had a beef over soups owed from a card game. Soups, candy bars and smokes were like currency in the big house.

Meservey came over to me and whispered what was going to go down, and I told Danny. Danny and I suggested getting a few officers to stop the cons before they started. Meservey didn't want to cause any waves, though, so he said that the three of us could handle any fight that broke out.

Jones came through the chow line, grabbed his tray and headed for his seat. Then Reyes came in and headed for the juice container. (It's called bug juice in both summer camp and in jail.) We watched both inmates closely; when Reyes came within a few feet of Jones, they both pulled out weapons from their pants. Reyes had a sharpened toothbrush and Jones had three bars of soap in a sock. They both started swinging their homemade weapons at each other, so Danny and myself tackled each of the would-be assailants and punched them a few times hard enough to make them to drop the weapons. This was where the lieutenant should have picked up the weapons so they wouldn't fall into another con's hands and be used against us. Instead, Meservey ran out of the chow hall as soon as the cons started to fight. The inmates were not that hard to subdue, but when there were sixty plus in the chow hall, the situation could get ugly, and fast. I couldn't believe that the lieutenant had run out on us. What possible excuse could he have for his behavior?

Danny and I had the combatants out of the chow hall by other officers so we could continue to keep control and cover the situation. When Meservey came back I asked, "Where'd you go?"

"To the bathroom," he said.

I replied, "Why, did you shit your pants?"

Danny wasn't so nice to him and called him every name in the book. The lieutenant walked away in shame, knowing he was just a coward. He couldn't even have written Danny up. It wasn't like Meservey had to jump into the middle of the fight; just his presence there would have been a deterrent in case one or more of the fighters' friends had decided to jump in.

Danny must have mentioned the incident to his uncle, as Meservey was transferred to minimum security and wouldn't have to worry too much about fights anymore. I was still really bewildered as to why a lieutenant in maximum security would run away and leave two officers on the ground, wrestling prisoners with weapons. Even worse for me was when Gobi became sheriff: he promoted the coward to captain. And Meservey had been doing some campaigning for Smith to boot! So why did Sheriff Gobi promote a Lieutenant to Captain, who ran from trouble, abandoning his officers during a fight with weapons and campaigned for the incumbent Sheriff, could anyone tell me? My feeling was that with the new sheriff, money spoke much louder than actions, especially cowardly ones. You could buy your way out of anything with this guy. It just ruined morale.

Sheriff Smith enjoyed his "donations," too, but he was really into promoting his family and friends first. This is where he lost me. One example was an officer with the nickname of Shooter—close to Scooter, but they were a little different. Supposedly, Shooter had been a sniper in the Marines for twenty years. He was a decent guy to work with and the inmates respected him, too. Then he started dating the sheriff's daughter, and within six months he was promoted to sergeant. I worked with him one day a week. We got along well, and I showed him the ropes and who was who in the block. When Shooter married the sheriff's daughter in the spring, he called in sick every weekend that summer to be with his bride. The deputy tried to reason with him, saying that he couldn't possibly discipline any other officers with Shooter calling in sick eight times a month for four months; but Shooter wouldn't listen. That's when the sheriff decided to put Shooter in special services in charge of keys—a newly made-up job with no accountability. But it suited Shooter just fine. He could come to work when he felt like it, or stay home and still get paid. And if you think that's not cushy enough, check this out. The sheriff's daughter needed more money from her new hubby. So the sheriff put out a posting for a lieutenant's position titled Honor Guard. He had thought that Shooter was the only one with the qualifications listed for the job; he had done a few parades in uniform for the jail during holidays and one at his Marine base. But little did the sheriff know that I had spent three years in Washington, D.C., doing just that. I was in the Old Guard, the Presidential Guard and Escort. Plus now I had more time at the jail, more time in as a sergeant, some life saving letters and college against Shooter's GED. Besides Shooter had two DUIs and some other iffy problems on his record. I was laughing because I knew the sheriff wanted to promote Shooter and didn't think anyone else would put in for it. Well, I did. I thought that somehow they would try and trick me during the interview, but they didn't. Afterwards two out of the three people on the board told me face to face that I had done exceptionally well. The Captain on the interview also said that Shooter had reeked of alcohol during the exam.

Shooter came up to me one day and casually mentioned that the promotion was going to take a while because the old man had to go through the state ethics commission. I thought to myself that those people must be the same ones who'd let the sheriff promote his family members. So I told Shooter that I would drop out if they would promote me to lieutenant on second shift. Shooter must not have told the sheriff about this, as it still took a long time to get back to us. And the winner was...Shooter. Shooter became the Honor Guard Lieutenant.

Now I was disappointed, and the disappointment became anger and frustration. I knew now that this was all a game.

From now on I was just going to do my job and nothing more. Furthermore, I was going to be a thorn in Smith's side.

My deputy gave me some sympathy, but he said, "You know how the game works, Mike. Either play it or get out while you are still young."

"I hear ya, boss. I just outdid Shooter in every possible category possible and still lost."

His next words surprised me. "Mike, I'm heading to Florida. I'll be on the books for six months using up my sick and vacation time. Good luck, kid." That was the last time I saw the deputy.

Now the sheriff had to fill my deputy's position. I could only hope he didn't pick some political hack. I was informed that there was a line of captains going into the sheriff's office, all vying for the deputy's job. I wanted to keep my head clear of all politics this week. So I called in sick for a few days. I called my captain, who let me use some vacation time. He was really good like that. A lot of the other captains acted like the earned vacation time was coming out of their own pockets. Not my captain. He was the best. I just hopped on my Harley and drove to Florida. I went to Daytona and enjoyed the beach and the warm weather. What a beautiful state.

Then I went into some strip clubs and started thinking about this dispatcher named Lauren. I'd met her when I was working second shift in the modular compound. She was wearing a jean mini skirt and had her legs outstretched on a desk in the dispatcher's office. Lauren had shoulder length dark brown hair and was very sweet. We each knew that we liked each other, but neither one of us made a move on it, even though a mutual friend of ours kept trying to get us together— the buxom, blonde officer who was with Captain Greenberg. She would say things like "Szabe, you should ask Lauren out.

She really likes you." I would act shy or faux insecure and say things like, "No, she probably has a lot of guys chasing her around," or, "She is out of my league."

But when I was in Florida I called the jail after a few hours relaxing on the beach and hitting a strip club. I knew Lauren would answer and I started flirting with her. She put me on hold a few times, which started to annoy me, but I knew the switchboard was a busy spot. Besides, she was intrigued that I had driven the hawg all the way down to Florida by myself. I told her that I was going to Disney and Universal for a few days each and she replied that she would give anything to be down there. I jumped at my chance.

"Well, Lauren, come on down!" She said that she didn't have enough money, so I told her that I would pay for her flight and the hotels. She couldn't believe it. I couldn't believe that she wanted to come down and share a hotel room, plus whatever else, without even going on a date first. She put me on hold again for about five minutes and I was just about to hang up when she picked up the phone and said that she could get the next eight days off. I told her that was fantastic and said I'd call her back after I called my travel agent and arranged the flights and hotels.

All went as planned. Lauren and I hit it off pretty well for the week. When it was time for her to leave on Friday evening, I had arranged for a shuttle to bring her to the airport; but she refused to travel to the airport without me because there was a thunderstorm and a tornado watch that evening. I didn't have a problem taking the shuttle with her to the airport, but she insisted that I wait until her delayed flight took off. Now mind you, it was almost midnight on Friday, I had a twenty hour ride on my Hawg, I had to take a shuttle back to the resort to get my bike and it was storming. But I waited for her plane to depart and left Disney in a bad storm.

I am an experienced rider, but I was barely doing thirty-five miles per hour in the breakdown lane on route four. I was so beat when I reached South Carolina that I fell asleep at a truck stop with my head on a curb. I slept through all the big rigs pulling in and backing out all around me. That trip probably took a year off of my life. I was driving like a little old lady going to church on Sunday. But I made it home, and Lauren and I continued to date for about nine months before I had to end it with her. I realized that at first I was infatuated with her in the jean mini and nice legs, but once I had that, it was pure boredom. In the nine months that we dated, she called me every evening to tell me about some dream boats from special services having vehicles towed for expired inspection stickers. I could have cared less about the officers with the little man's disease. When I went to her house we would just cuddle on the couch and watch home decorating marathons. I wished for that lightning storm again just to liven things up. She was a sweet and pretty girl, though, and when I ended it, it was almost like shooting a deer.

When I returned to work on Monday, I was somewhat surprised to see my new deputy, Greenberg, dressed like Regis Philbin. He had on a shiny maroon shirt with a sports jacket and black pants—the deputies were the only rank that didn't have to wear a uniform. You know he wanted the top brass to be pleased that they picked him. He tapped on the steel door and told me to let him into the block to check out his new area. After he made a quick run through, he summoned me to come out into the dayroom and talk to him. He tried to belittle me by saying, "Who runs this block?"

"I do, Deputy."

"You're a smart guy, right, Sergeant? Can you tell me why the beds aren't made at zero six forty-five in the morning?"

He was being quite the sarcastic punk, so I thought quickly to give it back to him without challenging his authority. "Well, Deputy, first of all, these inmates sleep in their bunks; it's part of the standard operating procedures. Secondly, we don't wake them until they eat at zero eight hundred. Deputy Lusignan should have left you the orders on how the block runs, sir."

Oh boy was he red. "All right, we'll see about this nonsense." And he stormed out of the block.

Within a week all the inmates were eating and had their bunks made by seven thirty. There was no way Greenberg was going to let me outsmart him. But far as I was concerned, a sleeping inmate was a quiet inmate. I could've care less about these guys making their bunks.

***

Billy O'Day was one of the officers who always worked in A-2. He was a smart person and had his single engine pilot's license. He worked in A-2 mainly because he was lazy. We even had a weekly award named after him. When the critics rate a movie as bad, they have a cartoon character of a man sleeping in a movie seat with "zzzzzz's" to symbolize that the movie is a snoozer. One of my coworkers enlarged the picture and called it the Billy O'Day award. It was pasted on the booth wall in maxi, and the person who did the least amount of work that week had his name placed on it. It was funny to receive it once, but more than once and people started getting angry. The sheriff took a look at it during one of his rare tours and laughed very hard, as he was friends with Bill's mother. Deputy Greenberg, of course, had them torn down.

Greenberg wanted to be recognized in the front office. He had a complex and wanted to be acknowledged by the sheriff and warden in the worst way. Basically, he turned into Slattery, the deputy who put cleaning ahead of security. Greenberg had murderers and other criminals who were going away for a long time dusting the gates and scrubbing walls only a few feet away from the last exit gate. One accidental turn of a button and they'd have let a dangerous felon out. I voiced my concern about that, along with having rapists cleaning out the secretaries' trash and mopping their floors. But Greenberg just didn't get it.

The last straw for him with me was the day of the state inspection. We had two of these a year, and the top people made a big deal about it. Every year it was the same minor gigs. Some inmate had an apple in his footlocker, or the water only reached one hundred and three instead of one hundred and eight degrees. It was pure bullshit. We were all working slower so as to be a little bit abrasive towards Greensburg's plans to kiss major ass. Just before the inspectors arrived in maxi, Greenberg handed me a brand new toilet brush. I told him that I would give it to one of the workers and have him go around to give each inmate toilet a once over. The deputy looked at me like I had just kicked his dog.

"No! I want *you* to go around and hit all the toilets."

I gave him a look. "That's funny, Deputy, but there's no way you'll see me doing that." I walked out without looking back and gave the brush to a worker, who reluctantly did as the deputy asked.

Freebie and I were in the booth just tidying up the place when Greenberg walked in. Freebie had swept under the desk and in the barbaric bathroom and put the trash in a pile. Funny thing, there was a broken toilet brush. It was old and the bristles were almost all gone. Greenberg looked at the broken toilet brush and I thought he was going to swing at me; but instead he jumped up and down on the broken toilet brush, thinking it was the one he had given me.

"Why? Why? Why?" he tearfully cried. "You guys don't care about anything. Do you? You just don't care!" The man had tears in his eyes. He left the area and went into the captain's office, put his head on the desk and cried. My goodness! Imagine having a breakdown over a stupid toilet brush. Freebie and I couldn't wait to burst out laughing—and we did.

I ended up going around with the inspectors, and the area looked wonderful. Freebie dared me to put a sign on the back of the heavier inspector. I told him no as that would have probably given them an excuse to look deeper into the block and gig us, which would have given Greenberg a lot of satisfaction. Then Freebie handed me the sign; it said, "Follow me to the buffet." This was amusing, since most of us in maxi were large guys anyways. It was too good to pass up. So I took the sign and palmed it.

When we were just about to leave the block, I patted the big inspector on the back and asked how we looked.

He said, "Nice job, Sergeant, you'll get our report in a week."

His partner saw the sign, however; so I faked a humbled look at being caught, and he snickered and let his partner walk to the next block with it. I was relieved that the inspectors were so cool. And it didn't surprise me that the inmate who pointed out the sign was Ritchie Renaud.

These next few tales aren't for the faint of heart. So if you are squeamish, flip a page ahead. I have to describe Ritchie. He was short and chubby with balding, blondish hair; and he had summer teeth—some are here and some are there. He was in for molesting his wife's sister, and he had a rap sheet at least ten pages long. Ritchie Renaud was one of the most famous in-house inmates that we had. He would swallow batteries, razor blades or anything else on a bet or if the officer on watch wasn't paying enough attention to him. It was Ritchie's way of manipulating the system. He would also shove objects into the end of his—brace yourselves—penis. Yup, that was Ritchie. He once lit a match that was hanging out the end of his penis and sang happy birthday to one of the officers, asking if he'd like to blow it out.

Pete and I thought that we should put the weirdo to work. Maybe some responsibility would nullify some of his crazy habits, we thought—but we were wrong. We gave him a broom and told him to sweep the tier. Well, Ritchie did exactly what we told him to do. The only modification was that he wasn't using any hands. He shoved the broomstick eight or nine inches in his rectum. What a sight! It was both funny and gross. He kept sweeping up and down the dayroom looking at us smiling. Sick motherfucker. I made Pete go get the broom and trade it to another block.

Ritchie would get four point restrained frequently, and as you could imagine he also went to the hospital frequently. Some of his other stunts included covering himself in feces when the officers were coming to take him away or to restrain him. He craved the attention. But on more than one occasion, Ritchie's cries for help would backfire. Razor blades in his stomach would slice away inside of him. One time he had a deep cut in his leg and kept making it infected. The hole got so deep that you could almost fit a cell phone in it. For a while, the hospital didn't know whether or not the leg would be lost. After promising to behave, Ritchie had unwrapped the bandage and put a cockroach in the wound unbeknownst to anyone then wrapped it back up. He complained to the nurse, so she asked to have him escorted into her office. She unwrapped the bandage and screamed when the cockroach came scurrying out. I don't believe that she worked at the prison much longer afterwards.

***

Okay, the squeamish people can start reading here. A few nights after we had broken up, I received a phone call from Lauren. I was surprised to hear her voice.

"Guess what?" she said.

"I don't know. What?"

"Your name is on the move list. They are moving a bunch of you down to the mods, and mods guys are getting moved out to make room for you guys."

She couldn't wait to tell me—just like a little kid. She had also told me that most of the officers going to the mods were the ones Greenberg had any type of disagreement with. We were all his enemies. I never really did anything to the man. I just realized that his methods weren't good for corrections. I was mad, but I also knew that I couldn't work for Greenberg so it was for the best. The only problem was that I was slated not only for the modular compound, but the segregation unit, or the hole, where the worst and most violent offenders in jail were kept. Officers had been getting hurt in this building every week. Good luck to me and my crew.

CHAPTER SEVEN
THE HOLE

I was a little intimidated at first even though I had been in for ten years by now. I was happy that I got to wear a jumpsuit, however. It was much more comfortable than those brown polyester monkey suits the rest of the jail wore. I also had some really decent officers working with me. These guys knew their stuff and were very professional, but with good senses of humor—and you have to have a good sense of humor when you are doing the real work in the trenches. We were the ones watching the dregs of society, the ones who used our handcuffs and leg irons everyday. We were the guys in the shit.

The seg. block was still called the "J" building. It was the same building where I'd worked five years ago when it was just a regular housing block, but now it had an eerie feeling to it. Like the walls and floor had seen a lot of bloodshed and action since I left. But that was ancient history. Stuff that happened last week was old news. There would be a new fight or stabbing this week.

The day shift officers were fast and efficient, while the second shift was muscular and full of testosterone. The third shift had a few decent guys and a handful of idiots. But they all had something in common: they were on someone's shit list. It was actually quite funny because some of these officers were the best; you could place your life in their hands and you'd be safe. It took me a while to get used to all the paperwork and the double checking and the computer work. State regulations required that these people, who had not only violated the laws of society but the rules of the jail, would be given three showers a week and one hour of tier time each Monday through Friday. But our jail misinterpreted that law, so we had to give those scumbags five showers plus an hour out each weekday.

These inmates didn't violate the little rules ones; they violated the biggies. They smuggled drugs, assaulted staff, or stabbed someone. These inmates were always handcuffed or belly chained, and wore leg irons whenever they were out of their cells. The cons would still try to fight with the restraints on, so we were only allowed to let out seven inmates of the same status at a time. It was a lot of work to learn the control panel, as each cell had its own switch, every five cells had a group switch, and the stairway exits had switches and so on.

I was still trying to grasp the control panel so I wouldn't accidentally let potential combatants out on my first day. There were five of us and a lieutenant who had been assigned, as the segregation lieutenant didn't hang out in the block all of the time. The lieutenant, or sergeant in the lieutenant's absence, was to report directly to the warden because the warden and sheriff didn't want didn't want a lot of middle management screwing things up, especially when dealing with potential life and death issues. But as you might guess, after a short period of time, the modular lieutenants, captains and deputy would stick their noses in and try to justify their positions. It was more like they were trying to kiss the top level's ass without ever working the building.

While I was still in the booth figuring out the switches, I received some flack from an officer who was handing out the morning meal. "Hey, Sergeant, we're all down here working. You know, feeding the convicts." He said sarcastically on the radio so everyone who was working the mods heard. I heard a couple of "duh's" directed at me via the radio. I thought quickly to redeem myself.

"Um, private, if everyone is on the floor, how are you going to get back into the booth? Corrections 101! I'll teach you." It was common knowledge that the officers would place a milk crate to keep the door ajar so that everyone could help out and feed the one hundred cons in the "J" building. The officers on the "I" side could have opened up the door anyway, as we watched out for each other. But this officer had wanted to challenge me, as he didn't care for anyone outranking him.

He was like Percy in that he knew every inmate, their charges and something about their personality. He, too, lived for his job and eventually went nuts. The last time I saw him at work was when a bigger protective custody inmate in the "J" building smashed his cellmate's head on the edge of the feed-in trap, a slit in the middle of the solid steel doors just big enough to fit a Styrofoam tray of food into. We also handcuffed the cons through this trap. It also had a lock and bolt to prevent any mishaps, but that made for a lot of work. You had to unlock each cell's lock, lift up the bolt, pull down the tray trap, have the inmates grab their food, close the trap back up, slide the bolt back down and lock the lock. Then, repeat the process to retrieve the trays fifteen minutes later, and all of this was done three times a day. This bigger protective custody inmate had played the system in trying to get a cell all to himself, pretending to have numerous enemies and refusing to have a cellmate. He finally agreed to take this one in particular, but ended up smashing the guy's head.

My smart ass officer was on duty there, and he called for help. When I got there, he had the assailant cuffed, and the victim was lying on the concrete floor with at least part of his brain showing through the copious amount of blood. I radioed for an ambulance and the nurse. His cellmate lost some brain function and had a hard time speaking after that.

About a year later, the state was pressing charges on the assailant, who ended up with a three-to-five-year sentence. I had to go to court for that incident, as the other officer who had been there told the District Attorney that he had asked me to move the inmate to another cell. I told the DA what really happened and my part was done. The other officer, who had "forgotten" the truth, left soon after due to some psychological issues. It's kind of a shame, as I had seen a lot of Percy in him. He kept the block running as smoothly as the segregation unit could have. He knew his job, but that must have been his downfall. He would call up while on vacation and ask if they'd received any new guys or how the logbook was looking and how many showers were done.

His locker being vandalized pushed him over the edge. He challenged everyone he thought was involved to a fight when he was on the property after his shift. They had him escorted off of the property; but the special services couldn't handle the situation, so the local police were called in—and that was it for another fine officer.

***

The building had areas for different status inmates. The first few cells had bars instead of doors where the suicidal or medical watch inmates were. There was an officer posted there just like on the lower left tier. For a while we had sentenced and pretrial inmates in the block, a clear violation of state regulations. But then, a lot of sheriffs only followed the laws when it suited their needs. When inmates complained, the sheriff could always claim that the jail was overcrowded.

That was the excuse for everything. Hangings? The jail was overcrowded. Gang fights? The jail was overcrowded. Drug overdose? The jail was overcrowded. Then the sheriff would say they needed more money to get adequate staffing, and would get the money using strong-arm or scare tactics. But amazingly, the more people they hired, we never had one more officer in the block. They would hire ten, twenty or thirty officers at a time, but these would get specialty jobs within a year or two; and if they didn't, they would replace an officer who did get a job outside of the block. This way, the sheriff could keep giving specialty jobs and the royalty checks would keep coming in.

One of my first inmate interactions in the "J" building was some crazy fifty-year-old drunk who was detoxing. Most of the drug addicts detoxing would get sick, vomit, eat sugar packets and in two to three weeks of cold turkey, they would be in fairly good shape. The alcohol detoxers would hallucinate, however, and these men were much harder to deal with. They would talk to imaginary people, try to tunnel through the walls, and attack the officers. This guy was coming off thirty years of at least a case a day. He threw a cup of urine in the direction of my officer, Tiger, and it hit the desk. Tiger, a good-looking officer with a shaved head and a physique that statues are made from, called me over to the desk. Tiger made you wonder if he was on steroids. His body was big and ripped, but not that huge. He also made it a point to sleep with most of the women on campus. They would fall for his smile and polite disposition. Heck, I would have fallen for the smooth talker.

Tiger said, "Sergeant, I believe this piss came out of inmate Ward's cell."

"Really?" I asked. "Mr. Ward, is this urine?" I was trying to tell without getting too close to it.

"No sir!" and Mr. Ward the drunk stood at attention saluting me.

"It sure looks like urine to me, Mr. Ward."

Ward was out of his mind and yelled back, "Oh, urine... no, it's my-in!"

I motioned to open his cell, planning to put the inmate in four point restraints. I couldn't have crazy cons throwing urine on my officers. When I opened the cell, Ward charged at me like a linebacker. I saw him running at me from the back of his cell so I embraced his momentum and pulled him into me, twisting my body and letting his own force drive him into the metal mesh designed to keep inmates from jumping off the top tier onto the dayroom floor. He cracked his head pretty good. Then I dragged him into the empty cell two doors down, and Gregory, my awesome booth officer, brought us the four point restraints. Inmate Ward put up quite a fight as we were tearing his clothing off. It was pretty much standard procedure that when someone attacks a staff member, they were placed on suicide watch too. That meant they kept just their underwear, blanket and a Bible. Tiger was very strong and tore the man's uniform top off like it was toilet paper. The man was restrained in no time and a week later didn't remember a thing, but he apologized for attacking me after hearing about the incident.

There were one hundred inmates in the segregation block. Each shift had to give out thirty-three showers. Some inmates had to be out by themselves due to the nature of their crimes, and showers were almost always interrupted by some shrink or other interview for a habitual criminal. So sometimes we gave out more showers and sometimes less. The more we gave the less the other shifts would have to give.

I was intent on setting a record, just once. One day, with the help of my lieutenant, I gave out seventy-eight showers and tier times during my shift. That number was unheard of. A new record was set. Some of the inmates would refuse to come out for their hour and just wanted to sleep their time away. Others would stay up all night yelling, since so many are street thugs and up all night looking for trouble anyways. That worked well for my shift, as it meant they were tired and slept in all day.

The second shift sergeant, Brion, was a hot-tempered guy who was into a cycle of roids for the summer. He bulked up fast. Sergeant Brion was in a bad mood one day after I had set this record, and at shift change he learned that on this one particular day I had only given out twenty-seven showers. As soon as he came into the booth, he got in my face and called me a shitbag.

I was stunned. "A shitbag?"

"Yeah, you're a fuckin' shitbag!"

"What's the problem?"

"No problem. You are nothing but a fuckin' lazy shitbag!"

That was enough, as far as I was concerned. "You know what, Brion? I may be a shitbag, but I've only been down here a few months and I've outdone you and all your juiceheads. So the way I look at it, you're lower than a shitbag. You can't amount to even being a shitbag."

Thank God that Frenchy Bousquet and Gregory were there, as Brion and I had to be separated. It was a heated argument gone awry. Frenchy pulled me away from Brion and Gregory jumped in between us while Brion's guys got him away.

When I was heading out the door still heated from the argument, Brion yelled, "Run away like the pussy you are!" I muscled my way back in and met a wall of officers. There were now eight between us. I pushed a couple aside, but the officers were getting mad at both of us and were yelling for me to get out and for Brion to shut up.

The next day at shift change, the deputy held a meeting. It had nothing to do with Brion and me, but Brion gave me, and my guys, an awesome compliment in front of the deputy, who was talking about changing a few items. Brion looked at me and said, "I give the day shift a lot of credit. They do more work than both of the other shifts put together in the "J" building. I honestly don't know how you guys do it." The deputy agreed, and I acknowledged that was the closest thing to an apology the sergeant could give. From that moment on, we kept our distance from each other, and talk was minimal; but the respect was there. Maybe Brion's coworkers had spoken with him and told him how I ran things when I did the occasional overtime shift in the seg. block. But deep down I was just chalking it up to a bad day on his part.

***

When we chained the inmates for showers and tier time, their hands were behind their backs, and they had ankle shackles or leg irons on. They would waddle around the dayroom floor and yell at the other cons. When the weekly fight would break out, it was mostly a lot of head butting. The cons had perfected the art of stooping down and popping their head up to try to hit each other con in the chin or on the side of the head. It was pretty silly to watch, but once in a while they needed medical attention.

The night shift seemed to have more fights than the day shift. Maybe that was due in part to the first and second shifts getting the easier and more easily manageable inmates out and showered. Sometimes we'd leave less work for the night guys, but it was still more dangerous.

Three of us would sit in the middle of the dayroom and watch the seven chained inmates hobble around and enjoy the time out of their cells. We would look at the sports page, do the crossword or word jumble. Then when it was time for the cons to go in, we'd all get up and put a couple inmates in their cells and let some more out. I become very proficient with the restraints. After we fed the cons lunch, two of us were allowed to go eat in the chow hall. The inmates were in their cells, so only one officer was needed to make the rounds every fifteen minutes. That was standard practice, anyways.

I was walking out of the trap on the bottom floor that leads into the other building and the yard to go grab a bite to eat. Bruce Morin, an inmate with a handicapped arm sees me in the trap and walks over to me from the "I" building. The "I" building door was opened, as they still had yard and programs going on.

Bruce said to me, "You, you're the one who wouldn't let me out of my cell."

I hadn't ever remembered him even being in the seg. block with us. "Kid, you haven't been in the 'J' building since I took it over—so scram!" I started to walk away, but he yelled at me for my attention,

"You think you're tough because you wear that jump suit? I'll punch your friggin' head in, big man!"

I turned around angrily. "What the—" The little bastard punched me in the right side of the neck. I didn't even move, and I actually thought it was funny, as he only came up to me chest. But the kid was in his fighting stance; he looked like he was mad and wanted to take another poke at me. I also saw a bunch of other cons looking and laughing. Grabbing the arm closest to me before he could hit me again, I did an arm bar takedown—just a basic self-defense move. But when I twisted

Bruce's arm, it felt and sounded like dry spaghetti breaking. The kid screamed and fell down, and I let go of his arm in shock. I stood back and put my arms up in the air. The cons gathering around were laughing hysterically. I wasn't sure what I had done, and I honestly didn't know what to do; so I told Bruce to stay down. I had the nurse and another officer escort him to the infirmary, and then he was locked in for assault. Now he could say that he had been in the "J" building.

Later he apologized and told me that he had mistaken me for someone else. Oh well, now he got to spend some extra time with us. I didn't want the kid to get any time for that, so I never pressed charges, but the jail did. He plea-bargained the time down to thirty days. But that's ancient history now.

The sheriff's election was coming up in two years, and we hadn't had a contract in the three previous years. That was why we had changed unions. I wasn't big into union activities until I learned how corrupt the politicians running law enforcement agencies could be. That they could transfer you, change your shift and your days off under the guise of the "good of the institution." We had changed unions because the people negotiating the contracts were employees. You just couldn't have that. The people negotiating the contracts would be offered a promotion or a cushy Monday to Friday job with weekends and holidays off so they would give leeway to the sheriff's proposals. They would more or less sell out, just like the officers giving checks and cash to their boss. Some folks don't realize that many people work on holidays or weekends out of necessity. They settle for a forty-cent raise for a year or two, and let the sheriff ignore seniority. Then they would get promoted, and the cycle continued.

So we switched to another union with a top-notch lawyer and a huge membership. These people would now do the bargaining for us. No more payoffs from the sheriff to appease the smaller union—or so I thought.

The union that we switched to was through the efforts of a few strong willed people. The one that sticks out the most was Officer Swenson. Gunnar Swenson was a stubborn, strong willed, Swedish man who took crap from both the administration and the naysayers. But he went around and gathered just enough signatures to endorse the new union.

I started to help Gunnar and Paul Murphy. Murphy was the president of the local at the jail, but he had to answer to the union officials on all matters and could only observe the bargaining process. Murphy had a military background, was sharp, squared away and he knew his business. He would file grievance after grievance, and nine times out of ten he received a satisfactory result. He was fighting for justice and wanted nothing for himself.

The only problem that Murphy felt was that he was struggling with his sexuality. He had dated beautiful women, but none could satisfy him. This place was loaded with testosterone, and he was the head of our local union and liaison to the mother union. He knew that he preferred the company of men, but he felt that he had to keep it a secret. The poor son of a gun was around all these good looking, muscular men in uniform and couldn't or wouldn't do a damn thing about it. It was tearing him up inside. But he had a job to do, and he did it well.

Gunnar did the legwork and Murphy did the secretarial work. The sheriff refused to come to the bargaining table with the new union, since he wasn't used to not getting his way one hundred percent of the time. In fact, he'd had the newly elected union officials handcuffed and escorted off of the property. Later that day he found out that it was public property, and they were allowed to be in the parking lot. I believe that stunt by the sheriff cost the taxpayers more money.

Time was running out for the fiscal year, so the officers started getting worried that they wouldn't get their forty-cent raise. The new union proposed that since we couldn't go on strike or slow down work (due to public safety) that we would have an informational picket at the courthouse. The idea was like the Mustard Seed Parable. It started off with some officers being gung-ho and other officers being scared. Some of the officers were loyal to the sheriff, which was understandable. But he had refused for three years to give them a contract! Can you name any other union workplace that would go three years without a contract? Some unions picket if they are out of a contract for a month.

The word spread and spread. Officers talked their buddies into it, and more and more were willing to picket. They union dangled figures at us, and the more they talked to us the more members promised to show up. The union also promised that they would have many officers from other departments there so we wouldn't stick out as much. There were some officers who were afraid; they knew that if we picketed the boss, there would be some repercussions. I could see their point, but if we all showed up, he couldn't possibly punish all of us. Other officers didn't want to spend their off-duty time walking around with a sign. They would rather sit back and reap rewards from the labor of others; then, if it failed, they could still cuddle up to the sheriff and let him know they had been against it from the get go. Then we got some help from above.

Shooter and some of the chosen few were selected to go to a weapons school just a few miles away from a popular ocean resort. There were five of them, including the sheriff's son and son-in-law. The night before the "training seminar" began, the boys decided to go out to a strip club on the beach. They parked an unmarked cruiser in the parking lot loaded with

M16s, large capacity handguns, shotguns and enough ammo to take over a small country. They left the weapons unguarded behind the strip club in the trunk and back seat with no one watching the car.

The boys went in and had a ball. They were all drunk, and everything except the ladies' tips was on the taxpayers' backs. Then Shooter went to get the cruiser and park it on the sidewalk to impress the women and pick up the rest of his crew. He thought it would be cool if he ran the lights and the siren at the same time.

The bouncer told him to get the vehicle off the sidewalk and park it in back or get out of there. Shooter, drunk and cocky, said, "Do you know who I am?"

The bouncer stood there with his arms crossed and said, "Get out or it'll be towed."

Shooter again ran the lights and siren. The bouncer walked over to Shooter and firmly said, "Get the fuck out of here now!"

There was a crowd gathering around the area. Shooter, not to be shown up by any local laws, asked loudly, "Do you know who I am? I'm the sheriff's number one man in the next county over!"

The bouncer said sarcastically," I don't care if you're the Sheriff of Nottingham!" He had the local cops there within a minute and a half. Shooter was arrested for drunk driving (his second offense), driving on the sidewalk, and disorderly conduct. Nothing was mentioned about the unsecured weapons. The event hit the newspapers, television and the Howie Carr show. It was just the boost we needed to gather more support of the picket. Sheriff Smith wasn't adept at handling the media like Gobi turned out to be. Gobi could fart and there would be a couple media people there saying how wonderful it smelled.

The picket went fairly well and did just what it was supposed to: draw attention and bad press towards the sheriff. Out of three hundred and ten officers and sergeants, about two hundred and eighty showed up during some part of the day. Some were there before work and some were there after work. My truck was parked next to the large courthouse with a four foot by eight-foot sign that read, "Qualifications not donations."

This was the beginning of the end for Sheriff Smith. He had been the sheriff for eighteen years and the warden for six before that. But he still refused to meet with the bargaining committee, and so we had three more informational pickets. The public was starting to get sick of the sheriff and his entrenched kingdom. His little perks, like living rent free and the free food and cars, "business" trips to the Caribbean, and his abuse of the company credit card started to surface; letters were written to local newspapers as the public started to realize what had been going on for years.

It was then that I went to visit Patrick O'Hara, Gobi's best friend who worked second shift at the jail. We needed someone with a big name in the area to run against Smith in the next election, and Gobi was a senator who had taken his retired dad's seat by name recognition. I asked Pat if he would talk to Gobi for me and see if he'd consider running for sheriff—which paid a heck of a lot more than senator, and the perks, of course, were phenomenal. Patrick got back to me a week later and told me that Gobi would consider running if I got the union and the members to back him.

The idea of a new regime made seventy-five percent of the staff giddy. "Wow! Having things run the right way sure would be a change!" That was the general consensus. We had special union meetings run by Paul Murphy, who was an awesome speaker. He could sell snow to an Eskimo. The main union heads were there to oversee the votes and the feedback. The only opposition to backing a new sheriff were the people in Smith's camp, the ones who had the cushy jobs and recent promotions. Thankfully, the lieutenants and captains had decided to pull out of our union and form their own association. They still wanted to be pets of the sheriff—and who could blame them? They had Monday through Friday jobs with most weekends and holidays off. They were also making sixty-five to seventy-five thousand dollars a year and didn't have much contact with the inmates.

The union meetings had heated discussions and the pickets had less and less members as they went along. Most thought, *why bother? We are going to have a new sheriff in a year and a half, so why waste my time now?* But we still had close to two hundred people at the pickets. We picketed at the courthouse and at three fundraisers for the incumbent sheriff. I saw some of my coworkers cross the informational picket line. I don't know what's worse: scabs or union sellouts. After the owners of the fancy country clubs and restaurants saw the amount of bad press and officers picketing, they asked the sheriff not to book any more events at their establishments. No good advertisement could come out of holding a fundraising event that was being picketed by officers and ex-military, especially when the sheriff refused to even bargain with the new union. His popularity and support was dwindling. But I still had a job to do, and now there was a target on my back.

CHAPTER EIGHT
SEG. BLOCK

Deputy Slattery, one of my former enemies, had developed cancer and was using his time to be with his family. My prayers went out for him for his recovery and for his family. Even with our differences, I could never be glad to see that happen to anyone. That must have made my deputy think about enjoying life, too, as he put in his retirement papers to go and pursue a music career. He was a hippy from the sixties and he once told me that he was the reason that the sheriff's department had a hair and dress code.

So now there were two deputy positions vacant. As Murphy's Law would have it, Greenberg had been sent to the mods. It housed the most staff and inmates, so they sent the most ambitious deputy down to run it. But he had just two years earlier sent down his enemies to the mods so he could mold his puppets in maxi. Maxi had turned back into a joke. The gangs took the place over again, and there were some successful overdose cases and a hanging that went unseen. All in the name of cleaning the block instead of basic corrections: care, custody and control—not clean, cower, and clean again.

Dumas was promoted to deputy with a lot of pull from Greenberg, and the other was a regular Joe named Haverty. Haverty was one of those guys who went on football trips with the guys and was rugged enough to tell you man to man what to do instead of hiding behind his badge or shield. Dumas took

Greenberg's spot in maxi and Haverty was sent to minimum security.

Greenberg knew that by coming down to the mods, where he'd unloaded his enemies, he was screwed. He spent the first week repainting the office and figuring out his plan to get the troops to work for him. There were one hundred and twelve officers assigned to the modular complex, split up as usual with the three different shifts and days off. We had twenty-six officers on during the day. When Greenberg came down for the first time he headed straight for the"J" building, which he knew was where most of the problem cases were. The officers who weren't afraid of him worked there as well. These officers had seen a lot of action and weren't going to be submissive to his cleaning details.

Greenberg walked into the "J" building through the trap door system via the yard. He'd started wearing dark sunglasses since the last time that I had seen him. He'd been dumped by the buxom blonde, for whom he had left his wife of many years; and if you coupled that with the pressure put on him by not only by the administration, but himself as well, you could understand why his face was red and he smelled of hard liquor. He'd also gone from being a Boston marathon runner to looking bloated. Hence the glasses were on to cover up his bloodshot eyes.

He thought in his mind that he was a perfectionist, and he would have been if he'd been an interior designer or cleaner. But he was not very good at problem solving with dangerous criminals.

When he came into the seg. block, we all gave him respect. Well, we didn't respect him, but we respected his rank and position and acted like we were working hard. Greenberg asked me to follow him around, and I did. He usually had five or six people walking around with him at all times. I'm not sure if it was because he was frightened or because he wanted to feel important. As I walked around with the deputy, he tapped on the glass of each inmate's cell and asked if they were doing all right. Every single inmate needed something, whether it was a pair of socks, phone call or a transfer to another facility because they weren't being treated like a human being. "You know me, Deputy Greenberg; I don't never give you no problems. They just got me locked up for some bullshit!" That seemed to be the standard, average response. The deputy replied, "See the sergeant. He'll get you your socks." He was good for promising things that he obviously never intended on doing; by telling them to see me, he put the burden on me. Nine out of ten times the cons had more stuff than they were supposed to anyway. Most of the time they would just be trying to get extra stuff to sell or trade with the other cons. It was just a game.

The deputy in charge of maxi and the modular deputy would often exchange prisoners that needed a change of scenery. You could only be locked down in one place so long before you went crazy. Obviously the deputies would try to pawn off the worst ones on each other. They each know the other's motives, and the cycle would just be a revolving door. But not with Greenberg. He would ask for the worst cons and boast to the front officer how he could manage the most violent offenders and make them into role models. That also made matters difficult for us. We would keep getting cons that wanted to stab or head butt certain other cons. Then we were loaded up with the wanna-be gangsters. This is where I met a couple of hardcore bikers—we'll just call them Mike and Steve.

The bikers knew how to do time. They didn't bother the guards, they kept to their own business, they never ratted and if they had to handle a situation, the officers rarely knew about it. More than half of the prison fights happened around the guards. Most inmates were afraid that if they were losing a fight, nobody would help them, so they started fights in front of us in case they needed us to break it up. But not my bikers. Steve was a prospect of a famous bike club, and we chatted about bikes, babes and silly jail shit. A prospect is the equivalent of a college pledge. He told me why he was in jail after learning that I was pretty cool and not a rat. He had just come from "church," the code word for monthly club meetings. There was a punk who tried to join the club, but couldn't do the things required of him. He didn't even have a bike but had borrowed his brother's bike to start hanging around with these dudes. When they found that out, they smacked him around a little and sent him on his way. The punk was such a bitch that he went to the police and gave them as much information as he could. Steve said the punk didn't know much, as he was just a hang around and wasn't privy to the business end of the club. But the local chapter president still wanted to speak to this kid, who had gone into hiding.

The prospect's mission was to find the rat and deliver him to the clubhouse. Steve knew the kid and they had an overlapping circle of friends. One evening Steve and a friend of his were going down a major road and spotted the kid. Steve tells me that he "accidentally" hit the informant with his car. It was nothing too serious. Then they wrapped his feet, hands and mouth with duct tape and threw him in the truck of Steve's car. They sped off to the clubhouse, which must have triggered the attention of a rookie state trooper—or maybe someone saw the Sopranos' style action on the side of the road and called it into the police. Regardless, the cop pulled them over and heard a muffled noise and some banging coming from the back of the trunk. The trooper almost fainted when he saw this guy wrapped up in duct tape in the trunk. Steve and his pal tried explaining that it was just a joke on their friend, but when the rest of the troopers arrived, Steve was arraigned along with his buddy. Steve came to my jail and his pal was sent to another county to try and prevent any formulating of alibis.

Mike came from a well-to-do family. They owned fairly large businesses and all had bikes, summer homes and were generally law-abiding citizens. But Mike told me that he'd always wanted to make the big, quick, easy score. He wasn't into the nine-to-five mode. Years ago, he was allegedly running weapons for a motorcycle club. The feds tried hard to nail him but always came up just a little short. Then they finally got someone close enough to him to gain his confidence. The undercover agent had pretended he was involved with big construction unions and promised Mike a very high paying union desk job. The feds went through some serious schemes to get Mike off of the streets. They rented out offices in high-rise buildings and planted agents as supervisors on large construction projects where Mike and the agent would meet and exchange money and drugs. Then one of the agents had Mike deliver a package to another agent on a construction site. When Mike took the money, they nailed him. Mike ended up getting over twenty years for the package delivery. He regretted being greedy and agreed that he should have just opted to work for one of the family's businesses. He would have been set for life.

These two bikers were ideal inmates with regard to the staff, and that was all I could ask for. If I had extra meals, they got them. They weren't the only ones that I took care of, however. If you were quiet and well behaved, I tried to make sure that you were given proper time out of your cell, phone calls and access to the social worker for any outside problems.

The two bikers were headed to another facility; but in the meantime, they owed my county a few months for some minor offenses. After they did their segregation time, I had them housed in the "I" building so I could use them to keep the building adjacent to mine quiet.

The "I" building had been having a small gang problem with young kids trying to make a name for themselves. My two bikers teamed up with the Spanish gang leaders, and soon the building was quieter than a nursing home. There were no fights, at least as far as we could see. No one was running out of there because they couldn't repay a debt, and there were no reports of room thieves, which were, as far as the inmates were concerned, as bad as skinners and rats. My two guys had made the area not only good for the convicts, but the officers' jobs were now easy, too.

Now, Deputy Greenberg had a hard on for Mike. It seemed that when Greenberg was growing up, Mike might have smacked him around a few times in the school playground. I told the second shift that Greenberg was going to set Mike up and have him moved because of his over inflated ego. I didn't want to cross the line between cop and con, but right is right. I told Mike to watch his ass, although he already knew. Two days later, Mike's cell was shaken down for contraband. They found an extra milk carton in his cell, and he was moved to maxi. When I came back to work I asked the second shift officer what had happened. He replied that he had been ordered to find anything in Mike's cell and move him directly to maxi.

"Who asked you to do that?" I asked him.

He said sheepishly, "I can't tell you, Sarge, but you know who

It was obvious to me by this point that Greenberg didn't care about safety or security. And this was just a personal vendetta of his! I got together with a few of the guys who'd had run-ins with Greenberg, and we decided to start giving him a taste of his own medicine. We started flooding his office with reports. They were legitimate reports, but of the kind that didn't need to be written. We started giving out twenty-four hour lock-ins for the most insignificant reasons. When Greenberg would tour through the buildings, the inmates would drive him crazy with complaints about these lock-ins. He tried to direct them to us, but we told the cons that only the deputy could override a lock-in. We gave out a lot more out on canteen day or visitation days. We also gave out the deputy's phone extension and told the cons to have their families call the jail and get the deputy's office. He started getting flooded with calls and paperwork. Some families were coming from Puerto Rico or out of state and only had one day to visit their incarcerated friend. Then, if Greenberg wouldn't answer or his secretary, a lot of people called back claiming an emergency and trying to get the sheriff or warden with their petty problems.

The top brass started leaning on Greenberg about the phone calls and lock-ins; he, in turn not wanting to admit that the pressure was getting to him, started more cleaning details to keep us busy instead of security and discipline. He started touring with the captain, lieutenant, a sergeant and an officer or two. He would wait to inspect the area until he had all his little ducks in a row behind him. His new fetish was "dust bunnies." That's right, dust bunnies. We were to look under each bunk three times a day to ensure that there was no dust. And if there were dust bunnies, the inmate wasn't to be locked in, but we were to go get the inmate a dustpan and broom. That was his way of getting us to slow down on the lock-ins.

One Saturday morning I had only been given three officers in the "J" building although we still had sixteen or so showers to give over the weekend. This was a no-no for me. I had signed post orders that we could not let inmates out for showers or tier time unless we had five officers on duty. I was off Sunday and felt that someone was trying to set me up. I told the compound's lieutenant and we decided that the second shift, although they wouldn't be happy about it, would have to give the showers, as they were at full operating staffing levels.

When I came back to work on Tuesday, I was escorted to special services, where they tried to get me to admit dereliction of duty by not doing the showers. I explained the staffing post orders to them, and then they asked why I had erased the shower marker board showing that they were done. I explained that I told the lieutenant on duty that the shower board had been the same when I left as when I arrived for work, and that since we were short staffed the next shift was supposed to do them.

"Well, they weren't done all weekend, and we're holding you responsible," they told me.

I said, "There were six sergeants in charge of the "J" building over the weekend. Why am I the only one to be questioned?" They couldn't answer that question. "It sounds like a witch hunt to me," I said. "When you have something worthwhile, call me."

I left their little interview room in disgust, walked into Greenberg's office and asked point blank, "Are you trying to hem me up? If you want me out of the mods, just trade me."

"Oh no, Mike! Things just got a little screwed up and that's all." He stuck his hand out to shake. I knew he was a sneaky, rotten backstabber, but I decided to let it go for now and shook his hand. Then I went back to my normal routine.

On the way back from dropping off some reports to the captain's office, I stopped and spoke with Steve the biker. My bike was backfiring whenever I would let off of the throttle, and he suggested that maybe the jets on the carburetor needed a little fine tuning or that my engine was running a little too rich. He told me of an awesome mechanic who was way cheaper than the expensive bike shop where I'd bought my bike. I was hesitant, but that evening I took my Harley down to the bike shop. The tall, clean-cut owner stopped me at the door.

"Can I help you?"

"Yeah," I said awkwardly, "ah, Steve told me that there was an awesome mechanic here."

"Stevie? Crazy Stevie? Well shit, bro, bring the bike on in, we'll fix her up in no time."

Three fairly large, extremely biker-looking dudes clad in leather and denim came out and worked on my bike right in this little store. The owner sold t-shirts, stickers and parts. There was a garage in the back, but they didn't bring my bike in there. They asked about Steve, and I told him that he was well, that I'd fattened him up more than he was. They fixed my bike up and asked me to hang out for a while, firing up the grill on the sidewalk in front of the store. I had a few burgers and watched the people walk in to buy a sticker or t-shirt. These guys treated me like family, like they were happy to see me. No charge for the bike, either. A couple of hours later, I shook hands with them and left.

When I hopped on, I noticed a bike club sticker on the right side of my bike just in front of the saddlebag. It was hard to notice unless you were looking for it. They called it "down-low." It wasn't a generic sticker, but the real thing. I thought it was pretty cool, but still, it was just a sticker.

The next day at work I told Steve about how decent they had been, and Steve never asked me for a favor other than a little extra food now and again. A week or two went by and I stopped in occasionally at the bike shop and just hung out for some food and laughs. I was there maybe three or four times. They were decent guys and never asked me for anything except when I bought a shirt from them with the bike shop's name on it.

Not long after, I came into work and saw cruisers and officers from many different counties in the parking lot. All my coworkers were grouped up into pairs and the pairs were grouped into groups of ten. I was instructed along with the other sergeants and lieutenants that we were going to shake down the entire modular complex. That was going to be a pain in the ass, but at least I didn't have to feed and shower the boys today. The night shift was being held over for that detail. I was getting my guys ready and we were discussing who was going to do what, when I heard a call on the radio for the defibrillator. That meant someone had dropped.

It turned out to be a kid I knew from the streets named Louie. He was in my block and only about thirty-five years old. How the fuck could he have keeled over? The officers and nurses worked to revive Louie to no avail. The ambulance got there pretty quickly, but Louie was gone. He was in the "J" building and had just gotten off of his disciplinary status and was awaiting a cell to open up in any cellblock. It was later found out that Louie had had a visit from his wife last night; she had delivered him a bag of heroin. He'd been clean for a while and the load must have been too much for his cleaned out body to take. When guys get clean from drugs, sometimes they go back to the same dosage that they used to do and it's just too much for them to start off on. I think any amount of heroine is horrible, but it's a big problem for society.

Greenberg now had to answer for the poor kid's death. The deputy would have given anything for me to have down there when Louie passed on. Then that snake in the grass would have been able to deliver me some punishment via the top brass. I would have been his prize fish stuffed and mounted on the wall.

We had about one hundred and fifty officers shaking down the entire modular complex. It was very systematic and thorough. The tactical teams from our department and from neighboring counties were there. They would go into the buildings as a show of force first, all dressed in black and one member in each squad had a riot shotgun with rubber bullets. The team leaders each had radio communication with the other teams and a lot of restraints should the cons get out of control. All the cons were in their cells yelling or making loud, heckling insults. The teams also brought in a few drug sniffing dogs—a day too late for Louie.

Once the team got positioned in each corner of the building, we would go into each building and systematically tear through the inmates' cells. I had five two-man teams. The sergeants stood outside of the cells while the officer teams stripped and searched the cons, handcuffed them and made them face the wall of the building; then they would go clockwise or counter-clockwise through the cells. That way the officers would be reasonably sure they didn't miss anything. Two officers did one cell at a time. I would be called to a cell only if there was a question about contraband. If the officers found anything I would jot down the whos, whats and wheres so the officer could write a report later and give the con a time out in the "J" building. A couple members of the tactical team would remove any inmate found with contraband.

Occasionally an inmate would act out to try to establish street credit. These were the weaker ones that wanted the other cons to think that they were crazy by taking on the well-equipped and numbered staff. They always lost in the end.

"You had better come ten deep if you think you're coming in this cell, CO!" one inmate screamed in the "L" building. The kid, Daigneault, was known to be a small time punk. He would steal from senior citizens or kids going to school. He had the look of a dirty thug. He was tiny, and had the "Moe" haircut. But in prison, he was a bitch for the taking. He wasn't a threat to anyone just more of a nuisance.

Five members of the team quickly walked over to the door, and the team leader firmly stated, "Inmate Daigneault, turn around, put your hands behind your back and wait to be hand cuffed!"

Daigneault, who was hungry for attention and a little street credit, yelled back so the cons would all hear, "Fuck you! You fuckin' pussies ain't shit! Just try and come in my cell!"

The team leader gave two more commands, and the inmate, who at this point was visibly shaking, knew that he now had to take his lumps. The first man in with the shield plowed the kid into the back wall, the other four team members right behind him. All you could hear was the punk making little crying sounds. Then mixed in was something about his lawyer. The team had the kid handcuffed, leg shackled and dragged out of the building within thirty seconds.

There were so many officers shaking down each cell and the multitude of prisoners in their underwear, handcuffed, that you couldn't just watch one particular area or cell. It was so surreal. The officers would throw out the inmates' extra uniforms that they had acquired by trading or stealing. Most of the time they used these to make a fluffier pillow. The prison mattresses and pillows were usually very thin, and the cons would slice the sides open and stuff more clothing into the pillows or mattresses to make them more comfortable.

While all this was going on, the brass was just joking and casually observing in the middle of the dayroom. I would occasionally hide in a cell and throw a roll of toilet paper or piece of fruit at the brass in the middle of the dayroom when they weren't looking. That started a small trend among some of the more daring officers. I remember seeing big Carl throw an opened carton of milk near the brass, splattering their boots and uniform trousers. He was looking at me giggling like we were sixth graders. We would pretend to be busy immediately after launching the projectiles. Occasionally we would hear a "that's enough, gentlemen" bellowed from the midst of the crowd of brass.

The dogs took a quick run through the cell after it was shaken down. Then we would scan the mattress with a handheld metal detector, looking for steel shanks. Finally the modular complex was completed. Only a few reports to write, maybe four shanks, some cons caught hoarding their meds, and a couple disciplinary problems. But Greenberg was going to be in some hot water for Louie's overdose. The deputy obviously couldn't be expected to control everything, but when a death occurred, someone had to take the heat. It would eventually roll downhill anyway, and he could pass part of the blame by handing out small suspensions to the visiting room officers.

The visiting room was strange. There were some beautiful women coming up to visit these cons—some were stripper quality. That's not to imply that they were smart, mind you, just beautiful. I guess that's why these con men could manipulate them from behind the bars. When I first worked at the jail, all of the areas had full contact visits. That meant that the con and his woman would be trying to get away with as much as possible. I would walk in there just for the entertainment value. The visiting room officers would be telling some not so well behaved children to stop running around, which acted as a diversion for a quick hand job or drug passing opportunity. Then after enough overdoses and cons hitting their women, the sheriff decided to make visits non-contact with the exception of the kiss at the end. Even then, a double wrapped bag of dope or pills could still be passed.

This leads me into an amusing story about inmate Daigneault. The evening after the big shakedown, there was a lot of cleaning up to do, and we wanted to ensure that the cons would behave. So they offered out quite a few overtime shifts. Most of the staff just wanted to go home to be with their family or drink their problems away, but there were a few of us known as "overtime whores." We would take just about any overtime that came our way. It boiled down to the state buying eight hours of your life, but it was easy money.

After his stunt earlier in the day, I wanted to ask Daigneault why he was trying to get street credit when everyone knew he was a bitch. I also wanted to rub it in that he'd put up about as much resistance as one of his third grade victims. We had been instructed not to give showers that day, so just a fifteen-minute wind had to be completed in the seg. The officers would take turns for two hours each, doing a wind every fifteen minutes. I told the officer slated for the next wind that I would do it since I wanted to inquire about Daigneault and his girlish sounds. I headed out of the booth with the stapler sized wind gun a little earlier than the fifteen minute interval called for. When I got around the first corner and looked into Daigneault's cell, I had to stop and refocus my eyes. The con was kneeling on the bottom bunk with the blue uniform pants down to his knees and his ass towards me. Freddie Maldonado had his forefinger and thumb in the kid's ass. I looked again, thinking I was seeing things. There was a light blue balloon covering a cigar shaped object stuck into his sphincter, and Maldonado was trying to dislodge it.

I called for the cell to be opened and for an officer to assist me in case these two tried to put up any resistance. When the door made the metallic clank, startled the inmates jumped up. Freddie had the partially shit-covered balloon in his hand. Daigneault's pants were still down.

I asked, "What the fuck is going on in here?"

"Oh, ah, nothing, Sarge," they both replied at different intervals. The tone alone indicated their guilt. Then Greg showed up and started to ask what was going on, but he stopped himself as he saw the balloon Freddie was trying to conceal behind his back and Daigneault's pants still down.

"Pull up your pants, stupid," Greg ordered, which I had forgotten to say, as my brain was still processing the recent events. The cons stood silent. Neither Greg nor I wanted to grab the balloon that was obviously filled with weed or dope. I told Freddie to toss it into the toilet and step back. He must have been figuring his odds of successfully not tossing it and trying to get hold onto it somehow. He took a few moments to think and wisely decided to toss it into the toilet.

Freddie was a very tough Spanish loner. He was known for taking things from weaker inmates and beating them down if they resisted. He wasn't involved in any gangs, as he didn't want to split the spoils of war with anybody else. Eventually, he died a slow, horrible death from AIDS. Near the end of his life, he wasn't able to defend himself and the cons that he used to muscle around finally got their revenge. AIDS had shrunk him into a scrawny weakling.

I peered into the toilet and looked at the blue object closely. The two cons admitted that it was weed in a cigar tube. I asked Greg what we should do; he said, "You're the sergeant." I knew he wouldn't write the report, and I sure as heck didn't want to write the report and search the object floating in the toilet. So I flushed it and had Daigneault moved to a single cell. If I had written a report about that incident, my coworkers would change the story or make up something like I was excited watching it or I pulled it out and sniffed it. They could be quite creative and cruel when they weren't involved.

As time went on, the crazy things that had happened didn't bother me as much. I became more callous. One afternoon, I was called up to special services during my lunch. I told them that I'd be right there, but I took my time. Why did they want to speak to me now? When I entered the room this time, there were four suits in there, as well as the special services lieutenant. The suits were from the big city's gang task force. Maybe they wanted some information about the cons in my block.

"Sergeant, we have some photographs of you and your bike that we'd like for you to explain."

That was not what I expected. "What?"

They had pictures of my bike and of the sticker that was on it. There were no pictures of me, as they had claimed, but they did have some telescopic pictures of my bike in front of the bike shop that I was hanging around in.

"We know that you have been hanging around with these guys and we believe that you may be a member of their club. This is unacceptable for a sergeant in the sheriff's department."

Obviously these guys knew very little about bike clubs. So I decided to take my little shots and try to belittle them. "Um…first of all, you guys are from the gang task force, so you know that the bike clubs wouldn't even consider anyone who is in or has applied to a law enforcement agency. Secondly, if all you have is a club sticker, and you are harassing me about my sticker, then you are violating my first amendment rights...as you are well aware of."

They looked around at each other, knowing that they were indeed violating my first amendment rights. "We just want to make sure that you aren't compromising any security, Michael," the apparently smarter officer in the group responded. They tried to force me to write a report about my dealings with the bikers, but I wouldn't. I wasn't involved with any club, nor would the club want me. The suits were pissed that I wouldn't write anything about the club, but I could have cared less. They should have known that law officials weren't allowed in the real bike clubs. Maybe they did know and were just trying to find out anything, or just fucking with me. But who was trying to screw with me? Who was trying to get me into trouble? Greenberg? The sheriff? Someone I had made fun of? Who?

They advised me to take off the sticker, but I informed them that I would only do so if the club members wanted it back. "We'll be in touch again, Sergeant." On that note I left the office.

I thought it was hilarious that they thought I was an outlaw biker. And I found out who had taken the pictures of my bike. It was Officer Smith, who had helped me smack around the wise mouthed Verdini when he wouldn't buy me a soda. Why would Smith have done that to me? He was in special services as a keep quiet favor from the sheriff. One evening he'd left MSF to go look at one of the K-9 dogs he was buying from the sheriff's department. The chubby lady officer who was best friends with the sheriff's daughter had landed a job with the K-9 unit. Hmm...cronyism? Smitty and the woman got into an argument about training the dogs.

"You don't know what the fuck you're talking about you fuckin' c@^t." I guess the c-word triggered a bad response because she pulled out her 40 mm and pointed it at Smitty's head. She was in proper form and aiming dead center on Smitty's forehead. He couldn't get out of there fast enough.

But Smith played the roll well, as he'd had a fellow officer along to witness the silly act by the female officer. Smitty went home and headed for some alleged counseling, playing the victim up nicely. He wasn't coming back to work because of mental distress. The sheriff made a deal with the two. Smith would be reassigned to the special services unit as a sergeant and the gun-toting female officer would get the transfer to a smaller, more desirable Oceanside county jail if they both would keep their mouths shut. They both agreed and received the promised jobs, but thankfully there was Smitty's friend to spread the noteworthy event.

I had just happened to run into Smitty at a local gas station. He came up to me like he was my best friend. "Hey, Sergeant Mike. How's it going?"

I grabbed him by the throat and pushed him up against the gas pump. "You're a fucking loser! Why are you taking pictures of my bike?"

He could barely speak, as my grip was fairly tight. "I didn't do it, Mike," he choked out. "It was Tommy. He's trying to set me up. You know I'd never do that to you. Didn't I give you my gunbelt and holster?"

"Smitty, if you're lying…" I let him go, as I didn't want to be on the gas station's surveillance tape beating him up. When I ran into the older special services cop named Tommy, I just asked him why he'd done it; he told me that Smitty was ordered to do it by higher ups. He also reminded me that Smitty was the sergeant, not him. It kind of made sense. But which story should I believe? I knew that both these guys were snakes. Tommy had been kicked out of a few agencies for pretending to be an undercover officer when in fact he was just a patrolman, using his badge to get freebies off hookers and women buying coke. But the jail was good for him as he could just pay his tithes to the sheriff and keep his cushy job.

Sergeant Smith's first special services interview with a convict can shed some light about the caliber of the department. Smith and Moroney were interviewing some scrawny, small time, drug dealing con. The drug dealer, Stratton, was being questioned by the two special service officers in a small room next to the classification department. They were trying to intimidate the little thug into giving up some names of people he had sold to. But the two officers were way out of their league. The kid, who wasn't handcuffed, picked up the telephone receiver and clocked Moroney five or six times in the skull. Instead of diving on Stratton to subdue him, Officer Smith ran out into the hallway screaming for help. The drug dealer beat Moroney to the ground then flipped the filing cabinets on top of him. Smith could have prevented a lot of permanent damage to Moroney's head, but he fled for his own safety against a scrawny punk.

Thankfully, many other officers subdued the assailant. I received the story firsthand from Stratton, who ended up in my "J" building. He told me, "Yeah, Smitty couldn't get out of the office quick enough. The fat bastard could have just fallen on me. They both tried to be tough guys, but they have no balls when you come right down to it. One couldn't fight and the other was too scared to fight."

I shook my head in disgust. These officers, according to the sheriff, were well-trained and supposedly better than the regular screws (COs). I ended up bringing the kid to the transportation crew, and he ended up with a few years for the assault—about the same amount of time that Moroney stayed out of work.

***

This is about the time of the story I started off the book with about Officer Hartwell. His nickname was Chipper or Chippy. The only thing I can add is to emphasize how much urine was thrown on him. From the booth some sixty feet away, I could see the urine dripping off his arms and his chin. It was pretty gross.

I had torn the ligaments in my left forearm and elbow when I carried the scumbag inmate up the stairs, smacking the kid's head off of the railing all the way up into the cell. Then Bousquet and I tore his clothing off and chained him up. The piece of shit never did that again. I went to the hospital that evening when my arm was burning, and the doctor told me to stay out of work until it was one hundred percent better. I stayed out a short while but decided not to milk it too long, as I knew that there was a target on my back already. When I returned to work I was called into the special services office again. This time there was just the lieutenant of special services, who was a small town's selectman. If you thought that was another gift by the sheriff to garnish support from the neighboring towns, you'd be right.

The lieutenant was fairly cool this time with some small chitchat about chicks. He asked me about Tammy, a beautiful short-haired blonde. She was always dressed with class and came from money. Her family was loaded. She was also quite chunky, but her beautiful face, cheerful personality and sophisticated dress more than made up for her being heavy. I ran into her and two other ladies who worked as clerks and secretaries while they were out drinking one Friday night. One of the crazy lieutenants had seen us leaving the club, and the story made its way around camp that we'd had a wild orgy. What had really happened was that we were trying to get the older lady, Susan, into a cab, as she was too drunk to drive and would only get in if I kissed her. I had my sights set on the other secretary, who had the body of a lingerie model. I was hesitant to kiss Susan, as I didn't want to blow my chances with the secretary. But Susan absolutely refused, so I went to give her a closed lipped kiss. She stuck her tongue into my mouth. I was a little grossed out; her breath was bad from a night of partying and eating pizza along with the customary cigarettes. But she got into the cab and off the driver went. I made a small joke to him about how she thought he was hot and would tip him well at her house. I'm not sure if he got the joke, but now I had a chance to land Jackie, the hot secretary.

Tammy excused herself for a minute, so I started flirting with Jackie. She told me that she had to get home to her fiancé, and I knew right there that was a dead end street. Jackie shook my hand and hugged Tammy goodbye. Then Tammy, whom I had never considered being with, asked me for a ride home. It's not that she was too big, but her divorce wasn't finalized, she was living with another guy and she was dating a maintenance officer to boot. So I'd just figured she was taken. She hopped in my truck and we made the usual chitchat about work. I asked her where she wanted to go, and she said that she wanted to swing by the maintenance officer's apartment that she was dating to ensure that he was home. I thought that was a strange request, as she was living with another guy, but I obliged her wishes.

The maintenance officer's car was at his apartment, and she seemed relieved. Then she had me bring her across the city to another bar where her car was. We arrived at one forty in the morning. When I leaned over to give her a kiss on the cheek goodnight, she turned her head and started licking my lips and face. We started making out; I could barely contain her tongue in my mouth.

I started getting very into it and said, somewhat out of breath, "Tammy, you had better get to your car now. I'm way too excited."

She panted back, "You want to fuck me, don't you?"

"Tammy, if you don't leave now, I'm going to have to."
She licked my neck all the way up to the top of my head and said seductively, "Get those jeans off and get on top of me." As I was furiously trying to get my boots off to pull my jeans off, too, she opened up her blazer, pulled down her lacey shirt top and exposed a huge pair of breasts—at least forty-two double Ds.

"I use these to get what I want, and now I want you." She slid under me and did most of the work from the bottom, obviously having done this before. She was absolutely wild, licking my face, grinding into my every thrust! Her legs were wrapped around me, pulling me in closer than I thought possible. What a wild woman.

We both had intense orgasms, and then her kissing got me aroused again. The night was incredible. We finished up after the second round, and then I gave her the goodnight kiss that I had originally intended. On the drive home, I pondered what her relationship was with those other guys.

The next time I saw her at work, she gave me the biggest smile—and she had an awesome smile to go with her personality. We never hooked up again, though. I'm not sure if it was because that we worked together or that she lived with someone; but I'll bet it was because I wasn't rich enough. She had come from money but was working at the jail as a finance lady. Why wasn't she working for her family? I didn't want to push the subject, but we always flirted with each other after that. She would frequently fish for compliments: "Do the guys think I'm old? I feel fat. I look ugly today, don't I?" I would always boost her confidence whether or not she actually needed it. I should have asked her out, but I felt that since she was in a relationship or two, she should let me know that she was interested in dating. But what a memory!

So I told the special services lieutenant the about this torrid sex scene, he said, "You probably know what this is about."

Here it came. "No, Lieutenant. I don't."

"We are ordering you to write a report about your involvement with the bike club."

I couldn't believe it. What a bunch of assholes trying to get me on anything. I thought for a few minutes and looked at the blank report form and pen in front of me. *So*, I thought to myself, *I have to write a report, but they can't tell me what to write.* So I wrote that I wasn't in the club and had never been to the actual clubhouse. I also wrote that any good law agency would know that I couldn't join or visit the clubhouse anyway. I handed it in to the lieutenant and said with a chuckle, "There you go, Lieutenant. See you again soon."

I was back to the grind of the "J" building while the union meetings became more and more popular. Most meetings would only host around four or five officers, but now they were holding over one hundred, and there were two meetings to accommodate all three shifts. The officers were getting excited about Gobi becoming the sheriff. He had previously worked at the jail for a couple of months when he had run for senator in his dad's seat. He'd won the senate election by name recognition. Now he was going to formally announce his candidacy for sheriff. We were elated, since Sheriff Smith was out of control, promoting his family and manipulating the former weak union. One day, I brought the wind gun up to the Greenberg's office to be read and replace the batteries, as was a normal everyday procedure. He wasn't there, so his secretary did the printout and I wrote a few things in his private bathroom wall. He had told Gobi a long time ago that Gobi wouldn't amount to shit. So I wrote a few things on the bathroom wall and signed them "Gobi." Greenberg had his nervous breakdown a month later.

When things were quiet, the lieutenant and the officers would play cards in the booth. I would play the occasional chess game in between my winds. I usually played with Tebo, a former boxer who now tipped the scales at slightly over three hundred pounds. He had a belly, but his arms were the size of most peoples' legs.

A few years and a few less pounds ago, Tebo had won the state police boxing championship and destroyed the ten-year reigning champion. Tebo hadn't been as heavy as he was now, but the picture showed this beer bellied, barrel chested man fighting a ripped bodybuilder type five or six inches taller. Tebo's punches were so hard that the champ had to spend days in the hospital.

Thankfully, he was never the aggressor in person. He would just retaliate when he was antagonized by us acting like school kids. I always kidded him about working for a computer company, which was his dream. Tebo was a brute, but he was also very book smart and computer savvy. He always had his head buried in a book about computers or messing with the ancient jail computers. I kidded him that someone at the computer company would think he was just some big, slow, fat guy and give him a ration of shit until Tebo gave the unsuspecting nerd a quick jab to the head without even looking up. He would do this to us when we'd occasionally make fun him.

One time a friend Ritchie and I decided to take Tebo head on. I hid behind my friend, who said he'd take the lead if I would tackle Tebo by the legs. The plan sounded good at the time. I used Ritchie as the shield and we got an arm's length away; then Tebo realized what we were up to and swung at

Ritchie. Ritchie ducked, and the right cross landed on my temple, spinning me around one hundred and eighty degrees. I had my fists up in the air aimed at the wall, like the stunned cartoon character saying, "Duh! Just passing by."

I was incoherent for a good ten seconds but somehow managed to stay on my feet. Then I heard, "Mike, I'm over here." The few people in the area were laughing, and I was fairly certain that they were laughing at me.

"Mike, good thing I hit you with my weaker arm," Tebo said. I thought it was a good thing he didn't hit me twice, or I would have still been asleep.

So we would play chess once in a while between rounds or giving showers to my cons. Tebo worked the "I" building with which we shared the booth. One day I was sitting with Tebo and saw my lieutenant and three officers arguing with an unchained inmate at the far corner on the top tier of the "J" building. We were never supposed to have inmates out who were not handcuffed and leg ironed. But Tyrell Watson was definitely unrestrained. I decided to head out and quell this little disturbance.

The lieutenant was trying to get the inmate's extra sheets and blankets. "Watson, you're not keeping three blankets and four sheets. This isn't the laundry." He grabbed one of the sheets and a tug of war broke out. The sheet remained in Watson's possession. Another officer tried to go around Watson, who was standing in the middle of his doorway, but was blocked by Watson's leg. Watson wasn't even fighting and these guys were losing. Maybe they just didn't want to write a bunch of reports justifying the use of force. Bousquet and Greg were there, too.

Finally the lieutenant bargained, "All right, you can have the sheets but I'm taking the blanket you're using as a rug out."

I said, "What?" Normally I could care less and would probably even been the one giving the extra stuff out, but when a ranking official orders a prisoner to do something routine, the prisoner should do it.

The lieutenant stuck his leg around Watson and tried to drag the blanket/rug out by his boot. Watson shoved the lieutenant into Greg. Deciding that the niceties weren't working at this time, I stepped in front of the losing officers and popped Watson with a jab that stopped him in his tracks. The punch was just enough to let him know that was it. He looked stunned, but then gave me a half assed upper cut to the chin that took me by surprise. I wound up and cracked him good with about a nine on the Richter scale by way of a left handed knock-out swing. Watson's head went back and his eyes closed. Blood, part of his lip and I'm guessing a tooth landed on the back wall. Then I picked up the defeated con, threw him on his own bed and handcuffed him. The booth officer brought down the leg restraints to ensure the safety of the officers—no one wants to be kicked by some thug.

The lieutenant ordered over the radio that he wanted a cell set up for Watson to be four point restrained until he calmed down. I thought, *Calmed down? The thug is almost unconscious.* Frenchy and I carried the kid, who refused to walk. As I was carrying the kid to the vacant cell around the corner, I noticed that my pinky finger was pointing to the ground while my other fingers were horizontal to the ground. "That doesn't look right!" Frenchy had told me after the fact not to punch the kid's head, since his head was like a cinder block.

We placed Watson on the bunk and I was looking at his face, hoping that he wouldn't spit blood at me. All he said was, "Damn, Sarge! You got a hell of a punch!"

"Look at what you did to my finger." My finger and two other knuckles were visibly broken. But it hadn't started to hurt yet. The officers were grossed out by my finger pointing ninety degrees away from the rest of my hand. Up to the infirmary I went. They arranged a ride for me to the hospital. The nurse told me my broken hand was good enough for "Doctor Summeroff." I started grinning—you weren't allowed back to work with a broken finger or hand. When the jail had previously ordered people back to work with broken bones, a few of the officers ended up getting hurt or re-breaking their old injury. The lawsuits ended up costing the taxpayers millions. So now the sheriff wouldn't bother you until you were cleared by a medical doctor.

Gobi changed this policy as soon as he became elected. He had guys with casts on their legs just sitting in their cars on third shift. They were called parking lot attendants. It was a clear violation of state laws and the contract he signed. As you will see in the next chapter, there were at least thirty of us campaigning for him while we were out injured on duty. It was probably morally wrong, but not legally. You had to be one hundred percent to work in a contact area, but only about fifty percent to hold a sign or gather a signature from the voters. Gobi knew this and utilized us every day.

I was patched, splinted and given a few painkillers. They told me no work for six weeks at least, but I did go to the next union meeting at the request of Gunnar. This is where we were asked if we'd endorse Gobi for sheriff. There was an overwhelming support for a change in the regime. But there were also a few guys who questioned Gobi's background, as he had only worked at the jail for a month or two.

Some of the officers were there to spy on those of us that were loud and vocal, and they reported back to the present administration. Gobi would later use these guys to spy on us as well. These officer rats gave Gobi checks to keep their jobs once he was elected. They knew the game of politics. This was something that Gobi had promised to do away with, promising that donations would be replaced with qualifications. He probably got that from my sign at a picket. I should have known better than to trust the politician.

Gobi had sent a letter to the union to read at the meeting. It stated that everything would be based on seniority. No more buying your positions. We would have the best contract and new, comfortable uniforms. The inmates would no longer get all the milk and cookies that they wanted. Gobi promised a lot, and most of us fell for it. I would say about sixty percent. The rest was broken up between the die-hard Smith fans and the officers who didn't want to get involved at all. There were a few that wanted to endorse a college professor with a background in law enforcement. He was very smart and had some good ideas, but he just didn't have the name recognition needed to outcast Smith.

And Smith had to go. There was no question. It was cool at the time. You could see a light at the end of the tunnel. The vote passed overwhelmingly to endorse Gobi. The following week Gobi called me and asked if I could gather as many officers as I could to endorse his candidacy in a few other towns. He told me that we would be on television and in the newspapers. I was excited and honored that he had asked me to do that.

Gobi gave his speech in five different towns and cities, promising to do away with the current administration's nepotism, cronyism and lack of accountability. I posed for the newspaper by holding the union's banner with big Carl, making it a point to stick my bandaged hand over the banner to let everyone know that I was out hurt and still helping the candidate. During the months that followed, we went door-to-door gathering signatures, holding signs in big intersections and writing letters about embracing to the editor. There were about two hundred madmen running all over the largest county trying to get people to pay attention to our plea for a new regime. Most of the time we were met with understanding, but maybe twenty-five percent were die-hard Smith fans. I persuaded a few with the story of how I had lost out on a position because I wasn't married to the sheriff's daughter. When I mentioned the sheriff's son-in-law, it rang a bell; and Smith lost more votes. His family and friends were his own worst enemies. They cost him many, many votes.

I worked hard that summer. Gobi would call me once a week to do some sign holding in a particular town. I was thrilled. When it came to getting sign locations across the county, I worked like a busy beaver. I was solely responsible for four towns, and I kept planting signs everywhere, asking business owners and people with prime locations for permission. Then I would send out thank you cards to everyone. We were on a roll.

Soon my finger was healed, however, and I didn't want to be accused of milking the system. So I went to the doctor and was given the green light to go back to work. I wouldn't normally be happy about this, but the election wasn't too far away. I was also enjoying the feeling that we were going to beat the embedded sheriff and get the people fired who had ruined the jail in the first place, or at the very least put out to pasture where they couldn't do any more damage. Morale was high. The captains and deputies were all campaigning for Smith. They had to. Most of them didn't have the balls to tell the sheriff what was wrong and how to fix it. They were just puppets. These men and women didn't care whom they bribed or donated to.

I know that most of you will say that's life and politics. But it's still not right; it goes back to the movie *Braveheart*. What would you do? Would you fight for freedom? Or would you cower and pay homage to whoever was in charge? Would you hide and wait until the outcome was decided? Would you fight for equality of others, or just for yourself? These are tough questions; and until you know yourself and what you are willing to do and risk, don't even guess.

CHAPTER NINE
BACK TO WORK (STILL SUCKS)

I had almost forgotten that I had a new deputy since Greenberg's breakdown. I guess I hadn't given it too much thought, as my new deputy was Greenberg's protégé, Dumas. He was the overly conceited version of Greenberg. They both had the same quirks and attitude, and they came from the same side of the bridge and screwed with the staff as much as possible. The only difference was that Dumas was a black belt and in pretty good shape. He would be a lot harder to break down.

I brought my note into the personnel department. They accepted it and I was given a return to work slip for the deputy. I walked over to his office, which overlooked the whole modular compound, and he greeted me with a smile and a handshake—not with a kiss, like Judas, but it was pretty much the same thing.

"Welcome back, Michael."

"Thank you, Deputy."

"All right now, let me see. You are going to third shift in the 'J' building."

I looked some sign that he was joking. He was wearing sunglasses indoors, as his mentor Greenberg had done, so it was tough to get a quick read. "What? You're joking, right, Dep?"

"No, Michael. You would have been in your old spot, but they promoted someone from special services to sergeant and he's in your spot now. Third shift was supposed to be Sergeant Prunier. He came back from being injured two weeks ago and was going to fill there, but he has called in sick for two weeks after I spoke with him."

"So I have to go on third shift because Prunier reneged on his deal with you?" I was not happy.

"Mike, it'll just be until Ray comes back. A month at most. There's a ton of overtime available for you."

I knew that was just a band-aid for all the bullshit. They had promoted an officer from special services that had never worked the blocks. Then, to top that off, I had to go on third shift because they wanted the new guy on days. Or was this the long arm of Greenberg, or the sheriff still being mad for me making him go through the ethics commission to promote his son-in-law?

Reluctantly, I said, "Okay, I'll play your little game. I guess you can take Greenberg out of the jail, but you can't take Greenberg out of you."

"What the heck are you talking about?" Dumas asked.

"You're picking up right where Greenberg left off. You two are peas in the same mod."

Dumas shook his head. "I'm nothing like him."

"Deputy, you are the same thing as him, just in better shape. You're him with a black belt."

Dumas just chuckled, but he was just as I had said. I decided to push him a little. I didn't think I could take him, even though my coworkers said that I would destroy him. I asked, "What would your karate training tell you to do if I jumped over the desk onto you?" I had a goofy smirk on my face so as not to make him think I was for real.

"You know, Mike, I thought about that when I heard you come in. A big guy like you, I'd take your legs out from under you. Then I'd get out of here."

The night shift in the "J" building was hell. As I've said before, this was when most of the cons were awake. Since this was an around the clock working building, most of them were up and yelling across the tiers to their buddies in other cells. The building echoed like crazy, and there were a lot of fights at night. We had to shower the cons that the other two shifts hadn't felt like doing. I knew that they usually leave the worst ones for the night shift, since I'd been on days for quite a few years. And we had to be really careful with these guys—not because they were dangerous, but because they had to work the system.

Some inmates committed horrible crimes, but the laws stated that we had to protect them. When we were holding a child molester, he was safer with us than if the victim's family were to see him. But if we didn't bow to his needs or wants, he'd call his lawyer and make a frivolous lawsuit. Most of the time the lawsuits went away, but sometimes an eager lawyer or reporter would snowball the story and make the officers at the jail look like monsters. There was one huge incident where the maxi officers under the command of Deputy Slattery were holding an illegal immigrant that had raped and murdered a four-year-old boy. The immigrant was throwing urine on the staff, so they placed him in a restraint chair. The con later claimed that the officer who'd put him in the chair had thrown hot water on him and burnt his stomach and genitals. I wasn't in maxi during the Slattery reign, but the wrong guy was charged with the crime. The court threw one officer into another penitentiary because they thought he was protecting someone, and the person he was protecting didn't have the guts to come forward to keep another man from taking the fall for the hot water incident. The sergeant that was blamed wasn't even in that block when the water incident had taken place; he lost his house, job and his wife, who left him due to the stress. The cowardly officer, on the other hand, was promoted under Gobi's administration. But I'm jumping ahead here.

We had an inmate like Ritchie Renaud in the "J" building. He was one of those inmates that needed attention, and if he didn't get it, he would do something stupid. Jimmy Kasaras was like a bigger Renaud without as much inbreeding in his blood. Kasaras would wait by his cell door when it was time to do a wind. He wanted to talk to anyone. If you didn't stop and chat with him, you could almost be assured of having to write a report for your next wind. It was like a child sent to his room as punishment, yelling for water or food just for attention and nothing more.

Kasaras' tantrums were a lot worse, though; he would do things like Kasaras: rubbing feces on the walls or himself to get attention. What can you do with a person like that? Chain him to his bunk for a few hours until a higher up tells you to let him up. By then he's peed and crapped on himself and you are now ordered to give him a shower. That's what he wanted in the first place: the company of an officer. You have to be around these special needs inmates all the time or they'll do something crazy and you'll spend more time writing reports than the punishment lasts.

Like Renaud, Kasaras was in for some type of sex charge. He was also from the area where a poor teenage girl had been missing for years. We would have charity bike rides for the family every year. The disappearance of this teenage girl fit the mode of operation for this Kasaras skinner. When I mentioned it to him, he asked me nicely to shut up about it. I felt by saying it, I could try and read his reaction. . I felt as if he was hiding something. So I wrote a report and turned it into the special services unit out of respect for the girl and her family and friends. I still don't know if they ever passed the report along or tried their own investigation, or if they just threw the report away because it came from some block sergeant.

Kasaras was being his usual punk self one night and spat in the face of my favorite third shift officer. I only worked with Timmy two nights a week, since we had different nights or days off. When Timmy called for me I really didn't want to go, as I knew I was going to have to endure some kind of mini hell and write reports.

Kasaras was laughing and Timmy said, pointing to his face, "Look at what Kasaras did!"

"He spit on you?"

"Yup, the dirty motherfucker! I'd like to punch his head in!"

Kasaras was laughing knowing that the odds of a special needs inmate getting beaten up were very slim. And then if he did get hit, the next day he would have a ton of attention with the brass and special services interviewing him.

"Do you really want to kick his ass?" I asked.

"Yeah, absolutely."

"Do you think you can take the mongrel?"

"Yes, I do," Timmy said with a smile.

I called for Kasaras' door to be opened, and Timmy went into the cell a little timidly. He tried to out-wrestle the fat skinner but wasn't doing a very good job of it. I'd thought Timmy was stronger than that, but sometimes these skinners had to be pretty strong to hold their victims down. I know that sounds callous, but they have this mental strength that kicks in when they are excited.

I saw Timmy starting to get pushed around so I put Kasaras into a headlock and told Timmy to go get the chains. I had no problem making the skinner drop to his knees and place his arms behind his back. We put Kasaras into four point restraints and wrote two very nice reports. While Kasaras was in four point restraints, we were supposed to have another officer watch him, but that would mean compromising the security of the block because for some strange reason we had one less officer on the night shift. Funny thing—I never gave a rat's ass about the shortage of staff on that shift until I actually worked it.

So I had to improvise. I had the officer covering the suicide watch cover the spitter. Then I had the booth officer wedge the trap doors open and hit the winds every fifteen minutes. That left Timmy and myself on the floor to start giving showers. We had to write our reports, monitor the showers and tier times, and cuff and uncuff the thirty-something inmates for the night.

The last shower was at about three-thirty in the morning. It was one lone inmate who was a real punk, but hated Kasaras. Timmy and I had finished our reports and the inmate on the dayroom floor was just hobbling around in his restraints, winding down for the night. We went into the booth and I asked the new officer on watch to keep an eye on the last inmate so Timmy and I could put our reports into the computer. We sat on the metal tables near the showers and made sure that our reports were bomb proof. I didn't want to give the brass any more ammo to get me.

Then I heard the booth door shut. It was the newly academy trained officer. "I gotta take a quick leak, Sarge."

"Okay. Did you put the other kid in?"

"No! It's not time yet."

I looked out and saw the shackled inmate hobbling towards Kasaras' open cell with a broomstick. "Oh shit!" He could do a lot of damage to Kasaras who was restrained on the bed and unable defend himself. Kasaras was a punk, but I would be in big trouble if this kid whacked him or stuck it into him—or God forbid shoved the broomstick into the skinner's throat.

I ran out of the booth and fell as I ran around the corner into the cell. The inmate was going to dive with the broomstick into Kasaras' face when I reached out and just caught the leg irons, pulling them towards me. He fell unexpectedly and the broomstick snapped under his body weight.

"Thought you were pretty slick? I got you, punk!" I shouted, thankful for the save.

"I'm sorry, Sarge," came from behind me. The new officer hadn't realized how bad that situation could have been. He was very regretful, and since he was on probation for six months—as are all new officers—he begged me to have someone else write the report. I called him stupid a few times but lessened the severity of the potential hazard in the report, writing that the kid was stopped outside the cell as I was doing the wind. It all worked out. There was no harm and therefore no foul. But the rookie owed me big time.

We had twin convicts in our block, but they were never in at the same time. This led me to wonder if they were really twins or just one con with duel identities. Ben and Jose Fernandez were always in the "J" building at one time or another during my five years in the hole. They had enemy concerns with members of their own gang. They were from Chicago, or so they claimed, and were members there of the Latin Kings. But the Latin Kings around this area weren't impressed with them, while the Fernandez boys thought the members around here weren't involved enough.

What amazed me was that the twins each knew how to manipulate the cell door's locking mechanism and jiggle it off its track. That meant they could open the door whenever they felt like it. Ben would sometimes open his door and taunt a shackled, and therefore defenseless, inmate, who was out on the tier enjoying an hour of semi-freedom, with a razor blade.

We weren't aware of this until one day we noticed on the control board on the booth that there was a red light instead of a green on Benny's cell. Green meant it was okay to go, while red meant stop and think; these assholes are out. Greg had noticed it when I was on the day shift. So he went out and checked it. Sure enough, the lock was sliding freely. That time, Benny was smart as not to let the officers onto his stunt. I wrote a report and Greg wrote two, but the administration didn't believe us so they ignored the problem.

One night I had two smaller, big-mouthed gangsters out yelling stuff about Benny being a poser and not having the balls to go out into the population. They were insinuating that he was a coward and thereby not a real Latin King. I told them to keep it down and was walking one of the cons back to his cell and I heard a high-pitched scream. It was the other gangster reacting to Benny swinging a razor at him. I felt the burning rush of adrenaline as I ran over to protect the little gangster. The thought of this razor-wielding wildman slicing me didn't scare me as much as the thought of him getting the little loudmouth who couldn't protect himself. I guess my sense of duty was more prevalent.

Benny was swinging wildly at the other con, who was ducking and backing away as much as possible. I saw the inmate go to my right, and, knowing that Benny would soon follow, I took a chance and dove where I figured his legs would be in a half a second. I was wrong; Benny cut back, I landed on the floor and heard quite a few laughs from the cons. At least none of my fellow officers were witnessing the action.

Benny leaped over my legs and I looked back; it felt like everything was in slow motion. I kicked his ankle into his other calf and he fell to the floor. Then I flopped over onto him and held him down, keeping my strong hand on his razor-wielding arm. He didn't want to wrestle with me. The other two cons were now brave and yelled for all to hear, "Look, he can't even win an unfair fight against a chained real Latin King! You ain't shit!"

My guys saw me escorting Benny back to his cell and came out to help put the other two back in. I think Benny just wanted to scare them. Otherwise he would have just jumped on one and started carving. But I knew that had had to do something about the cell door. I worked overtime the next morning and told the captain and lieutenant about it. They decided to move Benny a few cell doors down, thinking maybe it was a mechanical glitch in the door.

The next morning the first shift decided to shower the cons I'd had out last night, figuring that they would pass and the officers would make their quota of inmates before noon. An inmate who refused a shower was still counted as having one. It was a numbers game. This would give the officers a break and more time for cards. But the inmates who had been almost attacked decided that they wanted to come out just to taunt Ben for not getting them. They just never learned, I guess. These guys were yelling about how slow he was and that he had no game. Benny waited until they had quieted down before making his move. He jiggled the door off its track and ran down the stairs after the pair.

Thankfully, we were all watching and waiting. The officers made a semicircle around Benny, who didn't want to hurt the officers, just scare the loud-mouthed gangsters. Officer Gardella, who was behind Benny, hit him over the head with a large metal trashcan. Benny dropped and Tiger lunged on top of him. The captain had seen the inmate open the cell, so we moved Benny down to a cell with bars and slapped a set of restraints on it. The restraints went to the bars on the next cell door, so if he jiggled the door he couldn't open it far enough to squeeze through.

When the captain asked Benny how he'd done it, he replied, "You listen to how the latches fall. After a long time in jail I can tell where the levers are. I lift up and over to the left. Then I lift up again and over to the right. If you put me in a cell with the lock on the other side, I do the opposite."

"You are a smart man, Fernandez. Why don't you do something constructive with your life?" the captain inquired. He had the top brass come down and check out the potentially dangerous situation, but the maintenance department didn't know what to do. Did you reconfigure the locking system on all the cells of the jail? Benny and his brother were the only ones who had ever been able to mess with the locks, so they ended transferring Benny to another institution. Maybe the change would be good for him.

The next few months brought about a few changes. Ray Prunier decided to come back from his injury. He'd been out for two years from a back injury helping lift up an inmate in a wheelchair so big Carl could change his uniform. Now I'm not a doctor, but two years? Now that he was back, Dumas was going to punish him, as he had me, by placing him on the third shift in the "J" building. So Ray took my spot and I was given my day slot since the newly promoted sergeant from special services was promoted again to lieutenant of second shift. This guy wasn't even off his probationary period as a sergeant.

I had applied for the promotions, but I knew it was a losing battle. My evaluations were always done by my lieutenant at the time, none of whom could ever say anything bad about my performance or handling of high-pressure situations. No matter how many times they tried to get me, my evaluations were excellent.

One of the sheriff's daughters was in charge of personnel, and Dumas told me that she had called him and mentioned that my evaluation grade was too high and that they should change it. Dumas actually did me a solid man-to-man act of good faith. He told her no. He said regardless of what the sheriff thought about my political stance, he did a terrific job in the segregation area.

The sheriff's daughter was mad. "Well, this mark is just too high for someone like him!"

But I thanked my deputy, thinking, *Maybe this guy isn't as bad as I thought he was.* But maybe he was just worried about the possibility of a new sheriff and wanted to be good to those us who were close to Gobi. I'd find out soon enough.

The guys were happy to see me on days again as I wasn't a ball buster and they knew that I wasn't a rat. I got back into the groove of slinging chains during the daytime. Although, if there hadn't been clocks or regular meal times in the "J" building, you wouldn't have known what time it was. There was no sunlight beaming through. As a matter of fact, sometimes thunderstorms would pass by and we wouldn't even be aware of it until we left the building and saw that the runway was wet.

Early one Monday morning I looked at the list of cons slated to go to court. I had twelve of the worst inmates going— Benny's brother Jose, who came to us just as Benny was leaving; a white gang member from the Hooligans; three Latin Kings; three sex offenders; a wild kid who fought anyone who wasn't white; Kasaras, who would make the fourth sex offender; and two regular cons, one that was notorious for assaulting staff. It was our job to get these shitbags showered, fed and chained up. I also had to keep them separated according to their status. And the escorting staff who handled the cons from the prison block to the receiving area always seemed to be short-staffed. The officer in charge had asked me if I could escort some of the cons, as these guys went to court before the rest of the jail's inmates.

One of the night shift officers helped me get them ready and we began escorting them. We got ten of them out without a hitch. Kasaras didn't want to go, but Jose, who had been manipulating him for food and other items, yelled at him to quit giving us a hard time. Finally my coworker got him chained him up, and the fat skinner came down the stairs where Jose and I were standing. He had a huge smirk on his face. I kept my body between the two cons to prevent any horseplay, but they were determined to touch shoulders, as was customary in the "J" building when wearing restraints. Then we all headed toward the pedestrian trap to exit the building.

I looked at Kasaras and noticed a lot of blood running off his cupped and cuffed hands. I stopped him and looked more closely; his wrist was cut, and cut deep. Jose stepped away as fast as he could with the restraints on. He started cheering and making some loud noise like an automatic weapon.

"I got that punk-ass bitch! Yeah! L.K. forever three sixty, complete circle!" It was some kind of gangster rap.

I was pissed that they had done this to me. I was the cool cop. *What the fuck*, I thought to myself.

"I need the nurse and an officer on the 'J' dayroom floor immediately!" I hollered over the radio. I let Jose hop around the dayroom floor while I sat Kasaras down on the steel round table. There was a lot of blood coming out of his hands and wrist. I was so pissed off. As the other officers were putting Jose back in his cell, I yelled, "I won't forget this, you shitbag!"

He just looked at me and laughed. "Don't be stupid, Mike. It's all good." Whatever the heck that was supposed to mean.

The nurse arrived and I walked her over to Kasaras. "Yup," she said. "It's a definite hospital trip." I was so mad. I had another officer wait with the nurse, who was patching Kasaras' wrist up enough while they waited for a cruiser to take him to the hospital. Then I brought Jose up to receiving myself. I kept asking him, "Why? Why the fuck would you do that to me? I've always been good to you motherfuckers!" I might have manhandled him along the way and he might have been squished a couple of times against the walls.

When I dropped him off at the receiving area he whispered to me, "Mikie, it's all good. Things ain't what they seem." I had no clue at the time what he meant, but I didn't care. It was probably just some mumbo jumbo from his gang. I was heated. But I went back to see Kasaras and asked him about the incident. I noticed special services there taking pictures and getting information out of him. I looked at his bandaged wrist and down at the blood. Then I saw a small metal object next to his foot and behind him. It was a broken razor blade.

Kasaras noticed me looking at it and tried to step on it, but the chains hindered his legs.

"You son of a bitch!" I yelled. "You cut yourself because you didn't want to go to court!"

Kasaras looked down for a moment and then at the special services officer. "I'm sorry. I can't go to court today."

"Well, I guess you're not going today," echoed the nurse. "You rather risk bleeding to death than going to court?"

"I didn't realize how deep it was because I couldn't see my wrist behind my back."

The investigating officer said, "Excellent job, Sergeant Mike! You solved this little caper."

I recalled what Jose said to me. That son of a gun. He wasn't guilty of slicing the fat bastard, and he hadn't even said anything while I was bouncing him around like a pinball machine.

When I returned to the block Greg told me the Captain wanted to see me. I figured he was going to thank me and ask for details. My Captain was pretty cool. I entered his office on my hands and knees bowing to him as a joke.

His first words were, "The deputy said to send you home."

I looked up. "What? You're joking, right?"

"No. He said you should have known better than to have anyone out on the floor with Jose. Now Jose cut another inmate and you were there in charge."

I protested, "Captain, Kasaras cut himself. He didn't want to go to court. Special services has it all on tape. I found the razor he used."

He shrugged. "Well, the deputy wasn't aware of that, but he wants you to punch out and go home."

I lost it. "Well fuck him, Captain! I was going above my duty escorting the worst twelve inmates ever to go to court; and then I solve an assault case that turned out to be a self mutilation, and you are sending me home?"

"I'm sorry, Mike. Maybe you can call the deputy and tell him your version."

"No fuckin' way, Captain! You can tell him if he's man enough to meet me in the locker room and we'll settle this like men!"

"Mike, wait."

"I'm outta here!" I was so mad I was getting palpitations. I changed in the locker room and went home. No sign of Dumas. I drove around for a couple of hours trying to cool off, but it didn't help. I went home and paced back and forth for another hour. Finally the phone rang. It was my Captain.

"Sergeant Mike, the good deputy said that you can come back to work tomorrow."

"Fuck him! I'm not coming back until he apologizes!" Click: I hung up the phone on the captain, who was kind of caught in the middle.

The phone rang again. "Mike, don't hang up on me again!"

"Sorry about that, Captain."

"Come back into work tomorrow and we'll talk."

"Sorry, Captain, but I'm not, and I repeat not, coming back until the deputy apologizes to me. I did more than I should have."

He hesitated. "Are you sure you want me to tell the deputy that?"

"No, Captain. Tell him he's a piece of shit having you do his dirty work. And tell him that he should get his facts straight before he jumps the gun."

"Okay, Mike, but I think you're making a big mistake."

I stayed out of work for a week, calling in sick just to cover my ass so I wouldn't be considered AWOL.

When I returned to work the guys were wondering what had happened to me. I told them nothing but I did mention my phone call with the captain. Dumas called me to his office and said that I could bring union representation. I told him I didn't need it as he was in the wrong.

He said, "Well, come on up to my office, then."

When I arrived he used the *make 'em wait* tactic. This was supposed to make an enraged person lose some of his or her steam when going to see a superior officer. You were to wait outside the office, so the civilians you rarely see would start chatting with you. You ended up being more pleasant.

Finally Dumas' secretary said, "Michael, the deputy will see you now."

When I got into the office, the deputy said, "Have a seat, Michael. Look, you knew better than to have Jose or his brother out when anyone else is out. It has been a standing order from way back."

I wasn't about to budge. "There's no written order with either one of their names on it, boss."

"Well, Michael, I'm not going to split hairs with you on this. You should have known better than to have any of the Fernandez boys out with anyone else due to their reputation."

"Does the court house shut down when they are in there?" I demanded. "Does the police station close its doors when they receive a Fernandez boy?"

"Well, we're not the courthouse or any other place," he said, frowning. "There is a written order somewhere down there, so I just want to get back the eight hours you had off at home probably watching 'Everybody Loves Raymond' or something."

"Deputy, I was so pissed that day, I couldn't even sit still. But you can take one of my overtime slips and tear it up. Or you can take six hours, not eight, off my books since I left at nine. That's all I'm willing to give. You should be saying what a good job I was doing. If it weren't for me, you guys would still think it was an assault when instead it was Kasaras cutting himself to get out of going to court."

"I will say thank you, Michael," he gave me. "You do a wonderful job down there, but I still feel that you shouldn't have had those two out at the same time. My decision still remains at a one-day suspension. Do you want to appeal it?"

"Yeah, I do. Mark my words; I'll resign before I take a suspension for this."

"I'm sorry to hear that. Sign here where it says *I wish to appeal this decision.*"

The appeal process took about a week and a half. Gaff had retired and the new number three man, McNally, was one of my training officers. He was smart and reasonable. The only thing he didn't have was time with the inmates. The story was that he got scared after a fight and tried to quit, but his uncle got him a job away from the inmates. So many people act tough, but when it's time to be one-on-one with the cons they are just as scared as the cons are with an officer.

This time I brought Gunnar with me, as I wasn't going to take even a one-day suspension. Not for this. There were plenty of things that I could and should have been suspended for, but this wasn't one of them. McNally invited us into his office and offered us a soda, which I gladly accepted. Then he made some small talk about the Red Sox, which lightened the mood.

"Sergeant Szaban, or Sergeant Mike, as you are widely known, I did some research on this case. There was a memo put out at roll call, but you were out injured that day, and month, and almost all summer, for that matter. I guess I should have you in for a workman's compensation issue."

We all chuckled a little, as it appeared to be going my way.

"I was going to stick by the deputy's decision," McNally continued, "but since you were out and there is no official posting about the Fernandez boys, I'm going to let you off with a written warning that will be placed in your file. How's that?"

Gunnar asked if we could step outside and discuss the verdict and McNally told us to take our time. Gunnar said his offer was decent; he hadn't expected him to lower the deputy's suspension. But Gunnar wanted to get me a verbal warning, since there were no written warnings in my file as of yet. We went back inside.

"Deputy McNally, can you give Sergeant Mike a verbal warning? I mean, he did go above and beyond what he was called to do that day."

McNally thought for a moment. "I don't believe that Friese will go for that. But I'll tell you what. I will write a very nice warning indicating what a good job you did, but that you had one little slip up; and you can petition to have it removed in six months."

We all shook hands and I signed on the dotted line. Then I raided his refrigerator and we left. I was feeling a little better. I knew they'd been trying to get me for a while, and if this was the best that they could do, then so be it. Back to work.

CHAPTER TEN
THE BEGINNING OF THE END

The elections weren't too far away. It was a huge year for politics. There was the presidential race, the senatorial races, many local, small time representative races and the county sheriff's election. The sheriff's position was for six years at a time. Sheriff Smith hadn't had an opponent in eighteen years. This year was something new for the seventy-something-year-old. Lawns across the county were splattered with signs. There were as many signs as there were mailboxes. If you didn't have a sign in your yard, you could bet two out of three of your neighbors did.

Like I mentioned before, I was in charge of putting up signs in four towns, and of course my town took precedence. I had signs in virtually every lawn for two miles either way. The only problem I had was that a lieutenant, whose ex-wife lived diagonally across the street, had a huge Smith for sheriff sign. I wouldn't have been bothered by it except that it wasn't pointed so the traffic could see it; it was pointed directly at my front door.

This guy was being a punk. He was your typical tall, dark and handsome guy with slicked back hair and a greasy tan. The guy had never worked a day in the block but was promoted to lieutenant with just five years on some cushy desk job. He was divorced because he had been caught having sex with a fairly pretty young social worker who monitored either the ankle bracelet or home detention programs. The deputy had walked in unannounced and caught the two in the midst of the afternoon delight. Not wanting to dismiss the sheriff's cash cows, he didn't write the two up but rather told a few friends, who in turn told a few friends.

The lieutenant's job was now to drive around and make sure the inmates pissed in a cup every week to screen for drugs. The only problem with him being on that job was that his Expedition was always parked outside his ex-wife's house. The vehicle was there morning, noon and night. I planned to rip his sign down, as it taunted me every day, but I didn't want to get into a sign-stealing war. I had way too many signs out in my town and the three others. The signs seemed to be more of a psychological battle than a political statement at this point.

There was a neutral, town-owned area on the main street in a high profile area where everyone placed signs. There were signs for candidates of all parties and levels of government, from the school committee elections to the presidency. I had noticed that mine kept disappearing. Well, not mine, but Gobi's. But this was my town and I was going to win this town and win it big. I kept replacing the signs that were taken. The signs were in such demand by the voters that at first I figured out that it was just someone who wanted the cool looking black and gold signs.

I went over to the vendor across the main road and he laughingly questioned, "He got your sign again?"

"Who's he?" I questioned back.

"You know the tall, lanky guy with the shaved head, black pickup with Smith's bumper stickers on the back window."

"Oh, that dirty thief." It was K.C. He lived in the next town over and drove out of his way to pull my signs out. For the next two weeks I plucked at least twenty of his signs, tore them up and threw them into the back of his pickup truck.

He worked second shift outside the modular buildings in the yard. That wasn't a bad gig unless it was extremely hot or cold. Regardless, K.C. didn't mind because he was an outdoorsman, a big hunter and fisherman. He was used to the elements and enjoyed being out in the yard watching the cons.

After work I was usually the last or one of the last first shift guys to leave. One day not long after the sign fiasco, K.C. came over to me in the locker room while I was sitting on the long pine bench taking off my boots. "I need to talk to you."

"What's up?" I knowingly asked. He was visibly shaking; I wasn't sure if it was because he was mad or scared of the confrontation.

"If you ever touch my signs again, I'll gut you like a pig!"

I laughed, but I wasn't going to let him get away with talking to me like that, especially not in the locker room. "You drove out of your way to steal my signs. Don't even try denying it; I have witnesses. So unless you're man enough to fight, get back to your post, bitch!"

I figured that would either end the conversation or begin the fight. K.C. leaned over me, looking distraught but still shaking. The staff thought he was nuts because of his extreme hunting and fishing stories, but when I looked at him I saw a tall, lanky liar. I braced myself in case he punched—and punch he did. He hit me on the right ear with the same amount of force as my dog running into me. It was about a four on the Richter scale, just enough to make me stand up and give him two jabs to the nose. The first one stunned him and the second drew a tiny bit of blood. He swung a couple of quick but ineffective punches at the side of my head and shoulders. I wanted to end this quickly in case someone came in, so I kicked him in the stomach and he went down. I punched him one more time with just enough force to put him on the ground without hurting him. He was holding his stomach anyway; he wasn't going to fight any more. Now it was my turn to speak again.

"K.C., if I am missing any more signs in town, I'm coming after you. I don't care if it's you or not. I'm going to assume that it's you."

Lying in the fetal position, he moaned, "Mike, I won't touch your stupid signs. Can you just leave my big one by the golf course?"

"That's a deal, K.C." As I was finishing up getting dressed in my civilian clothes, he got up all wobbly and said without looking at me, "Hey Mike, just remember that the devil you know is better than the devil you don't."

I didn't want to get into it with him any more. Who was he to be badmouthing the politician to whom I had devoted a year of my life and a lot of hard work? I had written letters to newspapers, held signs on every major street corner, developed high blood pressure and gone out of my way landing spots for almost one thousand yard signs—and this guy was going to tell me that he was a devil. I should've still been hitting him.

I campaigned hard because I wanted things to be fair, not because of some ulterior motive like so many others were doing. I wasn't looking for a promotion or a Monday to Friday job as so many of my coworkers did. But I didn't know their motives at the time; I thought they were fighting for the same thing I was: fairness. Had I known that these men and women were only helping Gobi to gain titles and cushy jobs, I would have fought them instead. They could have "donated" to the incumbent sheriff and achieved their goals without all this bullshit of campaigning.

Gobi held a one hundred dollar a plate fundraiser, as he said that the campaign signs had drained his funds. I went namely for the food, as I would eat a lot, and secondly because if I believed in a cause, I would give it the shirt off my back. At the fundraiser I told Gobi about the sign-stealing incident but omitted the officer's name.

"Good job, Mike. I want you to drive down route nine and get all of Smith's signs out and into a dumpster."

"Consider it done, boss." I was actually worried about doing it, but Gobi *was* going to be the new boss. Maybe, just maybe, it would be fun.

Election day was finally here. I contemplated calling in sick. But my work was done and now in the hands of the voters, so I went to work. Gobi called me that morning and asked if I could get some people to hold signs at my hometown elementary school where the voting would take place.

"Well, boss, I'll be there at three after work."

"No, Mike, I need someone there early to show support when the early bird senior citizens vote."

"Okay," I promised. "I'll have someone there." My grandmother, who was in her eighties, said that she would go up, sit in her chair and chat with the seniors while holding a black and gold *Gobi for Sheriff* sign. She enjoyed being out of the house.

Work was like a ghost town. As many officers and staff who could get the day off to lend a hand to either Gobi or Smith. Smith's people were all off; there was no one above the rank of sergeant at the jail that day. My coworkers started rumors like, "We are down in all the cities," or, "We are losing two to one" But they were just being ball busters. I was thankful when my shift ended and that I didn't have to work overtime. I went straight to the school in my town and relieved my grandmother, who was pooped. Standing next to a couple of ladies holding Smith signs, I asked them why they were there. One lady said she had been paid to stand there for four hours, although she didn't know either candidate. I shook my head in disgust.

But it was nice seeing people I'd grown up with driving by and tooting their horns at me waving my Gobi sign, indicating that I was getting another vote for Gobi. Finally the polling closed. I hadn't heard anything from anybody, but the results would be posted in a half hour. I went home took a quick shower, and then phoned my grandmother to thank her again for her time. She said that she'd really enjoyed seeing some of the older townsfolk and reminiscing.

I hopped on my Harley and rode with eagerness to the polling area. My town had better win—and not just by a few votes. The tally was up; Gobi had won by a landslide. I was elated. I had the type of smile that just couldn't be erased. I was so happy about my town crushing Smith that I forgot to see who the townspeople had voted for president. Instead I rode with the results to our fancy meeting hall.

The place was already packed. It was a good thing that I had my bike, as parking was non-existent due to the amount of people. I was greeted with hugs, and Carl had watery eyes. "We did it," the big man said. "We kicked the emperor off his throne."

"Oh boy is this great!" I copied the line from *Animal House*. Everywhere I went, people were hugging, some tearful over the joyous victory. Television crews interviewed some of us, and reporters from the paper were there doing their jobs. We had defeated Rome. The most powerful emperor in this rich state had finally been defeated by our hard work.

Then Gobi came in and the place roared. People were yelling and thanking God. Gobi made his speech; when he mentioned Smith, a large percentage of the crowd booed. Then

Gobi, being the politician that he is, said, "No, no, I respect Sheriff Smith, and I don't want any badmouthing of him or his people." Then we celebrated the night away. Sheriff-elect Gobi came over and shook hands with Carl, Gunnar and myself, but dropped us like a bag of dirt when a pretty and curvaceous social worker approached him. That was it for thanking us. But I went outside still giddy and hopped on my bike, as I had to work the next morning. No one from Gobi's camp was going to call in sick since we wanted to see the facial expressions on the opponent's side. Maybe we would rub the victory in all the Smith ass-kissers' noses.

Before I left, Carl and a rookie friend of mine told me that the Smith people were at a bar just down the road. I joked with Carl's testosterone and said, "Let's go down to Smith's party and punch out a few people."

Carl grabbed my shoulder and lifted me off my bike seat. "All right, we're going down there and there's no half-assing it. We fight every one of those motherfucking scumbags. We are not going to let any of them walk away. Got it?"

"Carl, I'm kidding," I said hastily. "I'm not going down there to get arrested for beating up some crying coworkers."

Carl was actually disappointed, but he let me go. The big man had a few drinks in him and was feeling a little punchy.

***

In the next few weeks, reality sank in. A couple deputies retired, and Smith promoted as many friends and family as possible. This was when you didn't want to become promoted, however. The new administration would know that you were on Smith's campaign trail. He should have promoted his enemies instead so we would be targets for the new administration. We were hoping that all of the ass-kissing deputies would be fired and Smith's people would be at the very least demoted.

Then Gobi came out with another fundraiser. Why would he need more money? The election was over. He had one a week until he took office, and the brass was all there paying tribute. I didn't go, as I felt that I had done my part and now it was up to Gobi to do his. I heard of Greenberg going to the fundraisers, and Smith's family were also at the sheriff-elect's party.

Gobi made a speech that was relayed to us. He stated, "It's not a time to divide, but a time to add." That didn't sound like a leader whose men and women had just conquered Rome and wanted to clean it up. That sounded more like a politician who wanted to take donations from the Smith supporters. Gobi never called me again. He even changed his phone number. Apparently he'd had numerous phone calls from the men and women that I had campaigned with wanting specialty jobs, which was just stupid. Now they were doing the very thing they had fought long and hard to do away with. And it made them worse than Smith's cronies, as they were hypocrites and liars.

I decided to wait and see what happened. I wanted my enemies fired, as they were a big part of the problem at the jail. But when Gobi took over, he let Greenberg come back and put him in charge of my area, the mods. He did demote Dumas, sending him to another part of the jail, and Smith's family had all resigned except for Shooter. He was demoted because of a planned run-in with Lieutenant Prince. The lieutenant was promised a day position if he got Shooter on paper; and being the puppet he was, Shooter was nailed for disorderly conduct to a superior officer. Shooter was demoted to private and put on nights.

One of many Gobi campaign promises was to eliminate nepotism. But he hired more father and son teams and brother teams, and many, many of them were hired as deputies.

Dumas came up to me as he was leaving. "Well, Michael, you got what you wished for. I'm demoted."

"I actually wanted you fired, sir. But now I have Greenberg again."

"See; be careful what you wish for, Michael."

Dumas was right. Here I wanted him gone and I got it, but now Greenberg was going to be my boss for the third time.

While I was eagerly awaiting the posted promotions, I had to keep my nose clean. I didn't want the new boss to have to deal with any nonsense coming from me or Greenberg drawing attention to me. I was asked by the second shift sergeant to work for him, as he was being forced to work third shift in the "J" building. He was a good and quiet sergeant, so he talked me into it, on condition that I didn't have to work the "J" building. That way I could just read or catch a few zzzzz's. He told me I was all set for eleven p.m. Who would have guessed—I was stuck in the "J" building anyway. That was bullshit, but the regular night sergeant who had seniority didn't care that I was doing the second shift sergeant a favor. And to top it off, the tactical team had just had to restrain someone that was swinging a razor blade. Great! Now I had to monitor that troublemaker and do showers short-handed.

I saw the tactical response team leave except for my friend, Hercules, called that because he was a huge muscle man. But he didn't have the temper that juiceheads have. He had a wonderful personality and joked around a lot. He had nothing to prove to anyone and was stronger than anyone at the jail.

He looked around and said, "The scumbag we just chained, he's got a razor blade in his mouth."

"Really? And I'm supposed to get it out?"

"I guess my team leader didn't want to deal with it, but I'll call Deputy Haverty and let him know quietly."

I was angry but thankful my friend had let me know about this; if this kid swallowed it, he could die on my shift. I didn't want that.

Deputy Haverty and he called me ten minutes later. "Yeah Mike, I really need you to get that razor out of that kid's mouth. I don't care how you do it, just do it and please don't say anything."

I figured that he was covering up for someone and didn't want to make any waves with the new administration. I agreed and went to the young troublemaker's cell. He had a lot of blood around his mouth. Maybe they had tried to get it out, but couldn't and didn't want to risk him swallowing it. I went in and sat on the metal desk in his cell while he was chained to the bed with blood dripping out of his mouth. I made the usual chitchat so that he could sense that I was a cool CO. He stated that he was having woman problems and that was sort of why he was acting up. He also mentioned an officer that was pushing his buttons.

"It's just a game," I told him. "Don't let people get to you like that." Then we talked about girls and exchanged stories.

"Sarge," he said finally, "you're a pretty cool dude. I want to get rid of this razor. Can I give this to you and maybe get a shower?"

"I'll tell you what. You spit out the razor, chill out for one hour and I'll hook you up with a shower." I didn't want to unchain the kid too early; as word would get out that as soon as I got on duty I unhooked the kid. But I kept my word and the inmate wasn't a problem from then on.

I wasn't looking for a thank you or anything, but the only person who said anything to me was Hercules. He asked if I'd gotten it and I told him that I had. We then made the customary grunts and fake muscle poses at each other, shook hands and that was it.

This building was getting old. I had spent over five years here, and it was wearing on me. I was hoping for a promotion. There were a lot of them posted, and I had more time than most of the others who had applied, along with military, some college, excellent evaluations and many life saving letters. All I could do was hope that Gobi kept his promise to go by qualifications and not donations.

The following week my lieutenant called to tell me that I had to stay that night, as there was only one other sergeant on duty. There had to be two ranking officers on duty: one to be in charge of the compound and another just to run the segregation unit. I wasn't too happy, but this kind of thing was part of the job when you worked in the public safety sector. He asked if I wanted to work the "J" building or be in charge of the modular compound, which would mean I would be in charge of many officers and many more inmates, but with fewer problems. I opted for being in charge, but mentioned that I needed to step out and grab a sandwich. I didn't mind eating the food in the jail, just not for all three meals. It was customary for someone working overtime to go get sandwiches and bring them back, and the lieutenant said that since I was in charge, I obviously could step out and bring food back.

So I ran all the inmates to chow; and after they ate, they were all locked in their cells from five fifteen until six o'clock. I had the other sergeant cover for me in the unlikely event of a problem. When I asked around, none of my coworkers wanted anything; so I phoned the order in and gave my cell phone number to the two officers in the control booth. The girl there, Chrissy, was on the phone a lot that particular evening; I figured it was one of the few guys that she was dating. She kept saying, "No, not yet. Nope, I'll call you."

I went to pick up my order and walked back in with my good friend Drinkwater. Drinkwater was a proud Native American who hated sex offenders and punks that were into hurting animals. He was also a pretty good chess player, so when I worked second shift we played frequently. He was having a smoke on the landing by the entrance to the administration building, which leads to the control booth and the pedestrian trap to get in and out of the mods. I waved to the two rookies in the control booth, signaling that I was back and made a comment to the other sergeant that he could go rest as his ten minutes of being in charge were up. I received a couple of heckles on the radio about skipping a meal and not eating a whole box of doughnuts. Those smartasses.

I noticed that Chrissy was still on the phone and was looking at me through her peripheral vision. I was a good twenty years older than her. What was she looking at? Was she angry that I never paid attention to her? Had I yelled at one of the many guys she had dated? I didn't know. But I ate my sandwich with Drinkwater and we bullshitted about stuff that Lefty had pulled.

Lefty had been transferred down to the mods at my request. Lefty and Drinkwater were good friends, but they acted as if the French and Indian war were still going on. Lefty would put small toy blasting caps in the toaster so when Drinkwater made toast it would scare the crap out of him. Drinkwater would make reports out to mental health's suicide councilors that Lefty was having a breakdown. It was a vicious but funny cycle.

The night went smoothly, but next morning as I was punching in the captain looked at me and shook his head in disgust.

I inquired, "Did I do something?"

He said, "Man, you just don't want to keep a low profile, do you?"

"No, I don't. But what is it this time?"

"You left at five and didn't come back to work?" he asked in disbelief.

I laughed, thinking he was joking. But his demeanor showed otherwise. He told me that I had to go see Deputy Greenberg at nine o'clock and that this time I had better bring union representation. I took this as a joke since I knew Greenberg was trying to set me up with Gobi. Either he was trying to make me look bad with the new administration or this was his last shot at getting me.

I arrived in Greenberg's office a few minutes early with Gunnar. Greenberg had one of the bigger deputies with him as his witness, or protection. "Sergeant Szaban, I have received notice that you were absent from your post from seventeen hundred until twenty two hundred. You abandoned your post without authorization and you left no forwarding number. I had no alternative but to take away your stripes and suspend you for one month."

I couldn't believe that his last shot at me was this absurd. "First of all, Deputy, you shouldn't be trying to discipline me when you smell like hard liquor. Secondly, I was gone for ten minutes—maybe you could gain another five that I was on the landing. Thirdly, I gave Chrissy my cell phone number and had the other sergeant cover for me. This is all past practice."

"Ah. Nope. I have a report from special services. They interviewed some people and you are all done. Loss of rank and one month suspension."

"Why do you have such a hard on for me?" I demanded. "I never slept with your girlfriend. Many others did, but I didn't. Or is it that you are mad about having to sleep on the floor?

Are you mad that I do a much better job than you and you should be fired soon?"

His face was about to explode. I wanted to push more buttons, but Gunnar grabbed me and said, "Mike, let's get out of here before he loses it."

I was glad to finally confront the piece of shit Frank Burns (from "M.A.S.H.")/Captain Binghampton (from "McHale's Navy") type. But at the same time I was angry that I'd just let this guy try and get me for so long without any aggression from me. I'd always played defense, and it was getting old. Oh well, I knew I couldn't be officially suspended unless it went all the way up the chain of command.

Gunnar stayed with me most of the day to calm me down and to keep informing me that even if the truth won out, Greenberg could get me on being disrespectful. I'd take a suspension for that, but not for getting a sandwich! I would quit before they would get a day suspension out of me for that.

During lunch that day, I walked in to the inmates' chow hall after some grub and saw two deputies standing sheepishly in the corner—the number three man, McNally, and a lawyer who was also a deputy for the jail. What was going on here? These guys were never around, and I knew they weren't too keen on being around the cons. They were more of the white-collar types.

"What, are you guys slumming?" I taunted them.

"We just wanted to see how the chow hall operates."

Forty something years between them and they still didn't know how the chow hall ran, except on paper.

The other officers were standing as far away from the two deputies as possible, so as not to be labeled rats. I noticed an inmate standing up in the right hand corner near me. A couple of other inmates were smacking him on the back, but he was choking and starting to go down. I ran over with Gunnar and I wrapped my arms around him, squeezing out the Heimlich maneuver once. A little food dribbled out of his mouth onto my arms. It was gross, but the adrenaline was running and I didn't want this kid to drop. I squeezed hard and quickly, delivering a much more powerful Heimlich and the food released and shot out onto his tray and my arms. Gunnar was coaching me from behind; it was nice to have someone around.

The inmate regained his breath and Gunnar escorted the kid up to the infirmary just to check his vital signs. R.T. and some other guys said that I was trying to hump the young kid. Others said that the kid probably would die from broken ribs. It was all good humor.

Deputy McNally congratulated me and said, "Nice job, Sergeant Mike. We trained you well. I'm going to write you a little something."

I was kind of shocked. "Thank you, Deputy. I know you would have done the same thing if you weren't afraid of inmates," I joked. Then I went back to my post.

A few days passed, and Sheriff Gobi sent me a nicely written letter about my quick actions that saved a man's life. I didn't get the eight hours off, like under Smith's regime, but this was a nice start. Gunnar had received a letter also.

I also received a letter to see Deputy McNally about my pending suspension and brought Gunnar along because he wanted to thank the deputy for the nice letter from the sheriff. The deputy made the customary small talk and offered us sodas again. "Well, Sergeant Mike, we meet again. You know, you might have the record for being investigated. I'm going to have to check that out."

"Thank you, sir," I replied. "Of course they're all witch hunts."

"Now, I've read this report, and it says that Officer Ruggles from special services interviewed you and an unnamed officer. She wrote in her investigation that you admitted to being away from your post from seventeen hundred until twenty hundred hours. Now let's hear your reason for the appeal."

I said, "I never spoke to Officer Ruggles about this. And furthermore, the times keep changing. First I was gone all night, then I was gone until ten o'clock and now you're saying that I was gone until eight o'clock. What's going on here?"

"Well, Michael, what's going on here is that you left your post unmanned, and I have to agree with Deputy Greenberg about these charges. I'm not going to uphold the loss of rank, but—"

I interrupted him angrily, "No way, Deputy! I'm not going to take one day for this! You have a phony special services interview and a lie about the time I was gone! You didn't talk to the sergeant that covered for me the ten minutes that I was gone and the five minutes I was on the landing! Ask Drinkwater, ask Chrissy, and ask the sergeant who covered for me. And you know that this is all past practice."

"If I were you Mike, I'd be more concerned about the special services interview," he warned.

"No! I'm more concerned that you're taking a nut job like Greenberg's side without knowing the truth!"

We were both getting angrier and angrier. I'd never seen McNally act this way. He was probably as scared of the new administration as he was of convicts. Gunnar jumped in and told me to get out of the office. I could hear him talking to the deputy.

"McNally, I don't want this to end on a bad note. Can we just shake hands and do this at a later date?"

"Tell Sergeant Szaban that I will have to look into this matter further. I'm not happy about this phantom interview. That would be Mike's only leg to stand on."

They shook hands, and then Gunnar quoted some scripture to me and told me that everything would be fine. He said that it was in God's hands now. But he also reiterated that I shouldn't have been yelling or getting angry at the superior officers. Only the union representation could do that and get away with it legally. I told him that next time he was my liaison, he had better punch the deputy out.

My mind was whirling. Why would Ruggles have said she interviewed me? The only time I spoke with her was when we were discussing the sheriff's election. I'd told her that if Smith won the election I would resign. She agreed. I would have lived up to my part. Now she was writing fake interviews for Gobi's team. I didn't like this at all.

We were called back in at the end of the day. I was intent on quitting if I were to receive a day suspension or anything else. There was no way that I would put up with the continued headhunting by Dumas and Greenberg after all we had done to oust the former sheriff and his crooked ways. Any deputy could dish out the punishment, but only the sheriff could approve it.

Gunnar and I went back into McNally's office. I had decided to let Gunnar do the talking for me.

"Gentlemen, I hope we can get through this as painlessly as possible," McNally began.

We both nodded and mumbled, "Yes sir."

"I have gone back over the past few years investigations and noticed that you have been the target of some frivolous inquiries. I was very angry with the special services department. I spoke with Officer Ruggles, who admitted to not speaking to you directly, but rather being instructed to write your admissions. I will deal with her later. However, you did leave your post. We may disagree on the time, but left, so I'm going to recommend just twelve days suspension."

I smirked, looking at Gunnar to speak.

"Deputy, you know as well as I know that it's common and past practice for someone to go grab a pizza or a sandwich. It's done all the time. As for leaving his post, Mike had permission from the day shift lieutenant, and he had another sergeant cover for him. Can't we just make it a written warning?"

McNally shook his head. "I wish I could, but Mike left his post. The new administration wants to set a new example for accountability."

At this point I had to chime in. "Deputy, look out your window. There are five people out in the parking lot having a smoke. If leaving my post is the problem, then why don't you enforce the rules on those people out in the parking lot?"

"Well, Sergeant, why don't you write those people up?"

That was it. "You're trying to suspend me for leaving my post when there are five people in the parking lot who walked right past your window to go have a fifteen minute cigarette break? You are on Greenberg's team, aren't you? You pick and choose who you want to screw. Don't you? Mark my words; I won't take one day for this action!"

McNally was done. "Okay, Gunnar, take your client out of my office."

I was heated, but I had figured that these deputies from the old regime would stick together. They were probably angry that their time was coming to an end. Their days were numbered with the new administration, and when the new boss figured out what type of people they were, they'd be gone. At least, that's how it would have been in a perfect world. These are the same people who made the morale low at the jail to begin with. They would pick on the weak; but if you were strong and didn't kiss their ass, they would try to get you some other way as Greenberg had for so many years. Why did he have such a hard on for me? Was it because I was friendly with his buxom blonde of an excuse for leaving his old lady? Was it because I took care of the bikers? Or the biker that beat him up when he was younger? Or was it because I had made every block that I worked in quiet? Or more was it because Sheriff Smith was mad that he had to go yet again to the ethics commission to get his son in law promoted over me instead of just being able to say that he was the only person interested in the Lieutenant's position? It could have been any one or combination of those variables.

Gunnar and I went back to work. About a month passed, and Deputy Greenberg had asked if anyone wanted a transfer to the main jail. I raised my hand and said in front of the whole roll call (about twenty-six staff members), "I do."

"So noted, Sergeant."

When I walked by the deputy I whispered to him, "If I don't get transferred away from you, this place will look like Harlem."

Greenberg looked stressed out and reeked of booze. I was given my transfer orders within a week, which was fast. But Greenberg knew I wasn't going to try to make him look good in front of the new regime. My orders were back to Medium "C" block, my home. This was where I started. The only glitch was that Dumas would now be my Captain. But he seemed to be a different man. The day he had been demoted, he'd stopped wearing his sunglasses. Maybe he thought they made him look cooler, although we thought he looked silly wearing them inside the dark buildings.

I was happy with my new assignment. I only had four years left until retirement, and this could be a decent spot to wrap it up. I had been working my old block for a couple of weeks when Greenberg had another breakdown. I laughed this time, knowing Gobi was going to get him for his comments many years ago about Gobi not amounting to shit. So rather than face the music, Greenberg must have decided to play the mental breakdown card, again. I had almost forgotten about my pending disciplinary case when I noticed a ripped open envelope hanging in the window in central control with my name on it. I wondered who had opened it—some curious officer, my new deputy or Dumas? Oh well, it was no secret about my run-ins with the old administration.

The new warden, Turcotte, had had his secretary type a letter the same day I was supposed to appear in front of him for my appeal. I had held signs with this warden on the campaign trail, so he knew that I was straightforward and not going to beat around the bush. He also knew that I wouldn't back down from any type of argument. I went to his office feeling confident, as Turcotte and Gobi knew that Greenberg and his posse were pure evil.

I knocked on Turcotte's door and he spoke loudly, "Come in! Ah, Sergeant Szaban, have a seat. I'm sure you have heard about our beloved Deputy Greenberg, and you'll probably want a moment to say a prayer for him."

We both laughed, but I didn't want to open my mouth too much until he played his hand out.

"All right, Michael, you went for a sandwich because you were forced to work a double shift. I know that these guys have harassed you in the past and we're not going to condone that behavior. The only problem that I have is that you were in charge, and I don't want my people in charge leaving the property."

"Okay, Mr. Turcotte. What about this paperwork then?"

"Here's what I propose. Since we don't have any policy yet and you are my first case, I'm going to recommend that you stay out of trouble for three months and I'll rip this report up. How does that sound?"

"That sounds fine by me, boss, but remember that all my bosses are still Smith supporters, and they hate me for getting you guys into this cushy, high paying state job."

He laughed for a quick second and replied back, "How about you're on double secret probation just like in *Animal House*? No one will know, and it will have to go through me. Just don't do anything crazy for three months and I'll make all this disappear."

We shook hands and away I went. When I went by the captain's office he waved at me to come on in. Dumas asked me why I had to go into the warden's office. I figured that he was just playing dumb, so I played my game. "Ah, you remember Greenberg, how he was always trying to get me. Well, the new administration knows that he is a lying, no good piece of shit. So they squashed it."

Dumas said, "So you got your wish."

"No, I actually wanted you fired, too, but now you're my Captain. I hope we aren't going to have any problems."

He assured me, "Michael, I'm just going to finish my time out and retire." We shook hands, and Dumas did just that. He never bothered me again and actually tried to become one of the boys.

I was heading to the chow hall when I heard a muffled, panicked sound on the radio coming from the temporary housing unit in the gym. The gym had been cut in half, half for working out and half for fifty bunks containing pretrial detainees placed in a partitioned off part of the gym. We had one officer covering them, and there was no way of confining the convicts.

I ran through the opened gate that led to the gym. I was third man in behind two coworkers, who tackled an inmate that was beating the housing unit officer in the head with the desk telephone. The officer was on the floor in the fetal position bleeding from his nose and ear. The other officers handcuffed the assailing inmate quickly and ran him into every wall and doorframe along the way to the lower left—and rightfully so. Not wanting the problem to escalate, I yelled to the rest of the cons to get on their bunks; most did. Some were trying to encourage the beating, but even they knew that was wrong

I wondered how the door in the partition was open if only the housing unit officer and the gym officer had the keys. Then I saw Officer Mungeon, a three hundred pound plus, portly gym officer, holding the door open for us. It didn't dawn on me until later that Mungeon was just standing there watching his comrade get his head beat in by a little scrawny convict. Mungeon could have just lain on top of the kid and squished him. It shouldn't have come as a surprise to me that he acted this way. During the whole election, this big-time political hack didn't take sides, claiming that he was too involved in his niece's neighborhood election. She was running for something like school committee or neighborhood watch chairperson, something small. But Mungeon was just too scared to pick a side. The former sheriff had given him a sergeant's position in the gym with weekends and holidays off. He was also in charge of the scheduling, so he could take any other day off that he wanted. And he was friends with Gobi and had helped him take over his Dad's spot in the state senate. This man knew every politician in the city and was at every major campaign—except for the sheriff's election. He was too scared. I had a pool with his coworkers that as soon as the election was over he would put a Gobi sticker on his truck. I had one week in the pool, but I was beat by the smartass who'd said that Mungeon would have a sticker on the next day. And Mungeon didn't have just one Gobi sticker after the election, but three on his truck windows and two on his bumper. I had hoped that Gobi would see the transparency of Mungeon's deeds, but he was more interested in the man's donations than his cowardice.

***

Finally, I was enjoying my new assignment and was starting to count down the months to retirement. One Sunday that I was in charge I stopped by central control to see the officers in there. They had a small television in the control booth and would sneak a peek at the football game. It was no big deal. They had been doing this since the jail opened. Michael Jones, who was probably the toughest guy ever to have worked at the jail, was in there watching the game. He was third shift sergeant but loved to work overtime on weekends. Jonesey was about six foot two, three hundred pounds of mostly lean muscle, and a black belt in two different denominations—the only person who could put Tebo down for the count. Although he was lightning fast, he was very quiet or humble.

Sometimes when we would pass by each other I'd ask, "Are you ready to take the title from a slow white guy?"

His normal response was usually, "No, Szaban, it's all yours. You are the toughest." He would modestly just shrug me off.

This one particular day I jokingly asked, "Are you ready yet? I'm getting tired of no competition." With that he stood up and began trying to strike me with various hand movements. I blocked most of them, which seemed to be aggravating him. I only got in two counterstrikes, one in his ribs and another on his massive thigh while blocking his kicks. The officers in the room were amazed watching us two big guys spar. Then with my hand I blocked one of Jones' kicks that was going to my jaw. He was trying to drop me for the count. I could tell that something had happened to my hand and said, "Jonesy, I give. You are the master."

I turned and walked over to my buddy Dave. Jones sat back down like nothing had happened and continued watching the game. I quietly showed Dave my right ring finger, which was bent almost backwards. It didn't hurt too badly, but I knew it would, as it was definitely broken. Dave almost gagged just from looking at it.

I waited for the next hour to pass until my shift was over. When I went to the hospital, they said that my finger was broken but there wasn't much they could do since it was just one knuckle. By this time I was starting to feel the pain. They put a small metal splint on it and gave me a script for a few painkillers. I called in sick the next few days and told the captain that I'd broken my finger on one of the exit doors. I wasn't going to get Jones or myself in hot water for some horseplay. Then I'd get a real beating. Besides, I didn't want to let Jonesy know that he had broken my finger.

***

I just have to brush on this one sergeant with whom I worked. We were in the academy together, promoted together and now we finally worked together. He was called a Viking by his peers, but I love Vikings so I don't want to give them a bad name. Felix O'Shannon was as uncouth as they come. He would take his boots off in the booth and walk around in his dirty socks with holes in them. He would walk on the piss-covered bathroom floor with just his socks on. He would grab a pen, anyone's pen and scratch himself wherever he itched.

When we were in the academy they placed all twenty-six of us recruits on a large mat and told us to fight each other down to the sole person left on the mat. You could do almost anything to throw the other trainees off the mat. Finally, the three remaining officers were Brody, Felix, and myself. Brody was just sitting in the middle of the mat swatting officers away from him like a lion at the circus. Felix and I were doing most of the tossing, and whenever I thought I was close to being thrown off the mat, I would grab onto Brody's leg as an anchor.

Felix was a real roughian, but it was his vocabulary that amused us the most. He would mutilate sentences like Archie Bunker. "The next house I buy is going to be around conversation land." "I ran by the re-creation center last night."

Another classic occurred when I was driving him home one day after work. We just so happened to be talking about sex. He was trying to tell me about having sex with his wife during the pregame baseball show. "Yeah, last night ya know, Doreen gave me a prenuptial blowjob." I started laughing and couldn't stop. Felix thought I was laughing at his crudeness, but I was laughing at his vocabulary. So he felt encouraged and said, "Yeah, ya know, I'm gonna get another prenuptial blowjob tonight." I had to get him out of my truck before I peed my pants.

One time there was a pretty good fight in the inmates' chow hall and I didn't get there in time to jump in. One of the officers from maxi arrived, along with Felix, and a couple of my officers helped break up the bloody fight. The maxi officer got AIDS infected blood in his eyes and all over his hands. He went through the testing procedure and was eventually given a clean bill of health; but what a long six months, and he couldn't be as intimate with his wife as he would have liked to be.

Felix told me that he had kicked both combatants and made both of them bleed, and that he was responsible for breaking up the fight himself.

I asked Dave, who happened to be there, "Did Felix really bash the inmates' heads in with his boots? And did he really break up the fight all by himself?"

Dave laughed and said, "Felix was on the bottom of the pile screaming, 'Get off me!'"

I should have known. Felix had once told me when we both were passed over for promotions that he'd gone in and cleared the deputy's desk off. "I smashed his desk with my fist and said, 'What the fuck?' Then I took my arm and cleared everything that was on his desk onto the floor!" That story was true, but he forgot to mention that the Deputy wasn't even there at the time. What a character.

I was covering the inmates eating lunch with Bumbles. Bumbles had been given this nickname from the "Rudolph the Red Nosed Reindeer" show. He was a big, gentle giant. with a photographic memory, and I swear he read the dictionary. Any word or abbreviation that's in the dictionary, he knew. You did not want to play Scrabble with this guy. So we were solving the daily Jumble in the paper when I heard my friend Officer Sanchez call for help in maxi only a gate away. Bumbles and I called for the gate to be opened and raced down to help him. It was another one of those instances where an inmate tried to hang himself with a shoelace. Bumbles and I lifted the hanging con to relieve the pressure on his neck while Sanchez cut the shoelace with a pocketknife. Then we carried the inmate down to the infirmary.

Sanchez's partners still had not arrived. I couldn't believe it. They were usually much quicker than that. I wouldn't have been so mad, but the hanging inmate had pissed his pants and the urine was blotting my uniform. That pissed me off—or on.

Sanchez had one year left and he was set to retire. His wife lived on the Mediterranean Sea in Spain, and he was working overtime and two jobs, sending her as much money as possible to bump up their retirement nest egg. Sanchez ended up testing positive for marijuana and they placed him on administration leave. They never told anyone or offered him help. Not that it was a big deal, but it wasn't procedure. Then he was pulled over in a bad area of the city where he lived. The officer recognized him from working at the county jail and told him that he shouldn't be hanging around such a bad area that late at night. Even though Sanchez had been clean while on paid leave, according to his urine test, the jail's administration fired him for this incident. The union rolled over on him during arbitration and told him that they had tried, but that his conduct was unbecoming of an officer and they had to let him go. A month later the union president got his girlfriend a job at Gobi's jail. Quite a coincidence. I felt so bad for Sanchez, as he had only one year left to retire. All for a little weed.

I was working second shift one night for some extra cash and standing outside of the infirmary windows making faces at my friend Rosco. Rosco was a stone mason by trade and had a great sense of humor and disposition. He wasn't very big, but his arms were like steel and he had that rage every once in a while. We never thought of him as a tough guy because he was always laughing and joking. But we all knew how strong he was and that he had the rage inside of him if need be.

He was standing by his lieutenant with an inmate who was waiting to be seen by the nurse. The inmate was handcuffed in the front, and I saw him lunge at the lieutenant and grab his radio. Rosco pulled the kid by the shirt, but the shirt ripped. I ran into the infirmary and picked the punk up off the lieutenant by the hair; then Rosco and I threw the kid on the ground. The kid must have hit his mouth on the floor because he was bleeding. I didn't want to be wrestling on the dirty, germ-infested infirmary floor with blood on the ground. So we picked the kid and pushed his face into the white cinder block walls until he stopped fighting. When we let him stand on his own two feet, he looked at the lieutenant and spit a mouthful of blood on him. So I picked the punk up and wiped his face on the wall and tried to spell out the word *rat* with his blood using his head as a pen. Before I had finished with the exclamation point, Rosco decided that he was going to throw the kid across the waiting room and into the chairs. I wish I had known, as my hand was wrapped around the links that held the cuffs together. The whole pile of us went flying into the chairs as Rosco's pure adrenaline rush gave us the momentum. My finger snapped—the same one that Jones broke. We heard it snap this time.

"Was that you?" Rosco asked.

"Yeah, you mongrel! You broke my finger!"

Rosco was laughing and only said, "Oopsie."

I helped drag the kid down to the lower left, where he would spend the next several hours chained face up and hopefully realizing the error of his ways. We put him on the ground while a couple other officers set up the restraints. The kid kept trying to spit on someone. It didn't matter who. He just wanted to hurl blood on one of us. I would push his face into the concrete floor and say, "I'm touching you." Then he would relax, and I'd ease up and say, "I'm not touching you." I must have repeated this cycle about four or five times, to everyone's amusement. The crazy punk was finally subdued and only the lieutenant's clothing was stained. Except that my finger was broken. I stayed out two weeks on my own time, as this finger was really wrecked.

When I came back, I was given a letter from Turcotte that I was being transferred to minimum security in a week. That was a nice present, but I was kind of happy where I was. Minimum security, in my humble opinion, was for officers wrapping up to their retirement, not officers who want to search and destroy.

I had also noticed that the administration was promoting quite a few people. They were putting captains and lieutenants on every shift, as the day shift was top heavy with brass. They were finally doing something for the good. But the people they were promoting were not the best officers. There were quite a few who had run from trouble. They were known cowards. Sergeant Ray Prunier, who was no coward, was given a captain's position in special services. When I asked him about it he said jokingly, "It's too bad that I could only give five hundred dollars per person in my family. I had to write checks out in my wife's name, my three kids' names, my dog's name and now my goldfishes' names."

I chuckled back, but later that night I went to the state's website and saw that he wasn't kidding. All the people that had been promoted were giving a lot of checks. And that isn't to say that they weren't giving cash, too. I couldn't believe it. All the big, tough union guys I was fighting for equality with had rolled over and become exactly what we were fighting against. When I called them on it, they just laughed or tried to deny it. I had a printout of all their campaign contributions after the campaign, however. They were clearly buying their positions. I felt like an uglier version of Mel Gibson in *Braveheart* when he saw that the Scottish nobles were on the King of England's side. I was crushed. I'd had it with these crooked law enforcement politicians. All that work for nothing.

CHAPTER 11
THE END

Being sent back to MSF basically meant that I was being put out to pasture. I called in sick for a couple of days trying to grasp why my comrades had rolled over so easily. Then I went back to finish up my last week in Medium "C". When I came back, Pam greeted me like nothing had ever happened. Oh well, I wasn't going to start getting revenge on everyone who had been a backstabbing jerk. My God! I'd be busy for the next few years if I started getting revenge on all the sellouts and backstabbers.

Startled by a call from my booth officer saying that smoke was filling the upper tier of my block, I ran up the stairs and found all the inmates at the front gates gagging. The smoke was thick and spreading fast—the type of smoke that can fill your lungs and kill you quickly. I ordered the gates opened and had the inmates escorted to the gym for safe haven.

A couple of quick thinking officers arrived with fire extinguishers and Scott air packs on. My friend Jeff dragged one inmate, who had passed out to the infirmary. A couple others had to be treated for smoke inhalation, but I was concerned that there were more victims on the tier. Once I had the whole block evacuated and accounted for, we went from cell to cell trying to find the source. It turned out to have been some punks starting fires by the outlets and tossing smoldering mattresses on them to keep the smoke going. We had numerous fire fans going and all the exit doors open to alleviate the smoke. When it was all done, I wrote a report to the administration commending the officers that had helped. They had prevented what could have been a major loss of life and/or injury, which wouldn't look good for a new administration. The new sheriff wrote a nice letter thanking me, and a few of my coworkers, for preventing what could have been a major catastrophe. I had received another life saving heroic letter. I knew that it meant nothing, but I wanted my officers to know I believed effort was what counted. Not just donations.

MSF now had three buildings: the old main brick building, the new annex, and work release, which was down by the main jail's parking lot. I had to admit, it was nice to be around less problematic inmates for a change. The annex building was the easiest. These cons there were petrified of going anywhere else. There were some sexual predators there, but it was a minimum security building for cons that only had a short time left and couldn't make it anywhere else in the jail. I could write a whole book on the stories that these sex offenders have told me, but I don't want to make their crimes seem less horrific than they are by desensitizing readers. I worked three out of my four days a week there. The other day I was at work release where I was very busy logging inmates out to work or to community service projects. I wasn't a big fan of being that busy all day long. Besides, we had to take in clothes for the workers and thoroughly inspect them all day long, too. The workers were allowed shoes as long as they weren't steel toed, and they could have jeans and a t-shirt if they had jobs on the outside. That was a good gig for the short-term con. These guys would get up in the morning, eat, go out to their job and make money, then sleep at the jail and go back out the next day. Their time flew by.

Most of the time I enjoyed the annex building except for the constant complaining. There was a lot of homosexual activity there as well. I had always known that went on in prison, but these criminals were in an open Quonset hut type building with monitors that could zoom in on anyone anywhere. You could be sitting in the booth and read the same book that an inmate was reading at the far end of the building.

The day shift was run nice and quiet. There were very few problems other than the occasional lovers' spat or instance of a kitchen worker selling a little extra food for a deck of cards or something. The second shift was run by Sergeant Paul Murphy. He was the union's liaison to the main union's leaders and to the sheriff. He ran a tight ship. Maybe he ran it a little too tight. He'd been told to stop playing favorites and bringing in gourmet coffee and muffins to his pretty and muscular little inmate friends. As I've mentioned, Murphy had been fighting his feelings for men for years, and who could blame him; it was a tough field in which to "come out of the closet." Murphy was a recent promotion due to his selling of the contract for Gobi, a pretty big deal, as Gobi could make himself look wonderful in the paper by giving a union as big as ours a five-year contract including the two years that sheriff Smith had refused to negotiate.

We were in a hurry to settle the contract, as we had been promised that we would get the best one ever during Gobi's campaign. When Gobi got in, his first order of business was to give us a contract that would buy him a few years to get acquainted with the bargaining system. He had given Murphy and the union's secretary a letter from the state's capital stating that all departments wouldn't get more than a three percent raise—and that would be pushing it. The letter, which was read at the union meeting, was on official letterhead and signed by the state's comptroller's office. We couldn't blame Gobi for making it look as though it was the state's doing. We argued but finally agreed that, since we could only get so much for the next three years and nothing for the Smith years, we would try and get as much as we could. There were a few other incentives in the contract that amounted to a few dollars a month. The total amount wasn't even close to covering the rising cost of gasoline. When you'd been at a jail for seventeen years, you expected a raise of more than forty cents per year. But the letter that the union guys read from the state's capital swayed us to vote for the new contract.

A month after the contract was ratified the state police, court personal and a few other agencies were getting a twelve and fifteen percent raise. Where was that letter? No one could find it. The officers were pissed. We had been duped. The letter turned out a fake, and the union official who pushed it was promoted by Gobi to deputy. It had been a ploy from the new sheriff to get us to pass the contract. The union people who pushed the contract were all promoted, some two and three ranks. And Murphy was one of them. He was given a sergeant's position, and he was placed in charge of weak inmates who were aware of his sexual preference. It was a tough thing to hide around the showers.

Like I said, the day shift ran things nice and smooth, while Murphy had everybody on edge. He ran the minimum security building like it was Pelican Bay supermax. That would have been fine if he was in maximum security, but he had specifically asked not to go there or the "J" building, where his orderly fashion would actually be useful.

I had made friends with a super tough, fifty-year-old sergeant named Rusty. He took a beating from Tebo one day in the modular locker room. Tebo kept hitting Rusty with body shots that would have put almost anyone else to sleep.

But Rusty kept coming and even got in a few shots of his own; still, after ten or twelve gruesome horse punches, Rusty had to stop. I was also proud of Rusty: he had been called into the new sheriff's office and was given a promotion of lieutenant on second shift. But he argued with the Gobi that, since he was the senior sergeant, he should get one of the day slots usually given out to less senior guys. The sheriff wouldn't budge because Rusty apparently hadn't given as much as the others. So Rusty told him thanks but no thanks. Maybe a lot of folks out there think that may have been stupid, but it was probably the first time Rusty did something that honorable.

One evening I took my grandmother out to eat at a fancy Irish restaurant she was fond of. While we were eating, the newly elected lieutenant governor and our state senator came over to say hello to my grandmother, who was always involved in the state politics as she played a big part in her teachers' union. The politicians knew her. They made the usual small talk and fake smiles. Then they asked me how the new regime was at the jail. So I opened up my big mouth.

"It's the same circus; different clowns. You have to give money, sell out your coworkers or live in Gobi's town to get promoted. I'd like five minutes alone with my fat, redheaded boss!"

They looked at me like I was some sort of monster, said their goodbyes and quickly exited. I was half joking, but there was a lot of truth to what I had said.

We had some big state inspection coming up and I wanted my new assignment to pass with flying colors. I usually don't care about these things, but this was going to be my last stop at the jail before retirement. Rusty and I had the cons scrubbing the entire building spotless. I had seen one kid, whose name was Davis standing in the snow washing the outside windows inside the fence with holes in his shoes. When I asked him about getting new shoes, he said he had no money to buy a new pair of shoes, but that his mom could bring up a pair of sneakers during the visiting period. I told him to have her give the sneakers to me in the visiting room and I would inspect them. She brought them, I checked them out, and them handed them over to Davis, thinking no more about it. This is customary in minimum security and usually any worker gets clothes dropped off.

I always accommodated the visitors, as many of them were older relatives with health problems. Personally, I didn't understand why they would want to visit the jail two or three times a week, but that wasn't my concern. I just made sure that the seniors especially were treated decently and didn't have to wait outside in the cold past the visiting time. I had been getting a lot of complaints about the second shift treating the visitors poorly by making them wait, cutting their visiting time in half and belittling the visitors. I mentioned the complaints to Murphy, but he had his own philosophy. *Fuck them* was his motto. It seemed kind of funny coming from a man who faithfully attended church every week.

The building passed inspection, Rusty and I answering the inspectors' questions dutifully. Deputy Haverty gave us the highest verbal compliments, and our building had the best marks in the jail. But that didn't stop me from getting moved to second shift. Apparently there were a lot of union members that believed they were going to become promoted. Because of this, they decided against all logic and common sense to have an addendum put into the contract. Many union members thought that men or women who had time in service should have seniority of time in rank. For example, if had been were a sergeant for fifteen years and had seventeen years in, you would be junior to a newly promoted sergeant with a total of eighteen years in. Even though this sergeant would have no leadership experience, he or she would still be senior and thus be able to bump you out of your shift.

I found that to be absurd, quite the opposite of any other organization from the military down to your local volunteer fire department. It's just plain silly. But now I had been bumped from first shift to second. I would have to work with Murphy and witness firsthand his extracurricular activities. I couldn't help but notice that he was playing favorites despite his iron fist. A couple of the smaller, more ripped Spanish inmates would hang around the booth and flirt with him most of the evening. I found that to be rather unprofessional of him. Especially if another inmate came to talk to him, he would belittle the con.

When I looked at his cell phone contacts, I saw he had the home and cell phone numbers of the top three people in the jail. He was supposed to be fighting for us, as he had in the past. But now Gobi found his weakness: putting him in charge of a few cute, submissive inmates.

Murphy didn't like when I worked with him any more than I did. He felt that I was invading his territory. One night I saw him bring in some stuffed shells while Rusty was working overtime with us. Instead of heating them up and offering them to us, he took them and his "pet" into the back room for twenty-five minutes and did whatever it was he did to him. They both came out with red sweaty faces, so you do the math.

I pulled Murphy into the booth, pushed him up against the wall and yelled, "What the fuck are you doing? You've been warned about bringing inmates food and going into the back room with them! Knock your fuckin' bullshit off, now!"

He said back with an attitude, "I'm not doing anything. I'm just giving him some stuffed shells."

"You're stuffing someone's shells," Rusty injected.

"Didn't Gobi warn you about that crap?" I demanded

"Yes," Murphy defended, "but I'm not really doing anything."

"How about zooming in on the dudes in the shower? How about making them take off their towels when they are just getting in or out of the showers?"

"I'm just making sure that they aren't fooling around or having sexual relations in there."

I couldn't believe this was going on. "Murphy, don't do that shit when I'm here. And you should know better than to be alone in the back room with an inmate anyway!"

Rusty told Deputy Haverty, who asked me to write a report the next day. I refused to write a report, but I told him off the record that Murphy shouldn't be using the annex as his dating service. He laughed and I also told him that either he needs to go where his running of a tight ship would be needed or to transfer me. He said that he had tried to move Murphy, but nobody wanted him, as he is a liability. Murphy had been moved out of the building for a week due to his activities. But there was still no disciplinary action taken. But the sheriff knew. Murphy's saving grace was selling a lame contract and his family members donating a bundle.

"Mike, you are in charge. Don't let him do any of his silly little shenanigans. Just pop him in the mouth."

"Deputy, he could be your assistant and he'd think that he was in charge. He treats most of the cons harshly, while others he's bringing in gourmet coffee, muffins and whatever else. You also know that he's cutting visits short and treating the civilian school teachers like dirt; and he gets away with it because everyone in his family is on the list for giving five hundred dollars a whack."

Rusty moved Murphy's boyfriend out of there, for which I was thankful. But now there was a male stripper in our block. That meant trouble. The rookie lieutenant came down for his evening rounds, and I announced over the PA system that he was here. Murphy, however, was unaffected by his presence. For thirty minutes he lay half on the stripper's bed listening attentively to stories from the thug. The sergeant's expression was that of a teenage girl watching a boy band play without their shirts on. The lieutenant, however, was also a close friend of Gobi's, and hopefully this would be the kick in the pants that Murphy needed. We weren't asking him to change his sexual desires, just not to indulge them at work.

The lieutenant watched in disgust. Then he sent me out on the tier to get Murphy. The lieutenant told him that he'd better ask for a transfer or he would write his behavior up. This was at least the fifth time that the staff was aware of his activities. I figured this was going to be Murphy's well-needed transfer, which made me happy. I didn't want him to get into trouble, just give him a well needed change of scenery.

I had a class on my next day off. During break, a special services officer gave me a fancy envelope with a letter in it. I was to report to special services the next day at eleven o'clock. I figured it was about Murphy's activities, but I wasn't going to rat on the guy, just insist that he got a transfer. The next day, the two sneaky special services officers had me come in and sit down. There was a tape recorder on the table; they asked me if I wanted union representation, but I said, "No, I haven't done anything wrong."

"I guess you know why you're here, Sergeant Szaban."

"Um, yeah, I think so."

"Okay, then, we'll proceed. Did you accept a pair of sneakers for inmate Davis?"

I wasn't expecting this. "Yes, I did. It's minimum security. They're allowed and he is a worker."

"Did you accept any form of payment for the contraband?"

"Whoa, is this investigation about me?"

"Yes, Sergeant, you have been the topic of an undercover operation for a few months."

"Really? Then we aren't going to call sneakers contraband in front of me."

"We believe that the sneakers are contraband and therefore you are liable for introducing contraband into the facility."

"Sneakers are not contraband. If they were, you'd have fourteen hundred inmates with contraband, as almost every convict has a pair."

"Did you accept payment for the contraband?"

"There is no contraband. Let me ask you, am I the only sergeant under investigation here?"

"We can't answer that at this time."

The questions went on for about an hour. They tried to trap me with a whole host of word games. They kept saying that the kid's sneakers given to me by his mom were contraband. They had pictures of the sneakers and had made the mother sign an affidavit stating that I had been the person she'd delivered the sneakers to. They also tried to get me to admit that I let several ex-cons into the facility for visiting period. The only one I could think of was this kid O'Toole, who had asked me for a visit in the evening instead of the daytime. No big deal there. Even bunks were allowed visits during the day, and odd numbered bunks had them at night. No harm, no foul there.

When the interview was over I was told to go see Warden Turcotte. I thought this was way out of line, even for these rat motherfuckers. I headed up to Turcotte's office expecting the worst. When I arrived there he handed me a letter without saying a word.

It read, *Sergeant Szaban, you are hereby placed on administrative leave with pay. You will make yourself available by phone from Monday to Friday between eight and four p.m. You are not allowed on the jail's property until further notice.*

Now curiosity was getting the better of me. Was I just a cover until they got Murphy? Had one of my nemeses gathered enough donations to finally get me? Was it an ex-girlfriend that wanted revenge? Had the lieutenant governor told the sheriff about my comment on the restaurant? Why would I be on paid leave for something so minor? Why wouldn't the big man talk to me directly? Oh well. I hadn't done anything that bad. Nothing should come of this silly shit. I was leaning towards them getting Murphy out.

While I was on leave I received many phone calls from coworkers wondering what had happened. When I told them, they said, "No way! It has to be more than that." But that was it. That was all I was told.

While I was out, I read in the paper that Gobi had gone to a state park at the ocean and refused to pay the fifteen-dollar parking fee. He'd bullied this teenage girl who was just trying to make some spending money for the mall, waving his badge at her, threatening her and finally driving into the state park without paying. The girl, who was in tears, called the local police. Of course, Gobi's attitude changed then. He was then given a one hundred dollar fine for not paying the fifteen-dollar fee. When the episode made the paper in his home town, he shrugged it off and was quoted as saying, "I'm frugal with my money. Just like I'm frugal with your, the taxpayers' money." What a crock. What a line. Here he was, not paying the state and threatening a teenage girl, and I was on suspension for sneakers—fuckin' sneakers!

The jail called every number in the book trying to get a hold of me after a month of paid leave. They have a poor personnel system because Gobi hired his friends to run the department. Finally, the secretary reached me and asked me to come in at eleven o'clock. I went in and saw Mr. Turcotte.

"Have a seat, Michael," he said. "It saddens us that we have to do this to you. The sheriff is almost in tears."

"Do what to me? Do you even have the right guy? I mean, if this is about sneakers and a visit, that's a bit of an overkill."

"Michael, if this isn't a termination case, I don't know what is. We have signed affidavits and we suspect that there is more than this."

I couldn't believe my ears. "You would have to have more than this because sneakers and a visit aren't worth a slap on the wrist!"

"I'm sorry, Michael, but we are going to have to start the termination process."

I thought about my friend Sanchez, who had been fired and lost in arbitration because the union was in Gobi's pocket. The union counsel was even calling Gobi up for jobs for their friends and family. I couldn't go a year without a paycheck while they played in arbitration. I figured that if they were this intent on kicking me out, then fuck them. If they wanted a bunch of ass-kissing officers with no spines that just want to buy their positions, then I wasn't going to fit in anyway.

"If I resign, I want to use up my sick time and I want a check for my vacation and compensation time."

He looked relieved. "That's fine, Michael. If you ever want a reference for corrections or any other field, here's my card."

"No, I'm just going to grow my hair out, hop on my Harley and ride off into the sunset." I got up, turned my back and walked out without another look.

So if you are driving and see a long, blonde-haired biker, don't think of him as a scary degenerate dude; think of him as a solid, lifesaving man who has done nothing but good in his tenure. I know now that no good deed goes unpunished—and remember, be careful what you wish for.

Made in the USA